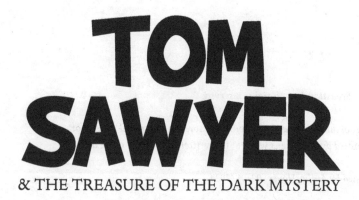

TOM SAWYER

& THE TREASURE OF THE DARK MYSTERY

SEBASTIAN JOE

EDITED BY: SUSAN LUBINSKI, RUSSELL ALLRED, AND KATIE HALL

authorHOUSE®

AuthorHouse™
1663 Liberty Drive
Bloomington, IN 47403
www.authorhouse.com
Phone: 833-262-8899

Published by AuthorHouse 02/08/2024

ISBN: 979-8-8230-1394-9 (sc)
ISBN: 979-8-8230-1392-5 (hc)
ISBN: 979-8-8230-1393-2 (e)

Library of Congress Control Number: 2023916589

Print information available on the last page.

Any people depicted in stock imagery provided by Getty Images are models,
and such images are being used for illustrative purposes only.
Certain stock imagery © Getty Images.

This book is printed on acid-free paper.

Special Thanks to Lillie Joe

A NOTE TO THE READERS

Hello, and welcome to the fantastic world of Mark Twain's Tom Sawyer. This project has been in the works for a very long time...15 years to be exact. I started writing this exhilarating story at the young age of 13, and I had always hoped that I could finish and publish the story for many others to read. Many of you, like myself, grew up reading Tom Sawyer and Huckleberry Finn as a young kid, either for assigned school reading, or just because it was recommended to you by a friend or an adult you knew. However, there could be quite a lot of you just reading about the characters for the very first time. To the former, I invite you back to the land of kid-like wonder and imagination with the widest of open arms. By now, I'm sure you're leading your own adult lives and maybe have kids of your own. Don't worry, we all grow up at some point; I just hope that you learn to love my book at least half as much as you came to love Mark Twain's original stories. For those of you reading about Mark Twain's characters and world for the first time, I say, WELCOME! You're in for an unforgettable tale of adventure, romance, and mystery that should keep you on the edge of your seats until the final page! However, if you have the time and interest, please consider reading the original books by Mark Twain. I tried to include some anecdotes from the original books to both remind older readers of what happened in Mark Twain's tales and catch up the newer readers to the continuity of the world of Tom Sawyer, but nothing quite beats reading the original author's work. I'll cut straight to the point: I'm not Mark Twain by any objective or reasonable measurement, and I didn't invent most of the main characters. But I fell in love with the world he created in his original books, and something inside me couldn't let the story end with the way he had finished it. But, much like how I grew up, I didn't want the world of Tom Sawyer to remain frozen in time, with everyone stuck in the same year and remaining the same age, and so, I felt the need for the characters to grow up just a little as well. Don't worry, I love Mark Twain's characters, and so I took the utmost care in preserving each individual's unique personality. I did my best to write the story like how I thought Mark Twain himself would have liked it written. I also tried to give more insight into the lives of some of the less discussed characters from the original books. I think you're in for a real treat, so turn the page, and join me on this spectacular adventure!

CONTENTS

PROLOGUE

HOW TIME PASSES

Tom Sawyer was an average kid who lived an average life. At least it was an average life when he wasn't searching for buried treasure, uncovering hidden secrets, or leading his friends on dangerous adventures.

Perhaps "average" is an understatement.

Though his childhood did contain a certain element of tragedy, it nevertheless deserves to be told. You see, Tom's mother and father fell ill during an infectious outbreak of tuberculosis. Both perished. Suddenly, six-year-old Tom was an orphan.

But he was not alone.

Kind of heart, his Aunt Polly, his mother's sister, graciously offered to take him in. And so, the young boy traveled to his aunt's house in the small village of St. Petersburg, Missouri. With tall trees, hidden caves, and the giant Mississippi River only a stone's throw away, Tom's new home was perfect for a little boy.

Aunt Polly was a handsome woman, whose hair shined a lovely hue of gray. She was gentle, loving, and prone to worrying about Tom. She treated her nephew as if he were her son and taught him to seek out the best of life. She took him to church, sent him to school, and admonished him with endless scolding, for he was endlessly into mischief. While Tom didn't love Aunt Polly's worry and the chastising, he loved her. Besides, her fretting and chiding were nothing compared to his annoyance with his whiny half-brother, Sid.

Sid was Aunt Polly's dream and Tom's greatest nightmare. Four years younger than Tom, Sid seemed to be Tom's complete opposite: He never got into trouble and always did what was asked of him, or at least that's what all the grown-ups believed. Sid wore big, round glasses and had black hair combed into an ugly hairstyle; at least that's what Tom thought. But Tom might be prejudiced, because it seemed to him that Sid lived to get Tom in trouble. Also, Sid was a snitch, and Tom couldn't stand snitches. Tom knew you couldn't choose your kinfolk, but he often wished he could have had a say in the matter.

Apart from the frustration of having Sid as a little brother, Tom felt his life was pretty worry-free. School could have posed a problem if Tom had cared a whit about studying or his grades, but he didn't. In his opinion, life was too short to worry about silly things like grades. Though Aunt Polly worried about Tom, she didn't know what she could do. Tom seemed impervious to her scolding.

However, Tom's grades did pose a problem for Mr. Dobbins, the quick-tempered village schoolteacher. While it was reasonable to assume that some of the class work Mr. Dobbins assigned would sink in, Tom just fell further and further behind. He was getting such bad grades that Mr. Dobbins had almost given up. Now, at the age of 17, Tom had grown to be Mr. Dobbins's biggest problem student. Tom Sawyer played hooky and pulled pranks.

He made jokes out loud during class, when he showed up at all, and worst, his bad behavior seemed to delight his classmates.

It seemed only natural that Tom had become best friends with another mischievous, yet goodhearted soul. In Huckleberry Finn, Tom Sawyer had seen past the worn-out clothes, and the drunken, unseemly father, and found a staunch, loyal friend, ready to drop everything for adventure.

Much like Tom, Huck's father was no longer alive. But anyways, Huck preferred to live on his own. The charitable Widow Douglas had taken Huck in and seen that he was given a basic education, but it was living on his own that brought Huck joy. Many of the village people often treated Huck as an outcast because he wasn't like the other boys in town, who had normal families, clean clothes, and good manners. But Huck didn't care. He found nothing wrong with sleeping under the stars at night and surviving on stolen food. Paradise didn't need much else, he figured.

Tom Sawyer also had a number of other close companions, one of whom had stolen his heart from the moment they first met. Her name was Rebecca Catherine Thatcher, though she preferred to be called Becky. She came from one of the town's affluent, educated families, but was as down-to-earth and kindhearted as any girl could be. Her father, Judge Thatcher, was one of the town's authorities and the president of Thatcher Bank. Becky was a year younger than Tom. Her silky, sun-golden locks and emerald-green eyes drew the envy of nearly every other young girl in the village, and the attention of nearly every other young man. Tom Sawyer had the sole pride and privilege to call her his girlfriend.

Another friend of his was Amy Lawrence, a cute, red-headed tomboy of 15. Amy and Tom had been friends for years. Originally his girlfriend, Amy was happy for Tom now that he and Becky were inseparable. Eventually, Amy became Huck's girlfriend instead. Unknown to most aficionados of Tom's life story, Amy also had been orphaned at a young age. She had a brother named Andrew, who was ten years older. Many years ago, Andrew had become an apprentice to a local carpenter. A few years later, flush with all of the skills he had learned, he took over the business from the original owner, which allowed him to comfortably support both himself and his sister. No one in the village knew much about Amy and Andrew's parents; their origins and their disappearance mostly remained a mystery, whose answers faded with each year.

Over the course of this last school year, time had passed quickly for Tom, Huck, Becky, and Amy. Their lives grew intertwined and close, and their friendships deepened. And today, as was the case for most school kids, the exciting days of summer vacation beckoned.

And so, it was on this beautiful, almost-summer morning that Tom Sawyer found himself walking to school, mischief in his eyes, totally unprepared for what was about to happen to his young life!

CHAPTER 1

SCHOOLTIME SHENANIGANS

With a practiced throw, Tom expertly skipped a smooth stone across the river.

"Sid," he crowed exuberantly at his brother, who walked alongside him, "I just can't believe that this is the last day of school; it's almost summer!" Just ahead was the schoolhouse. Despite its proximity, Tom was in a great mood.

He enthusiastically bound down the dusty lane, inevitably dirtying the bottom of his feet. Tom considered footwear a hassle and almost always went barefoot. But Sid was in a bad mood and couldn't have cared less about his older brother's rapturous declaration. Trampling a lovely lilac wildflower, he scowled at Tom.

The brothers' dispositions were as different as their looks. While Tom exhibited a happy, carefree spirit, Sid's pessimistic attitude could actually dispel rainbows. This was not an exaggeration: Tom had witnessed the sad phenomenon one time after an April shower. If grumpiness and grouchiness were catchable diseases, Sid would have infected the whole earth.

"That don't mean nothing...for you, anyway," Sid groaned, waving around his hands in an attempt to clear the dusty air caused by Tom's skipping strides. "You only showed up to school half of the semester, and I'm pretty sure you learned nothing when you did come. During the other half of the time, you were hanging out, swimming, and fishing with the likes of Huck Finn; he ditches school <u>all year long</u>!"

Tom recognized the truth behind Sid's statement, but he honestly didn't care. The way he and Huck saw it, when you grow up too quickly, you miss out on all the amazing, fun parts of life. Tom saw the moroseness in his brother and hoped it wasn't too late for Sid to change. But instead of denying the claims, he faced Sid and quickly defended Huck's insulted honor.

"Ok, Sid. Number one, you're starting to sound an awful lot like a kid raised by Aunt Polly **AND** Mr. Dobbins in the same household. Number two, there's different kinds of smarts, Sid, and Huck's taught me a whole lot of <u>important</u> stuff," Tom replied rather proudly. "Like this."

With that, Tom pulled a simple, wooden slingshot out of the back pocket of his trousers, loaded a single, steel marble, aimed at a nearby rock, and hit it square! He even caught the tiny, metal sphere in his hand as it bounced off the rock! Tom then copped a Wyatt Earp pose, reveling in his accomplishment. His attitude was, 'I answer to no one.' With a bit of flair, he spun the slingshot around his finger like a mighty gunslinger, holstered his weapon, and grinned at Sid, expecting a little praise for his skills.

Sid, however, wasn't impressed, either with Tom's hero worship of Huck or his stupid slingshot. "Name me one thing that you find <u>important</u> about that," Sid demanded flatly. "That parlor trick won't get you nowhere."

"Oh, that there was just for practice, Sid," Tom said slyly, ignoring the sarcasm. He then retrieved the slingshot from his pocket again. This time, he loaded two marbles into the leather strap at the same time; one was the same steel sphere from before, the other was a personal favorite from his collection. Taking aim, he shot both at the same rock. Dead on! As both marbles ricocheted back at him, Tom caught the first one but accidentally missed the second one! With dread, he watched as it flew past his hand, straight toward the schoolhouse! He didn't hear any glass break, so the window must have been open. But he knew he wasn't out of the woods. Sure enough, Tom heard a quiet snap, followed by what sounded like angry shouting from someone very adult. Shoot! Mr. Dobbins! And it sounded like he was having a fit!

"Uh oh," Tom muttered, his mind brainstorming escape routes.

"What do you mean, 'Uh oh'?" Sid asked suspiciously, not having heard Mr. Dobbins's commotion, and thus, having no idea what was coming.

"I gotta get to school," Tom announced breathlessly and hurried off.

"You know, if you'd hadn't stayed up till midnight yesterday we wouldn't be three hours late for school!" Sid called after the disappearing troublemaker.

The worn schoolhouse had withstood many young men not unlike Tom Sawyer. Though the wood had grown old, the roof

leaked from time to time, and the windows didn't always open completely, it nevertheless felt like home to Mr. Dobbins. Though quick tempered at certain times, the 55 year old man possessed a generally patient demeanor, as he had three of his own children to raise. Day in and day out, he taught a variety of subjects to the pupils, including arithmetic, science, and even music. This morning, he was in the middle of teaching a lesson in U.S. History.

"Now remember, class!" Mr. Dobbins intoned. "The two lanterns in the North Church tower served as a warning to Paul Revere that the British were coming by sea." While he was speaking, he was also writing bullet points on the chalkboard with a long piece of white chalk.

Just as the class learned the British were coming by sea, Tom's stray marble shot through the open schoolhouse window, careened off the blackboard, and struck the chalk in Mr. Dobbins's hand, shattering it into pieces!

Chaos reigned as the teacher jumped away from the chalk shards, which shot everywhere. The children in the row closest to Mr. Dobbins jumped out of their seats to safety. As soon as the reason for Mr. Dobbins's dancing became obvious, the children's facial expressions changed from shock to laughter. The expression on Mr. Dobbins's face, however, turned to fury. He bent down and retrieved the chalk stick, now in pieces, and the marble, which had rebounded with a loud clack against the chalkboard.

"Who did this?!" he demanded furiously, instantly silencing the room.

To ensure his displeasure was taken seriously, he held up the marble and marched heatedly around the room, like a military drill instructor, showing it to each and every student. He was too caught up in his anger to notice the subtle smiles appearing on the faces of the students.

Truth be told, each one of those students knew exactly whom that marble belonged to, but none were about to sell Tom out. Their loyalty to the mischievous Tom Sawyer was solid.

Mr. Dobbins continued to pace angrily around the classroom, attempting to deduce the culprit. Right then, he noticed that Tom wasn't in his seat, nor was his younger brother! Just as the lanterns in the North Church tower illuminated the reason for Paul Revere's ride, the lights came on for Mr. Dobbins. Tom Sawyer! That boy. Mr. Dobbins rolled his eyes and walked back to his desk. He picked up a wooden ruler and tapped it into his hand like a sturdy police baton.

"I should have known it. TOM SAWYER, WHERE ARE YOU?!" Mr. Dobbins shouted, his angry voice reverberating around the entire schoolhouse.

At that moment, Tom entered, casually carrying his schoolbooks, acting like nothing was amiss.

"Yes, sir?" Tom asked happily – almost too happily to be taken seriously.

"Tom Sawyer, this is an unprecedented first for you, mister. You're three hours late to school, and to top it all off, your crazy shenanigans have disrupted my school lesson! Somehow, I think it would almost have been better if you hadn't shown up today at all!"

Mr. Dobbins was speaking heatedly through clenched teeth, attempting to control the anger in his voice, but failing miserably.

"Well now, what on earth do you mean?" Tom asked innocently, knowing full well what he was being accused of. By now, in his 11th year of school, playing the innocent victim card came about as naturally to Tom as breathing air.

"I'm talking about this!" Mr. Dobbins yelled, as he showed Tom the destructive marble.

There could be no doubt about it, the White Alley shooting marble was one of Tom's prized possessions. It gleamed back at him, as if encouraging Tom to continue fighting for his acquittal; and fight he would. Tom knew that he would be in trouble if he didn't explain himself fast. Pretending that nothing had happened wasn't working. Besides, his lies could be much more convincing than the truth. At that moment, Tom glanced at the schoolhouse door. Sid had just entered. Tom narrowed his eyes. The time for payback had come due.

"Well, Mr. Sawyer, I'm waiting for a response," Mr. Dobbins pestered Tom, holding out the White Alley marble in his hand.

Without so much as batting an eye, Tom said, "Oh look, sir, you found Sid's marble. I thought it was gone forever. And I truly wish to apologize for my brother following in my mischievous way of living."

Still not quite sure what was going on, Sid opened his mouth to protest his innocence and correct Tom. Never before had he heard his older brother tell such an unbelievable whopper. But Mr. Dobbins silenced Sid before he could speak.

Mr. Dobbins knew that Tom lied with ease. But unfortunately, he also knew there was no way for him to know the real truth. He had no choice.

"Sid Sawyer," Mr. Dobbins began, carefully setting the marble on his desk.

"Y-y-yes, sir?" Sid asked nervously.

"Is there anything you want to say for yourself?"

And there Sid stood, not quite knowing what to do, overcome with the strange desire to let Tom get away with it. He thought maybe if he spared Tom Mr. Dobbins's rage here, then perhaps he could get Tom in even bigger trouble at home with Aunt Polly. "No, sir, I mean, I'm sorry, sir. It won't happen again. Can I please have my marble back?" he humbly pleaded with the schoolmaster.

Now Mr. Dobbins had allowed himself to be backed into a corner. He couldn't accuse both boys of lying. "Well," he began, "I never reckoned this day would come: The day a model student would slip up and follow along the dark path of his older brother. I see no hope for your brother, but I can only pray there is still hope for you. In the meantime, SIT UP HERE NEXT TO MY DESK WHERE I CAN KEEP AN EYE ON YOU!"

"Yes, sir," Sid timidly responded, as he sulked glumly up to the dunce chair next to Mr. Dobbins's desk - a first-time experience for the notorious "saint" of the school.

Tom, trying to keep the disbelief off his face, took a seat between Becky and Amy, even though he was supposed to be sitting with the boys on the other side of the schoolroom. He greeted Amy cordially, as a good friend would, and then gave Becky's hand a gentle squeeze to say hello. Having just gotten back from a three-month European tour, Becky had missed Tom dreadfully, and she covered his hand with her own.

Becky tried to focus on Mr. Dobbins. She didn't believe for a minute it was Sid's marble, but she certainly didn't want to give Tom away. Moreover, after being gone for so long, she had quite a bit of catching up to do in her studies. Her father hoped that one day, she might even consider attending law school, just as he had. Best to keep her wits about her.

Across from Becky, Amy twirled her auburn hair around her fingers impatiently, tapped her chalk against her desk, and glanced up at the clock on the wall: 12:00? Had it only been an hour since the marble came flying through the window? The end of the school day wasn't until 3:30. Amy let out a loud sigh. She was never going to make it: The boredom and the almost-summer heat would kill her first. If only she could get out of class early.

With that last thought, she hatched an unbelievably clever plan.

If Tom Sawyer was the expert of mischief, Amy may as well have been his apprentice. She had learned much from him. After a quick wink at Becky, she nudged Tom's arm. Getting his attention, she whispered quietly, "Play along."

Tom gave her a peculiar look before nodding. And without further ado, Amy put her brilliant plan into action. Dramatically standing up and complaining with a loud voice that it was too hot for her to bear, she then proceeded to collapse in an excellent faint.

Shocked at the young woman lying prone on the floor, Mr.

Dobbins found himself completely clueless to the brilliant acting taking place before him. Tom, however, caught on immediately.

"Mr. Dobbins, quick, do something! She should see the doctor. Do you want me to take her?"

"Yes, um, yes, of course," Mr. Dobbins stuttered. "Take Miss Lawrence to see Doctor Stevens. See if he can give her some smelling salts."

The act was almost complete. Only one more scene to go.

Tom pasted on a look of great innocence. "Absolutely, sir."

As Tom got to his feet to help Amy, Becky saw the golden opportunity as well and got out of her own seat. Without being asked to help, she bent down and grasped the recumbent Amy's lifeless hand. She looked Tom directly in the eye and told him in a loud voice to be gentle as they both lifted Amy up and supported her under her arms.

"Miss Thatcher," the teacher called. "You really don't need to…"

Too late. Before he could finish, Amy was already being carried out the door by her two friends.

It took the teacher perhaps five seconds to realize what had just happened. He'd been had! It was the greatest escape plan ever. Furious, he charged out the door to yell at them. But just as he began to raise his voice to call after them, he looked back inside and caught a glimpse of the calendar on the wall: It was May 31 - the last day of school before summer break.

Right then, he remembered the awful misery school had been for him growing up and how much he had yearned for summer. He mentally relived how hard his parents and teachers had pushed him, the late nights of study, and how he couldn't wait for the last day of school. So, instead of yelling at Tom, Becky, and Amy, Mr. Dobbins pulled the rope to the school bell and announced to all the remaining students that class was dismissed early for the rest of the day.

"I'll see you all next fall!" he called out to the jubilant pupils. "Try not to forget too much of what we learned!"

Back inside the school room, wondering about his own course of action, Sid tried to blend in with the other students streaming toward the door, but to no avail.

Mr. Dobbins saw Sid and caught him by the ear before he could escape. Turning him toward the messy school room, Mr. Dobbins spoke. "Mr. Sawyer, I have my own private opinions on what happened earlier, but someone must be punished. You, young man, took the blame. Therefore, you must remain here at school cleaning up this…." And here, Mr. Dobbins paused, gazing at the room, trying to decide on the right word, "…this disorderly mess," Mr. Dobbins finished.

CHAPTER 2

NEW PLANS FOR OLD TREASURE

After all of the excited students had left the schoolhouse, Sid repeatedly, and quite adamantly, cursed Tom Sawyer for having ever existed and began the unpleasant duty of tidying up the schoolhouse. In all honesty, he should have expected the devious behavior from his older brother, but he had found himself caught off-guard by how easily the teacher bought the lie. To a neutral observer, Mr. Dobbins might as well have been taking orders from Tom. Granted, looking back, he also couldn't believe that he had been dumb enough to justify taking the rap for Tom. But no matter how Sid looked at it, no amount of disdain for his brother could change his unfair predicament. So, he focused his energy on cleaning up the school and hoped that a brilliant idea of revenge would materialize in his mind.

Elsewhere in the village, not knowing of the early dismissal, Tom and Becky continued half-dragging, half-carrying the 'unconscious' Amy away from the schoolhouse. Truthfully, they probably could have set her down a while ago, but they found that they were having too much fun.

"I can't believe that actually worked," Becky giggled happily, delighted to have taken part in a prank, something she rarely ever did.

"I know! Mr. Dobbins ain't never gonna learn that we kids are smarter than we look!" Tom chuckled.

They continued down the road a ways when along wandered Huckleberry Finn, carrying his fishing pole over his shoulder like a focused militia man with his musket. Huck's destination was the local fishing pond, which sat just down the road from the schoolhouse. Though he had heard the school bell dismissing school, he didn't understand why school had let out so early in the day.

"What gives?" Huck called out. "You guys don't get out until at least 3: …"

At that moment, he saw that Tom and Becky were carrying Amy. For one brief moment of confusion, he actually thought she had died, and that Tom and Becky were part of her funeral procession.

"AMY! Good Lord! What did you do to her?!" Huck asked incredulously.

"Nothing at all," Amy smiled, raising her head up innocently.

Huck was so overcome with shock that he tripped and fell backwards, almost snapping his fishing pole in two and effectively causing an enormous eruption of laughter from his friends.

"Why on earth did you that, Amy?" Huck gasped. "That there's a surefire way to make a guy's heart give out."

"Well, I'm sorry, Huck, but I wanted to get out of school early," she replied, causing Tom and Becky to nod their heads in agreement. "So, I faked a possum. Tom and Becky were carrying me to the doc for smelling salts. At least that's what Dobbins thought!"

"Wish you could have witnessed it, Huck," Tom remarked, smiling broadly. "I done swear that Amy's taking after me more and more."

Huck eyed Tom with a look of annoyance and reacted to Tom wishing him back in school. "You know darn well that I'll never set foot in a schoolhouse again, so long as I have a say in the matter. I know how to read and write, and that's all a guy like me needs. At any rate, though, it looks like your plan worked," Huck remarked, checking out the old town clock in the distance. "But, boy, you sure had me worried," he finished, relieved that Amy was all right.

"Well, now that we got out of school, what are we supposed to do for the rest of the day?" Becky asked everyone.

"I don't know," Amy shrugged. "Didn't really plan that far ahead."

"Let's go fishing," Tom suggested, picking up Huck's fishing pole and handing it back to its rightful owner. "I heard talk that they finally fixed old man McCabe's fishing dock."

With heads nodding in agreement, the four set out for old man McCabe's dock.

For the next three hours, they all shared Huck's pole and tried their hand at fishing. As they sat on the edge of the dock, feet swinging leisurely below them, mere inches above the calm, quiet water, friendly conversations sprang up among the young couples.

"Well, I don't have myself any high hopes on catching

anything, Becky. Wanna tell me about your trip to Europe?" Tom asked cordially, as he passed the shared fishing pole over to Huck. "It's been a lonely three months without getting to give you at least a hug."

Becky smiled at Tom's lovely confession of his feelings for her. He rarely ever opened up to such a level of emotional closeness, and she loved it when he did. "Europe was interesting," she admitted. "But there was such an expansive amount of history to learn that I thought my mind was going to break down at some point. I got to visit some of the places I've always wanted to see, like Italy and Spain. And ever since we left, I can't stop wanting to go back to Paris, France. They have a gorgeous art museum called the Louvre. I've never seen such breathtaking paintings and sculptures."

On the other half of the edge of the dock, Huck and Amy shared a tender moment of their own.

"So, been to any art museums lately, Huck?" Amy asked.

Huck turned to Amy and gave her a perplexed look, almost as though she had just spoken an alien language that no one in the world knew how to speak. Amy kept the genuine look of interest on her face for about five more seconds before she cracked and let out an enormous laugh. "I'm just messing with you, Huck. I wouldn't ever actually want to bore you that badly."

"Yeah, I was wondering what you were getting on about there, Amy. I don't know anything about art, but wanna hear about the time I almost caught a full-grown bull-snake? I swear, that thing must have been almost seven feet long and could have choked me to death!"

Snakes were icky, but Amy kind of wished that she had been a part of such a fearsome encounter!

At the end of the third hour, though, everyone had just about given up. Even for a seasoned professional like Huck, the fish just wouldn't bite. At about 3:30 that afternoon, they packed up their gear and gathered to decide on the next part of the day's activities.

"I'm not one to complain," Becky admitted, turning to Tom. "But isn't there something better that we could be doing right now?"

Tom was ready for her. Adventure glowed in his eyes as he laid out his next scheme. "I've got a great idea," he suggested excitedly. "Let's look for treasure!"

"Still dreaming 'bout treasure, Tom?" Amy asked him curiously. "Most treasure hunters wind up dead, you know."

"I reckon it's worth the risk," Tom replied nonchalantly. "Ya'll remember where this came from, right?"

He reached into his pocket and pulled out a solid gold coin, showing it to everyone, bringing forth not only riches, but great, vivid memories of the past.

All of them remembered the fateful day when Becky and Tom had become lost in McDougal's Cave, the very same cave in which the infamous criminal, Injun Joe, had made his hideout. When at last the two children were rescued, Judge Thatcher saw fit to seal the entrance to the cave to prevent more people from vanishing. Only by witness of Tom Sawyer did the village learn that Injun Joe still remained inside at the time. Though the village tried to get to him, it was too late. Injun Joe had starved to death. Despite the tragedy, there had been a light at the end of the tunnel.

Shortly after Tom and Becky had been found, Tom and Huck discovered an incredible stash of treasure hidden inside the cave! Under the wise influence of Aunt Polly, Judge Thatcher had set both boys up with savings accounts for the $6,000 they each had retrieved. And while Tom certainly enjoyed being mildly wealthy, Huck didn't enjoy the repercussions it brought to his life, like having to go to church, take baths, or use table manners. So, rather than lead a clean, dignified, well-mannered life, he instead gave his share of the money to the judge, in exchange for a single, measly dollar, and soon returned to his 'comfortable' way of living.

"Well, how could we forget?" Becky asked, drawing Tom out of his flashback. "For a long time, your wealth was the only thing the village talked about."

"Yeah," Huck murmured. "The villagers treated us all real nicely. I mean, most of them probably wanted a small piece of the wealth for themselves, but they were still nice."

Amy nodded and laughed. But then, she felt inwardly pressed to ask Tom a question that had been on her mind for a long time. "Tom, where did the gold even come from?"

Tom mused about it and replied, "Well, as I recall, Injun Joe was the one who hid it in McDougal's Cave and…"

"I meant, where did he get it from?"

"From another gang is what I think he mentioned."

"But the coins you showed to everyone in the village looked mighty old, like they came from someone else before the gang, Tom; where did they come from?"

"I…well they could have…hmm…" For once, Tom was at a loss for words. He didn't know the answer to her question, and honestly, it kind of bugged him. Curiously, he looked down once more upon his golden token of victory. "I honestly don't know, Amy. There's not really anything special about the coin; it's just a plain gold coin."

"What about the chest?"

Everyone turned to Becky.

"What do you mean?" Tom asked.

Becky shrugged. "I don't know if it's true or not, but I've heard legends of pirates marking their treasure chests with their own unique symbols. You know, as a way of knowing what treasure was theirs and which belonged to some other pirate crew."

Judging from their lengthy silence, she realized that none of them had ever heard of this. "What?" she asked. "You learn a lot when you study European history. Anyway, I could explain myself more easily with an actual treasure chest. You still have it, right?"

Huck only shook his head in embarrassment. "We done left the chest in McDougal's Cave. Tom and I brought the gold coins back to the village in bags, and we used a wagon if I recall correctly. The treasure itself weighed too much to carry out in the chest."

A long silence followed. Then, from Tom: "Well, there's only one way to find out the answer, then: I reckon we'll need to revisit the scene of the discovery."

Huck and Becky nodded affirmatively in support.

"Becky, after the village buried Injun Joe's body, did your dad ever seal the cave back up again?" Tom asked curiously.

"No, Tom, he didn't," Becky answered. "Even though it scared him that people might continue to get lost in there, he was even more frightened by the idea of accidentally locking someone in there again. To the best of my knowledge, he left the cave open."

"Well, that's certainly good to hear," Tom said, sounding relieved. He then looked directly at Amy. "Do you want to come with us?"

Amy's eyes flashed back and forth between her friends, like an indecisive customer at the general store. "What makes you believe there's any good reason to go back into that cursed cave? Still creeps me out to think that old Joe's soul might be haunting those endless caverns."

Huck, never one to get the heebie jeebies over the undead, sided with Tom in a heartbeat. "A pirate never buries his booty in the same place twice, Amy. Why, I'd reckon that even the great Buccaneer Blake himself couldn't resist hiding a little of his loot here in America. And no curse, ghost, or adult's warnings would ever keep me away from that place," Huck vowed mightily.

"Well, if we're going to look for the chest inside the cave, then it couldn't hurt to bring some tools along, just in case," Becky suggested.

"Amy, think we could borrow some supplies from your brother?" Tom inquired.

"Of course, Tom," Amy answered, rather puzzled.

"Well, could you trouble him for a rucksack with a couple coils of rope? It's been a few years since we've gone in there, and there ain't no telling what's happened inside that old cave."

Amy seemed more than willing to accommodate such a

request. "Just try to make sure you bring them back; my brother ain't Saint Nicholas, you know."

Tom agreed and nodded. "Huck, you bring your fishing pole; you never know when you might need it," he told Huck, before addressing his girlfriend. "Becky, do you have any yarn?"

She groaned, as though conjuring up the memory of an annoying former suitor. "Plenty of it; in fact, Papa makes me knit, sew, and crochet every single day! He thinks that that's what proper young ladies ought to do," Becky replied sarcastically, drawing laughter from the other kids. "But I usually just tie knots in the string to pass the time, mostly because I've never had any skill at any of those things."

"But how much yarn do you have exactly?" Tom asked.

"Oh, I'd estimate about 20 to 30 skeins," Becky guessed. "It's a real problem."

"Well, for the purpose of this expedition, I think we'll need you to just bring two," Tom decided.

"AWWWW, why can't I just bring them all? I'd really like to dispose of them somewhere my dad would never find them," Becky protested.

Tom chuckled to himself. Becky was really cute when she got annoyed.

"Well, bring two. I'll help you get rid of the others later," Tom decided, trying not to laugh. "And I shall bring flint, steel, a lantern, and of course, my brain."

And now, each with a task, the four friends began the short walk back into town. An exciting adventure awaited!

CHAPTER 3

REVENGE IS BEST SERVED
COLD...AND WET

The very next day, they began the short trek out to McDougal's cave. Each brought the items Tom had asked for. Tom had his flint, steel, and a lantern. Amy shouldered a leather backpack bearing a couple coils of rope. Huck carried his fishing pole over his shoulder. And Becky showed up to the location pushing an entire wheelbarrow full of colorful skeins of yarn!

"Woah, you weren't kidding about how much yarn you have," Tom joked in astonishment.

"I told you it was a real problem," Becky reiterated.

"I still don't get how you got me to come along," Amy interrupted, looking somewhat puzzled. "I thought you two got lost in this cave a while ago."

"Remember?" Huck reminded. "We need that treasure chest."

"True," Amy admitted. "Maybe we'll finally figure out whose treasure it was."

Not long after, the four approached the dark entrance of the cave. The ominous darkness inside whispered of potential danger, but also seemed to call out with a voice of hope and excitement. Needless to say, the balance between light and dark only strengthened Tom's thirst for adventure. That the journey was filled with almost certain danger mattered not one whit. Might even have made it a bit more exciting.

At the entrance, Tom called out to the others to join him. He needed to explain his strategy before they went in. However, before he could start, Becky whirled around and began pushing the wheelbarrow towards a nearby, small side-channel of the Mississippi River.

"Where are you going?" they called to her. All three were perplexed. But their questions were soon answered.

As they watched, Becky proceeded to dump the entire contents of her wheelbarrow into the river! Dancing with glee, she watched as the slow current carried away the burdensome string. No more sewing, no more knitting, and no more crocheting. She was free. She dusted her pale hands together in triumph. It was a job well done.

"NO!" Tom cried. "We need those!"

In his haste to save the yarn, Tom almost jumped into the river. But Becky quickly stopped him and revealed two skeins of blue yarn she had taken from the wheelbarrow and hidden under her skirt.

Once Tom understood that Becky had salvaged his plan, his labored, panicked breathing began to slow. Soon, laughter took its place.

"That sure was funny, Becky," Amy chuckled, "But you should have let him jump in the river."

Becky giggled, gave Amy a wink, and then held out her hand

to Tom, who graciously reached for her. Quick as a bunny, Becky gave Tom a giant shove, and into the river he went! He surfaced about ten feet away and grinned good naturedly at Becky, who winked again at Amy. At once, Amy whipped around and pushed Huck into the river as well! Finally, without any fanfare, Becky then pushed Amy into the water! Laughing out loud, Becky quickly pulled off her overdress and jumped in herself! "Now we're all soaked!" she cheered triumphantly.

"It's a good thing, because we've got ourselves a score to settle with you!" Amy laughed, as she started splashing Becky.

Huck and Tom joined the water fight quickly. With Becky distracted by Amy, Tom saw a perfect opportunity for revenge. He quickly took a deep breath and dove underwater. Silently, he swam under the surface of the river. With a strong, powerful kick, he surfaced directly behind Becky, picked her up, and swung her off her feet. Huck immediately followed suit and grabbed Amy.

Assuming a pose of great relaxation, the girls crossed their ankles and folded their arms behind their heads. But Tom and Huck had other plans for the girls. Nodding at each other, Tom and Huck then heaved the girls into the cold water, face first. While the girls flailed, both boys hurried out of the water onto the bank, out of reach of the girls, expecting the worst. But when Becky and Amy resurfaced, they were both laughing. In time, the girls also climbed up the riverbank to join the boys on the soft grass. Then, they all laid down on their backs to dry off in the warm breeze.

It was going to be a great afternoon.

CHAPTER 4

INTO THE DARKNESS

When everyone's damp clothes had mostly dried, Tom called the others together. In unison, they approached the entrance of the cave. When they were just outside the cave's opening, Tom asked Becky to tie one end of her yarn to a bare branch of a nearby hazelnut bush. She did so, and then rejoined the group, where Tom was explaining his plan. "You see, we're going to walk into the cave carrying the yarn with us. As it unwinds, it will create a trail in the cave. Then, when we find the treasure chest, we can use the yarn to retrace our path out of the cave. There's no way we can get lost again. I read about this in a Greek myth once. I believe the guy's name was...um...like... Odysseus or Priebius or something."

"Theseus," Becky corrected. "And now this plan actually makes some sense; I've got to give you creative credit for thinking it up."

"Thought you weren't really the kind of kid who read a lot of books," Huck remarked to Tom.

"I actually don't mind story books that much," Tom explained. "And I like books with pictures."

With his prior experience in McDougal's Cave, Tom knew that candles weren't always the best source of light; caves could be windy, which could blow out the flames. Nevertheless, the cave would be dark as pitch, and Tom knew they were going to need extra light. Earlier that morning, he had "borrowed" an old, brass kerosene lantern from Aunt Polly's shed. Now, at the entrance of the cave, he took out his flint and steel and sparked up the lantern.

Tom trekked into the cave first, leading the way. Amy and Huck followed, and Becky entered last, carrying the yarn in her hands, and keeping an eye on their surroundings as the skein quietly unraveled.

"What an awfully nice place this is," Amy commented genuinely. "It's so calm and peaceful in here."

"That's not quite the way I remember it from the last time I was here," Becky quipped uneasily, as she made her way carefully along the side of the cave. "It's nice to explore in here as a group, but it isn't much of a party when you can't find your way out."

As the light from the entrance shrank and eventually disappeared, the group entered a room that was covered from floor to ceiling with beautiful stalactites and stalagmites. The long mineral formations were situated among a number of shallow pools of water that danced in the light of the lantern. The farther in they went, the quieter the cave became. It was eerie. The only sound was the distant plop of water falling from the ceiling, hitting the pools beneath. Slight though the sound was, it reverberated down the corridor of blackness.

"Now stay close, everyone," Tom ordered, looking back at the others.

"TOM!" Becky shouted, "LOOK OUT!"

Immediately, Tom dug his feet into the dusty, slippery floor of the cave and came to a complete, abrupt stop. He tried to keep his balance, but his body swayed and tilted forward, and his arms windmilled as he found himself staring over the edge of a long drop-off! He could hear a few loose pebbles bounce past his feet; he was going to fall! And then he felt Huck grab the back of his overalls and pull him to safety.

That was close. Too close. Tom took a series of deep, startled breaths as he watched the rocks fall and disappear into the dark abyss.

"How far down do you reckon it is, Tom?" Becky asked, now holding tightly onto Tom. Their expedition had just begun, and already, she had almost lost him.

Tom shook his head and considered Becky's question. "From the looks of it, I reckon it's a long way down. Thanks for the warning, Becky."

After that incident, the four of them paid more careful attention to the paths they chose. As they began to hike out of the room, Tom noticed something important. He opened the door of the lantern and blew out the flame, plunging the room into total darkness. Unfortunately, Huck hadn't been prepared for the sudden loss of light and promptly bumped into a wall.

"Oof! How about giving me a little more warning next time?" he asked Tom, rubbing his nose in pain.

Tom quietly told everyone to look up at the ceiling. Hanging from the roof of the cave were hundreds of shadowy creatures with red eyes. They were watching the kids' every move. It took a while to figure out what exactly they were looking at, but Huck and Amy gasped when they realized that they were standing under a huge colony of bats!

CHAPTER 5

TOO FAR OUT OF REACH

While lost in the cave several years back, Tom and Becky had run into these same bats. It didn't end well. Armed with only a couple of small candles, Becky and Tom had to fight off the entire colony. Tom didn't want to relive that traumatic event. Hastily, he told everyone to follow him out of the room as he felt his way along the cave walls. Everyone stayed as quiet as possible. No one wanted to "disturb the residents." Once they were clear of the room, Tom produced the lantern once again and relit it.

For Huck and Amy, this trip felt like a grand new adventure, but for Becky and Tom, it felt like terrible déjà vu. Six years ago, both of them had spent a lot of time lost in the cave. It had taken them both more than a week to recover after they were rescued.

"Guys, we've got ourselves a bit of a problem," Tom announced. "The path splits up ahead."

"Huh? What do you mean?" Amy asked, confused, squinting into the darkness.

Sure enough, further ahead were three different doorway-like openings. The treasure chest they were hunting was surely through one of the openings; the problem was, which one? They had to choose carefully. For all they knew, one of the paths ended in another treacherous drop-off. With only one source of light, splitting up was out of the question.

"There's gotta be an easy way to figure this out," Tom mused. "We must have left behind some clue the last time we got stuck here."

One by one, taking turns with the lantern, each began examining the different openings. And one by one, each had a theory why a certain opening was the right one.

Eventually though, Becky gave a whistle. "Come on everyone! We should go this way!"

"How can you be sure?" Huck asked.

She confidently motioned for the others to walk ahead of her. "Trust me, let's just say I've got a good feeling about this."

As they passed through the threshold of the opening on the far right, Becky nudged Tom. Curious, Tom held up the lantern and peered up and down the cave wall where Becky was gesturing. What he saw brought a smile to his face, and a warm memory of the last time they had been there.

Tom Sawyer
+
Becky Thatcher

While they had been lost, Tom and Becky had found themselves growing steadily hungry and hungrier. Tom had shared a piece of cake with Becky that he had saved from a picnic. They had adorably agreed that it would be their wedding cake for when they got married in the future. He had drawn the heart and scraped the message into the cave wall to commemorate his first girlfriend.

Now, here he was, back in the cave with that same girlfriend. He gave Becky's warm hand a quick squeeze.

At this point, the first skein of blue yarn ran out. Becky hurriedly pulled out the second skein. A quick and secure knot attached the two bundles of string together. The daring quest resumed. Eventually, the teens made it to a room that shined mysteriously brightly from within with golden light. They entered the room through a stone archway. A dark cross had been engraved upon the keystone. The village had carved it into the archway as a grave marker for Injun Joe.

As the four made their way inside, they realized that the light was emanating from a hole high in the cavernous ceiling. Beautiful sunlight streamed around them. Becky, Tom, Huck, and Amy proceeded into the enormous room. To get to the opposite wall, they had to traverse a narrow, stone walkway. As they crossed upon the stone bridge, each wore a look of great expectation.

But danger still lurked. The last to cross the bridge, Becky accidentally tripped over a loose stone. As she caught herself, she dropped the skein of yarn! Over the edge it rolled. Four pairs of panicked eyes followed it in despair as it eventually disappeared from view! "Oh no!" Becky exclaimed. "How are we supposed to find our way out of this place now?" she asked dejectedly and started to sniff.

Tom knew that even with the benefit of natural sunlight, they would be very unlikely to find the yarn in the depths of the cave. But he knew that was not what Becky needed to hear at that moment. Instead, he put his hand on her shoulder. "Don't worry, Becky. We'll find another way to get out of here. I'm sure of it."

Becky couldn't help but smile at Tom's tenderness and his kind heart. As Tom reached for her hand, Becky gladly offered it to him. The four of them continued on, exploring deeper and deeper into the chamber.

The walkway led to the far side of the cave. But just as they were about to reach the cave wall, they came to a gaping hole where the walkway had broken apart. Huck, Amy, and Becky turned to Tom. Whatever were they going to do? How were they supposed to cross the enormous gap? Was their quest over already?

CHAPTER 6

PRANKS AND PRATFALLS

"Uh, Tom, when did that happen? Huck asked, scratching his head in astonishment at the huge hole. "I don't remember anything wrong with that path when we came here last time."

"I don't know, Huck, but we'll need to find a way across," Tom decided.

The four of them began throwing possible solutions out, each option more perilous than the last. Amy suggested a bridge made out of all the spare yarn Becky had brought in the wheelbarrow, only to remember that the river had probably washed it a great distance away by now. No one mentioned that a bridge built of yarn would never work. Huck stupidly suggested that he and Tom fling one of the girls across the gap, which only resulted in screams of fear and verbal scolding from both Becky and Amy. These, and other ridiculous notions, were shared amongst the group, delaying the needed continuation of their journey.

Slowly, Tom walked to the edge of the very narrow path and looked across the gorge. He shook his head. The dangerous gap spanned about ten feet across and dropped 50 feet down into the darkness. Even with youth on their side, they would be unable to jump over the chasm; and if they fell, well...Tom shuddered to think what would happen.

However, Becky happened to glance upwards, at the ceiling, and immediately saw their answer. The 25-foot-high ceiling had a long section of horizontal stalactite bars, stretching out from end to end. They extended far past where the broken edge of the walking path was.

"Everyone, look!" she called excitedly, pointing at the roof of the cave. "I'll bet that if we can secure a rope to those bars on the ceiling, we could swing over to the other side."

Looking up at the strange formations, considering, Huck eventually asked, "But do you think that it'll work?" His tone was skeptical. "I don't know much about rocks and caves, but I reckon those bars might not be sturdy enough to hold our weight."

"I reckon it could work," Tom guessed. "It'd be just like a tree swing."

"And besides," Becky added, "it isn't like we're going to put all of our combined weights on the rope at the same time; we'd cross over one by one."

"We're forgetting something, though: How are we supposed to get the rope up there?" Amy asked, throwing her two cents into the matter.

"I have an idea," Tom offered. "Amy, can I have one of the coils of rope?"

Amy, who was carrying the backpack, took it off her shoulder and set it down. Opening it, she took a coil of rope out and handed it to Tom. The rope itself was about 50 feet long, strong, but not too thick. It would be just fine for the job. Taking the rope from Amy, Tom uncoiled it, tied a medium sized stone with a bit of weight into a loop at one end, and swung the rope in a circle at his side a few times to gain momentum. Then, he launched the knotted rock at the horizontal bars. Luckily, the rock flew over one of the bars. Trailing the rope behind, the stone then fell to the ground.

Huck stepped up to the rope, removed the stone, widened the loop, and tightened the knot in the rope more securely. Then, he pulled it over his head, shoulders, and arms, and sat down in the loop. "We have to test it to make sure that it can hold our weight," Huck decided aloud. "Tom, hoist me up!"

Tom cocked his head sideways, questioning the wisdom of Huck's decision, but did as his best friend asked. With the assistance of the girls, Tom slowly lifted Huck off the ground towards the ceiling. And then, all of a sudden, both the rope and Huck dropped to the ground! One moment Huck was comfortably rising in the air, the next moment he was sitting on the ground, rubbing his rear end. "What happened?" he asked, painfully puzzled.

Tom started laughing: He had intentionally let go of the rope.

Realizing what had happened, Huck pulled the rope off of himself and chased after Tom, vowing revenge. Still laughing, Tom escaped his every attack.

CHAPTER 7

CROSSING THE CHASM

Eventually, Amy stepped in and put an end to the raucous game of chase between Tom and Huck. She thought they were lucky neither one had fallen off the high, narrow path.

"Ok, you two, enough lollygagging; let's get across already before we run out of daylight," she commanded the two boys.

"Right then, ladies first!" instructed Tom, making a low bow, and motioning chivalrously to the awaiting end of the rope.

"Why thank you ever so much, kind sir!" Huck thanked Tom, in a strange imitation of a girl's voice, as he strutted up to the rope.

Tom grabbed the back of Huck's overall strap and pulled the jokester back to where he was standing, then motioned for one of the girls to go ahead of them.

Becky bravely volunteered to go first. She had a genius plan in mind. She pulled the back of her long skirt under the front and tucked it in her green sash in front. Additionally, she took the second coil of rope from Amy's backpack and looped it around her shoulder. Finally, she sat down on the rope loop where Huck had sat originally. Working together, the rest of them pulled her up to the cave ceiling.

No one even "joked" about letting go of the rope that time.

Once up at the top, Becky grabbed hold of the stalactite bar above her and called for Tom and the others to give her a little slack in the rope. With the rope holding her up slightly less so, she then swung from one stalactite bar to the next, like a determined kid on a pair of monkey bars. This plan was brilliant because it allowed Becky to move across the ceiling, but it still allowed the others to catch her with the rope had her grip on the bars failed. The others looked on from below, marveling at how agile and strong she was.

When Becky got to the middle of the bars, she put her legs over the bar in front of her and hung upside down by her legs, like a trapeze artist. Inverted, she dutifully tied one end of the spare rope she carried to the sturdy, horizontal bar and threw the free end back down to the others. Once Tom caught the loose rope, Becky yelled for him to anchor it down with his weight. With the knot tied correctly and securely to the stalactite bar, she slid down the rope, just like a fireman's pole, landing gently next to the others. She then pulled down the first rope and wound it up, putting it back in Amy's backpack. The others awarded the successful mission with applause and catcalls.

Next, Becky made a loop with the hanging end of the new rope and stood on it, easily swinging across the chasm to the other side. This new rope wasn't as long as the rope she had used to ascend to the ceiling, but it was sturdy and held her weight without fail. Quickly, she swung the rope loop back to the other side, where Amy grabbed it, stood on it, swung across, and swung the rope back to the boys. Soon, everyone had safely crossed over.

They left the makeshift rope swing on their side of the path, so they would have an easy way to return when they finished.

The four continued on their trek and eventually came to the spot where the treasure had been collected. There sat the old, wooden chest in the same dirt pit they had left it in. But once they got up close, they realized that the cave must now be under the Mississippi River, because the treasure chest now also sat smack in the middle of a shallow pool of water!

CHAPTER 8

CLIFFSIDE CHAOS

Considering that the Mississippi River most likely resided above their current position, the only reasonable conclusion they could come to was that the water had leaked into the cave through the soil around them. It was a wonder that the cave hadn't become totally flooded at some point. Wasting not a moment, Huck reached his rough hands into the cold, muddy water of the pool. But even though the chest contained absolutely no treasure, he couldn't lift it. "Tom, give me a hand, won't you?" he called.

Together, both boys quickly pulled the wooden chest out of the pit, draining the muddy water to reduce the weight. Finally, it was clear of the pool. Setting it on a dry slab of rock, they examined the chest from all angles. Eventually, Amy pointed to some obscure symbols carved in the wood on the back. As they crowded around the chest to look, no one spoke.

The first symbol was a skull and crossbones. It was the Jolly Roger pirate flag. However, the chest also bore a second symbol, one that looked like a compass rose, but instead of intersecting arrows, there were intersecting cutlasses.

For a long moment, they all looked at the symbols. No one knew what to make of them.

Becky's congratulatory voice broke the silence, "Great job, guys! Once we take it home, we'll hopefully be able to figure out who owned the treasure you guys found."

And all at once, it dawned on them that they had really done it: They had found the chest! Their adventure had been worth it. Flushed with excitement, they quickly began the long trek out of the cave. Without the treasure inside, the chest proved far easier for Tom and Huck to carry. Still, its great size made the chest rather unwieldy. Several times, Tom and Huck had to strategically maneuver through the narrow passageways as Becky carried the lantern for them in front.

Getting into the cave had been easy; finding their way out would prove a bit more difficult. Along the way, they accidentally took a couple of wrong turns. Their return expedition led them through a forest of tall, thick stalagmites they couldn't see over or around easily. Eventually, disorientation and panic began to set in among the explorers as they engaged in the lengthy process of navigating through to the other side.

After perhaps 20 minutes, the group found their way to the other side of the columns, onto a large, flat drop-off overlooking the lower levels of the cave below them. This wasn't their intended destination, but at least they had a chance to pause and catch their breath. While pondering their next steps, something bright caught Tom's eye far below him. Puzzled, he walked closer to the edge. "Well, wouldn't you know," he said, almost to himself. Then louder, "Hey guys! Would you look at that?"

Everyone glanced at where Tom was pointing. There, lying

far below the drop-off, and across from a small, rushing river, sat the blue skein of yarn that Becky had dropped!

"How about that?" Huck remarked humorously. "It landed in the exact same place that we were headed. And it looks like we found it just in the nick of time too."

Excited as they were at the discovery, everybody knew that the yarn lay way beyond their reach, and that the climb down the ledge would be very difficult, if not impossible, even for experienced outdoorsmen like Tom and Huck.

"We're gonna need a way to get the yarn back," Tom solemnly realized. "This cave is like a labyrinth, and I know that without the yarn, we'll never get out of here."

Huck tapped Tom on the shoulder as he looked over the ledge again. "I guess that's what friends are for, then," he replied, as he whipped his trusty fishing pole from its perch on his shoulder. Quickly casting the fishing line forward, he lowered the fishing hook down the side of the rock face, swinging it in desperate hope for a catch. Unfortunately, the yarn still sat about 20 feet out of reach. "Shoot!" Huck muttered grimly. "I knew I should have wound myself a little bit of extra string on the spool this time!"

Pondering various solutions to this problem, Amy eventually stepped forward from the rest of the group. "I'll go and get it," she resolutely declared to the others, who watched her traverse to the edge of the drop-off. Taking off the backpack and retrieving the longer coil of rope, she tied one end around her waistline and tossed the loose end to the others.

"Naw, Amy, don't do this. It ain't worth it," Huck pleaded, attempting to dissuade her from this dangerous task.

Amy, on the other hand, wouldn't take no for an answer. "Then what do you propose? That we stick around in this cave until we meet the same fate as Injun Joe?" she snapped in an unusually frustrated tone. "Tom and Becky already proved that this cave is impossible to escape from without some help. Besides, nobody knows that we're in here, Huck."

Amy knew what Tom was about to say, and she swiftly beat him to it. "And no, Tom, that lantern's only got a small amount of oil, surely not enough to last more than a day."

"But you could get stuck down there, or worse, get swept away by the river!" Huck objected persistently.

"Well, I gotta trust that ya'll will keep that from happening," Amy reasoned calmly, shrugging her shoulders.

Not many things could make Huck shed a tear; he had seen too many horrible things. But what scared him more than anything was the prospect of losing the girl he loved and cared for with all his heart. He walked up and gave Amy a hug. "You can count on us, but you take care of yourself, and don't you take so many risks," he warned her.

"Wouldn't dream of it," she replied, smiling, walking over to the edge, as she began the slow task of rappelling down the side of the rough rock face.

With Tom and Huck supporting her weight, and Becky guiding the rope over the edge, Amy soon made it to the bottom with no injuries, barring minor scrapes to her clothing. She hopped the narrow river quite easily, actually, and quickly retrieved the skein of yarn, tucking it safely into one of the deep pockets of her jumper. Then, she hopped the river once more and tugged on the rope, indicating a desire to ascend back up the rock face.

Though the trip up was only about 30 feet, being lifted up the cliff face proved a difficult challenge. Because of gravity, it is not hard to lower someone down the side of a cliff. But without a pulley system of some sort, pulling someone up a cliff is much more difficult. The three others had to work extra hard to lift Amy back up the face of the cliff. Helping her move from ledge to ledge on the way up, Tom and Huck dragged the rope back and forth along the sharp edge of the cliff. Initially unbeknownst to any of them, the sturdy rope had frayed and thinned. By the time Amy was halfway up, only two strands kept her from plummeting to the cave's floor!

Becky spotted the danger first. "Oh my gosh! Tom! Huck! Pull her up faster! FASTER!"

Not understanding her alarm, Tom and Huck nevertheless began heaving Amy up faster. Soon, she was only ten feet from the top.

With Becky pointing at the fraying rope, Tom and Huck finally understood. Amy was in great peril of falling from the cliff face to the river and rocks below! They heaved and pulled as hard as they could. With only six inches to go, Amy and the others let out a loud sigh of relief. She was so close they could . . .

SNAP!

And like that, the rope broke! Amy futilely tried to grab at the clifftop, and screamed at the top of her lungs, as her support dropped out from under her!

CHAPTER 9

A CRY FOR HELP?

Becky, who stood closest to the edge of the cliff, dove into the dirt near the edge. She barely caught Amy by her hand. As the two girls clung to each other, the rope loop fell off Amy's body down to the ground far below.

"PLEASE! PLEASE! DON'T LET ME GO!" Amy screamed and began to cry.

"I can't hold her much longer!" Becky called out.

Meanwhile, Tom and Huck had dropped their useless section of rope and flung themselves down next to Becky. Grabbing Amy firmly by her other hand, both boys began to pull her up. Slowly, her body slid up and back over the edge of the cliff.

Once on solid ground, Amy held onto Huck and began crying in earnest. It took a good ten minutes to console her, but once her emotions returned to normal, they all began once again on their journey out of the cave. Now, with the assistance of the yarn, they were able to find a clear path through the stalagmites and back out of the cave.

They soon came to the cavern with the huge broken gap in the walkway. Using the rope still tied to the stalactite bar on the ceiling, Tom swung over the broken pathway, onto the other side

of the ledge. He then threw the rope over to the others. Amy caught it and looped it tight around the body of the chest. She then swung the chest over to Tom, who quickly released it from the rope. Then, Tom threw the rope back on the other side so that Becky could swing over. After Becky, Huck generously let Amy swing over, and then he swung over himself.

"Well, so much for returning the ropes to your brother," Becky joked to Amy. "We've got one rope uselessly tied to the ceiling of the cave and another one that broke the first day we used it," she finished humorously.

"My brother has more," Amy reassured her. "And I don't think he needs to know what really happened back in there to me," she muttered.

"Agreed," Tom and Huck spoke in unison.

Quickly, they continued to make their way out of the cave, retracing the string through the various rooms, until, eventually, bright sunlight appeared around the corner!

They were out!

But just as the boys set down the chest, outside, in the sunlight, the quiet atmosphere was pierced by a sharp, blood-chilling scream!

CHAPTER 10

THE ENEMY EMERGES

Everyone froze, then looked around for the source of the terrifying noise. From where they stood, they couldn't see anything or anyone.

Afraid even to breathe, Tom was the first to notice the unnatural silence. It was deathly quiet. Normally, the outdoors was alive with the sound of bullfrogs and birds, the rustle of the trees, and the hum of bumblebees. But now, it was as silent outside as it had been inside the cave.

Then, the piercing shrieks rang out again, causing a flock of birds to burst into flight from a nearby tree. All of the teens looked at each other. Despite their fear, Tom and Huck each grabbed one end of the chest, and then, all four began running. They were moving so fast, that they weren't looking where they were going. Blindly, they crashed into the town sheriff!

Though they were just kids, the four of them running together had generated a huge momentum. The chest they were carrying was as forceful as a battering ram. In a great tangle, all five of them painfully crashed to the ground. Collecting their wits, and dusting themselves off, the four friends profusely apologized to the peacekeeper for not minding their surroundings. But boy, were they glad to see him.

"It's all right, kids, but you should have seen it! I almost caught the rascal; the slithery varmint was in my grasp," the sheriff bragged, making grabbing motions with his hands.

"Who?" everyone asked, completely baffled.

"Dead Eye Dan, that's who," said the sheriff.

At this, three of them paled and stuttered, "D-D-Dead Eye Dan?! Who's that?"

Huck's eyes, however, narrowed in understanding.

"He's a notorious criminal," the sheriff explained. "He's currently wanted in five states for forgery, fraud, theft, burglary, extortion, murder, kidnapping, and impersonating a girl."

Tom, Becky, and Amy laughed nervously. They couldn't imagine a famous criminal wearing a dress. Even the sheriff chuckled softly!

Not Huck. Huck knew that Dan would do whatever it took to stay one step ahead of the law. His rotten father had once partnered with Dead Eye Dan, so Huck was familiar with the man. Huck's father was nasty, but even he had certain standards. Dead Eye Dan had no standards. There was nothing he wouldn't do. He was as vicious as they came.

The sheriff, knocking the dust from his hat, began speaking again, "And now, I've got no blasted idea where the snake even went. I saw him run right through the women's meeting in the park back there, but I lost him after that. He's as good as gone now. Dan's the most cunning criminal I've ever had to bring to justice."

Amy's mind flashed back to the frightening screams. She

asked, "Then who was that person screaming? Could it have been one of Dan's victims?"

"Actually," the sheriff muttered, embarrassed, "those screams came from my wife. She's supposed to be a fearless frontiersman's wife, and yet she became terrified when a colony of perfectly harmless ants showed up at her picnic today. That's why she screamed – ants."

"Well, that's really interesting," Tom remarked, looking up at the setting sun. "But we really should be getting home; our parents may be wondering where we've disappeared off to. Thanks for the warning, sir."

"Don't mention it! And make sure to always watch your backs! Dan could be lurking anywhere around here!" the sheriff advised.

Saying goodbye, the four of them picked up the chest and left.

As the late afternoon began to settle into evening, the forest began to darken. Though the almost-summer sun was still out, its light barely pierced the dense foliage of the treetops. Lost in their thoughts, the four teenagers journeyed home, shuffling along the dusty forest floor. Their intent was to take the chest to the local librarian tomorrow. She might be able to offer new insights on the chest's origins.

As they walked through the dimly lit forest, Huck's eyes cast from side to side, Dead Eye Dan on his mind. Suddenly, he noticed something, some creature, glaring at him through the underbrush. "Tom, look over there," Huck spoke quietly, nodding to a nearby bush.

Mirroring Huck, Tom peered into the foliage, where Huck had motioned at, but he didn't see anything.

"Tom, no, no, over there. Look over there!" Huck exclaimed again, this time pointing to another bush.

But once again, when Tom turned his head, he saw nothing.

Now, Amy began to get scared. "Is...is...that you, D...D... Dan?" she asked in a quivery voice.

"Don't be ridiculous, Amy," Tom said. "There's no chance or reason why Dead Eye Dan would come after **US**."

"Tom, look over there!" Huck shouted, motioning to yet another bush.

This time, though, Tom and the others whipped around in time to see what had caught Huck's attention.

It was a pair of bright, red eyes!

CHAPTER 11

FALSE ALARM

Amy screamed at the red eyes, which promptly vanished into the bush, only to quickly reappear in an adjacent bush, and then in another bush, and another bush.

"What do you suppose those are?" Huck asked, feeling rather perplexed. "Demons?"

"I don't think so, Huck; but something doesn't seem right about this," Tom responded.

Finally, Becky had had enough. "All right, everyone, the next pair of eyes you see, I want you to jump on them," she ordered fearlessly. "We're not going down without a fight!"

Almost immediately, the bush across from them shook a bit and then lit up once more. With that, the teens dropped the chest, sprinted over, and, with a wild shout, leapt mightily upon the bush together.

"Ow!" came a whiny voice from the bushes.

All immediately recognized it.

"Sid?!" They shouted in unison. Pushing aside the undergrowth, they revealed none other than Tom's annoying little brother. "What are you doing out in the woods like this?"

Sid smirked, satisfied with achieving his goal of completely scaring the living daylights out of the four friends. "That's for getting me in trouble with Mr. Dobbins, Tom," he sneered. In his hands, he held a Leyden jar (an old-fashioned battery), a few long strands of insulated wire, and several medium-sized, red light bulbs. By connecting one of the wires to the jar, the red-light bulbs, which looked eerily like red, glowing eyes, lit up in the bush next to them. "I had to borrow some of Mr. Dobbins's science equipment, but it was worth it to see the looks on your faces," Sid mocked, beginning to laugh at their expense.

Tom was angry. Just because some bad blood existed between him and his brother, it didn't give Sid the right to terrorize Huck, Amy, and Becky. Tom let loose with a mighty shout, and with a chop of his hand, he knocked the Leyden jar out of his brother's grasp. Then, Tom nodded at his friends. As soon as they got Tom's signal, they all leapt upon Sid, tumbling furiously around the forest floor.

The loud ruckus they were creating caused great dust plumes to rise high into the air. In fact, so thick were the plumes, they could be seen all the way from the village. From that distance, the plumes of dust strongly resembled enormous pillars of smoke. Thinking that a fire had sparked in the forest, the villagers quickly sent out the local volunteer firefighters to put it out. But upon reaching the forest, all the firefighters found was Sid in tatters, covered from head to toe with bruises, lying prone on the forest floor.

CHAPTER 12

A LEGEND DISCOVERED

Disgusted with Sid, the four friends had left him on the forest floor and continued on their journey back to the village, carrying the empty, wooden chest.

"You know what, Becky?" Tom proposed enthusiastically. "I don't know what this chest will show, but I wouldn't be surprised if there were more treasure out there waiting for us."

Becky rolled her eyes. "Oh Tom, really?" she asked caustically. "Do try to be sensible. What would you even do with the treasure? You're probably already richer than most kids your age. What exactly do you think will happen when we learn where this chest came from?"

"Actually, there's a lot of interesting information and history about this chest," announced Judge Thatcher.

It was the very next day, and the children found themselves busy at the local library, accompanied by Becky's father, Judge Thatcher. As planned, they had carried the old chest with them into the building, so as to be able to study the exact symbols, instead of just remembering what they looked like.

Having received assistance in locating a historical textbook from the librarian, Judge Thatcher had seated himself amongst the kids at a sturdy, wooden study table and had begun to peruse the worn, thin pages. A good hour later, he turned to a page that displayed an illustration that matched the symbols on the chest perfectly.

"Aha! On page 135, it states that these pirate symbols have close ties to the infamous pirate, Red Beard. According to legend, this swashbuckling scallywag looted ships and nations all over the world. It is estimated that he stashed treasure in over 50 different places worldwide."

At this news, Becky, Amy, Tom, and Huck gasped sharply. The judge thought for sure that his daughter was going to faint. Of course, she wasn't; she was completely healthy.

Nevertheless, Judge Thatcher hastily ran out of the library to get smelling salts, a pillow, and a glass of water for his "frail" child. While he was gone, the foursome returned the book to the proper shelf, thanked the librarian who had helped them out, and left the library with the chest. Tom was sufficiently excited about the possibility of new treasure that he couldn't help but smile ecstatically in that moment. However, he made Huck promise not to just hand over his portion to Judge Thatcher ever again. Huck agreed, but he swore to himself that, no matter what happened, he would never ever trade in the life he had now. Not even for more treasure.

CHAPTER 13

GARDENING IS BETTER THAN PAINTING

Two days later, as the sun continued to shine down brightly, and the weather grew rather warm, it seemed yet again to be an excellent day to go fishing. That morning, Becky, Amy, and Huck gathered just outside the front gate of Tom's house, waiting for their fearless leader to come out and go fishing with them.

Now, because it was Saturday, Tom wasn't quite up. Even with legitimately important investments of time, like school, he rarely woke up early. But on weekends, he had a reputation for staying up very late and sleeping in extra late.

It was around 11:30 AM when Tom actually did wake up and remember his fun plans for that day. Hopefully, he and his friends would beat the local fishermen to the lake and actually bring home something besides disappointment. He quickly got dressed and fixed his hair, making sure he didn't look too unkempt: Becky was going to be there. Then, he sped through breakfast. After a very quick repast, Tom grabbed his fishing pole and bolted towards the open front door.

Unfortunately, Sid had witnessed the quick breakfast AND the fishing pole. Being the irritating tattletale that he was, he screamed at the top of his lungs, "AUNT POLLY! Doesn't Tom have chores to do?!"

Sid's whiny yelling carried through the house, all the way to the front porch, where Aunt Polly sat reclining in a comfortable, wooden rocking chair, reading a book.

"Tom, just hold on for one minute, now," she commanded, halting his sneaky escape out the door. Deliberately, she bookmarked the page she had just read and set the book down on the table next to her.

"Sid, why can't you keep your unhelpful mouth shut for once?" Tom thought angrily to himself. Needless to say, Tom wasn't excited for what was about to happen. His biggest fear was that he would be asked to whitewash the long, white fence around his house. Again. That would leave him almost no time for his friends.

It had become a familiar pattern over the last few years. Sid would snitch, and Tom would have to endure the tedious work of repainting the fence, while Sid made a big show in front of Tom about how relaxed he was. It happened every few months. Sure, painting may not seem like much of a chore, but painting 30 yards of high board fence, with at least two solid coats, out in the hot sun, would reduce anyone to a bitter mess. And besides, Tom no longer had the luxury of gullible friends to trick into doing the work for him, not since the last time he had tried that clever scheme.

Just as he feared, Aunt Polly stood up from her chair and grabbed a bucket of whitewash and a long paintbrush off the porch floor. "Tom, before you leave, you do have a chore to do," she announced.

By now, Sid was standing outside, waiting to watch his older brother get what he deserved, and smiling with great satisfaction for doing his part at being the perpetual thorn in Tom's side.

Tom cursed his bad luck, under his breath of course, so as not to give Aunt Polly a heart attack. "Whitewashing again?" he asked, motioning to the familiar equipment in his aunt's hands. Tom was beyond annoyed that Sid had gotten him into trouble… **AGAIN**. "Aunt Polly, if this house were any whiter, the president would probably live here."

"Actually, I thought today it would be more appropriate for Sid to start doing that job," Aunt Polly replied, handing Sid the paint and the paintbrush.

Sid's eyes instantly widened in shock. What had happened? His plan had backfired! Immediately, he began complaining.

If ever there were a day that Tom was extra thankful to God, that day was today. "Well, shucks, Aunt Polly, I'm awful glad to hear that," Tom responded, more than a little relieved. "But wait, if Sid's painting the fence today, then what did you need me for?"

"Well, I wanted you to plant these," Aunt Polly explained, producing a packet of flower seeds from her apron pocket. "I found them in the cellar this morning, and I think they'll make the garden look so beautiful."

"Yeah," Tom sighed apathetically. Then he asked, "How come you've never planted them yourself?"

"Well, as I said, I found them just today; if that's too much of a bother, you can work with Sid on whitewashing the fence," Aunt Polly offered cheekily. "I'm sure I can find another paintbrush around this house, and I'd reckon your brother wouldn't mind having an extra set of hands to share the work with him."

With that, Tom's attitude straightened out quickly. "You really don't play fair," he grumbled, taking the seeds from her hand.

Aunt Polly chuckled as she settled herself back into her chair and reached for her book.

CHAPTER 14

A HIDDEN SURPRISE

After Aunt Polly disappeared to complete her Saturday errands, and Sid had started grumpily painting the fence, Tom kicked off his shoes and grabbed a small hand shovel and a tin watering can.

Outside, to avoid being confronted by Sid, Tom's friends walked quietly through the gate to where Tom was getting ready to start planting.

"Hey, Tom? What on earth are you doing? Are we going fishing or what?" Amy impatiently asked him.

"I'm sorry, Amy, but Aunt Polly had other plans for the start of my exciting summer weekend," Tom dully responded, holding up the packet of seeds and slowly waving them.

Huck peered at the faded label on the front of the seed packet, examining the flower illustration. "Sunflowers? I would have preferred a nice patch of roses myself," Huck admitted, trying to sympathize with Tom.

"That, or a plant that bears fruit I can eat," Tom agreed, cheering up. "But this was all Aunt Polly had."

"Well, maybe we could help you," Becky suggested. "I'm sure

that we could get it done in no time; I have some experience with horticulture, after all."

Tom loved his three closest friends; not only were they heaps of fun to hang out with, but, when they could, they would always offer to help him with the tasks he didn't like and share the unpleasantness.

"That's mighty kind of you," he said gratefully, taking a moment to mentally divide the tasks. "Amy, do you think that you could loosen up the dirt?"

"Well, alright," she responded casually, kicking off her shoes. "I kinda enjoy getting dirty."

"I'll dig the holes," Tom announced, indicating his task by motioning to the small trowel in his hands. "Becky, would you do the job of planting the seeds?"

"I suppose I can do that," Becky surmised, taking the packet of seeds from Tom.

"Huck, can you cover the seeds again with the soil we'll dig up?" Tom inquired.

"Sure," he replied, setting down his fishing pole on the ground where it wouldn't get in their way.

"Oh, one more thing, Amy. Since you'll be done first, can I bother you to water the seeds?" Tom questioned, lifting up the watering can.

Once again, Amy agreed to Tom's request.

Amy started turning up the ground with her bare feet to soften up the soil for planting, acting the role of a human plow. She was soon shadowed by Tom, who used his trowel to excavate small mounds of dirt and make holes deep enough for the seeds to take good root. Becky followed after, depositing a small seed in each hole, while Huck replaced the dirt. With the first part of her job completed, Amy soon followed with the watering can after her boyfriend, making sure that all the seeds got just enough water to thrive in their new habitat.

As Tom dug the final hole, his trowel scraped against something hard hidden in the dirt! Everybody heard the sound. In an instant, there were four curious heads peering down into the turned earth.

No one was prepared for what they had just discovered!

CHAPTER 15

AN EXCITING ESCAPADE

"What in the world was that?" Huck asked, confused.

"Probably a rock or something," Tom guessed, shrugging his shoulders, but still peering at the soil.

Becky shook her head, disagreeing with Tom's analysis. "That didn't sound like a rock, Tom: Rocks aren't hollow."

With a couple of careful digs of his trowel, Tom began unearthing the mysterious object. In the hole he had created, there appeared to be a faded wooden board hidden beneath the dirt. He dug around deeper and loosened the unknown object in the soil. Lifting the item free, what appeared to be an old, wooden chest with rusty steel handles emerged.

"It looks like...a chest," Becky gasped. "Another chest!"

"Yeah," Tom spoke up. "It does look like a chest, or like some sort of...containment device," Tom declared, not really knowing what a containment device was.

"Like I said, a chest," Becky reminded him rather sharply, not impressed with his attempt to sound smarter.

They all took the time to examine the container more closely.

"Huh, I wonder what could be inside?" Huck asked rather

dumbly, making everyone wonder whether or not he was being serious.

"That's what we all want to know, silly," Amy joked, poking Huck in the stomach.

Tom looked at the front of the chest, staring at the old, rusty padlock which guarded the mystery contents inside. The lock looked almost as old as the chest, possibly even older. A generation spent in the moist soil had worn down the lock's metal exterior - and likely its internal structure and sturdiness.

Amy picked up on this. "The lock doesn't look very strong anymore; heck, I think I could even break it off," she said.

With that, she picked up the small shovel that Tom had been digging with and brought it down, at a sharp angle, onto the padlock. The padlock broke easily, almost as though it had been made of dust.

After removing the lock, the four tried opening the lid of the chest, but they found that they couldn't lift it. A further inspection revealed that the lid of the chest had actually been nailed shut!

"Wow," Huck marveled. "I reckon that there ought to be something important inside if the security is this tight."

Without saying anything, Tom sprinted back to the house and soon returned carrying a long, sharp axe. "All right, everyone! You might want to take a step back!" he warned. Then, with all his strength, he brought the sharp blade of the axe down onto the lid of the chest. The aged wood splintered upon impact.

In his excitement, Tom hadn't thought about what was inside the chest or if it was fragile. It would have been most unfortunate if the chest had been filled with crystal wine glasses or porcelain dinner plates.

They all looked eagerly into the chest. But their eagerness soon turned to disappointment: The only object residing in the chest was a rolled-up fragment of paper. Huck pulled it out and gazed at it with frustration.

"Tom, what a joke. I can't believe I got my hopes up for a stupid scroll," Huck groaned, as he prepared to throw it into the nearby bushes.

Amy rushed to stay Huck's hand. "Huck, are you crazy?! You haven't even read it. What if it's something important?"

Huck, reconsidering, handed it over.

Little did they know that the piece of parchment that Huck almost threw away would lead them on their greatest adventure yet!

Amy gently unrolled the paper to reveal a highly decorated surface. Tom and Huck's eyes widened as they looked upon the intricate markings.

"I . . . I can't believe I almost threw this away," Huck stuttered regretfully. "This here could be really valuable."

Tom just nodded, still staring at the parchment.

"Would someone mind explaining to me what this fancy piece of paper is?" Becky's voice broke through the boys' reverent stare.

"Yeah," put in Amy. "If it's not an ordinary scroll, I want to know what it is."

Tom rolled his eyes in exasperation. "First of all, I really can't think of a country that still uses scrolls anymore ever since we invented the book," he began, looking to Becky for support, which she gave with a slight nod of her head. "And second, this looks like a real copy of Red Beard's treasure map that will hopefully take us to the location of Red Beard's treasure!" Tom finished happily.

"How can you be so sure that it's Red Beard's map, Tom?" Amy prodded. "Surely there have been other pirates in history, right?"

All it took was for Tom to motion to the crude, scrawled images on the left side of the paper to put Amy's curiosity to rest. A familiar icon of the Jolly Roger sign paired with a cutlass compass rose reminded everyone of the chest they had recently retrieved.

"But I thought you guys already found Red Beard's treasure in McDougal's Cave," Becky pointed out. "And anyway, Thomas Sawyer, don't you already have enough treasure to last a lifetime?"

Tom felt a little embarrassed to have his full name used, especially by the girl that he was sweet on. "Oh, what's another half a million dollars or so?" he asked. "And anyway, what we found in the cave was probably only a portion of Red Beard's total treasure. You remember what your dad told us, right? Word says that Red Beard buried treasure in over 50 places worldwide!"

"I guess we could try and see where the map takes us, as long as it's fairly close by," Becky decided, before muttering under her breath, "It isn't like I could talk you out of it anyway."

"But I have a question," Huck spoke up. "Where does the map begin and end?"

Tom looked intently at the map in order to answer Huck's question. "From the looks of it, and the small fragments that

I remember from Mr. Dobbins's geography lessons, I'd reckon that we're looking at an outline of the upper part of the State of Missouri," Tom determined.

"That close to us?" Amy asked. "Seems mighty foolish to put too much of your treasure within such short distances of each other; I mean, you and Huck already pulled a fortune from McDougal's Cave. Why would Red Beard hide not just one but two treasure chests way up here in Missouri?"

"Well, don't forget, the treasure didn't really start out in the cave, Amy: Injun Joe moved it there from someplace else. In any case, even if the treasure's hiding spots were local to each other, Red Beard must have had a good reason for doing so," Tom solidly reasoned, and kept reading. "We can look into that later in the quest. In any case, the map doesn't really appear to have a starting point, but I can also make out an outline for what looks like Jackson's Island," Tom announced.

"Hey, you're right! That's the tiny island a few miles down the river from here where we stayed during that awful storm," Huck suddenly responded, reliving the terrible incident in his head. "And where does the map end?"

Tom looked high and low for an X on the map but couldn't seem to locate it. "I don't know, but it ain't here," Tom concluded. "The X might have faded away, or there could be more than one piece to this map - probably the latter, I suppose," he deduced, motioning to the torn, jagged edge on one side of the paper.

"Well then, why not try to find the other pieces of the map? We could go to Jackson's Island!" Huck suggested brilliantly.

"But do you think that we should leave St. Petersburg?" Amy questioned. "What with Dead Eye Dan on the loose?"

"Well, we haven't run into him yet, and besides, there's no good sense in just waiting around hoping the treasure will come to us," Becky enthused, getting caught up in the excitement. "After all, it is not in the stars to hold our destiny, but in ourselves!" she finished courageously.

Tom rolled his eyes. "You took that line from Shakespeare, didn't you?"

Becky found herself most impressed. "You've read his work?"

Tom shook his head. "Nope. All that Old English nonsense makes my head hurt. But that speech is too fancy, even for you. In any case, is everyone on board with Huck's plan?"

By the end of a few minutes' time discussing, everyone agreed to at least give the expedition a solid attempt.

"Oh, one last, big request," Tom added. "Amy, do you think that you could ask Andrew to build us a sturdy raft for the trip?"

"I'll definitely ask him, Tom. The chances are good that he'll want to accompany us on the journey," Amy responded cheerfully. "Hopefully we won't waste the raft like we wasted his ropes," she joked.

"Well, that'll be fine," Tom said, thinking. "We could always use an extra pair of hands to help us on the trip."

Eventually, they agreed to stage the trip in approximately three weeks' time.

They were headed down the Mississippi!

CHAPTER 16

TYING UP LOOSE ENDS

On the day of the trip, Tom didn't even bother to ask Aunt Polly's permission to go to Jackson's Island. If he did, Sid would find out, and that would be a problem. Besides, he knew she would say no. Too dangerous. While he liked that she cared about him, an inconceivably thrilling adventure like this only came around once in a lifetime. He couldn't afford any parental setbacks.

As the afternoon passed, and day turned into night, he mentally prepared himself for what awaited him outside the front door and down the river. He and his friends might discover treasure! Again! They would be legends. Their exploits would be recounted for generations to come. It would be great!

That night, time passed slowly for Tom as he lay in bed, waiting for the house to grow dark and silent. The wait gnawed at him like a dog on a bone as his sense of excitement grew. Around 2:00 AM, positive that everyone was fast asleep, Tom jumped softly out of bed, got dressed, and crept toward the front door. He kept to the shadows in a valiant attempt to remain unseen. Almost out the door, he remembered the picnic basket full of food he had put into the icebox earlier that day. After all, what's the point of an intrepid expedition without lunch? Aunt Polly rarely used the basket, so he figured she wouldn't miss it.

Turning around and walking away from the door, Tom was almost at the kitchen, when suddenly, he noticed an eerie shadow moving across the wall! Quickly, he backed away and retreated behind the doorway. His heart was pounding. Burglars? Demons?

"Darn!" He muttered to himself. It was neither burglars nor demons: It was Sid.

He dared a quick peek into the kitchen. Sure enough, it was his little brother. Tom had forgotten about Sid's regular late-night snack excursions. He could hear his kid brother mumbling to himself, while pulling open the cabinets, as he searched for a snack. With annoyance, Tom watched Sid pull **HIS** picnic basket from the icebox. Rats! That was supposed to be for him and his friends! As he watched, Sid began curiously rifling through the contents of the basket, surely wondering at the bounty he had lucked into.

"Argh," Tom mumbled quietly. The grand adventure was going to be over before it had even gotten started. Tom quickly made up his mind. There was no way he was going to let Sid work his way through the delicious contents of the picnic basket **HE** had packed. As his brother remained focused on the food, Tom crept into the kitchen, sticking to the shadows.

Sid was holding up a large serving of meat and talking to himself. "Yum. Smoked ham. But who packed a smoked ham into here?" Sid asked, confused. "Aunt Polly would never pack for a Sunday picnic this early."

Silently, Tom reached up to the wooden kitchen rack, where Aunt Polly kept the metal cookware. Ever so carefully, he withdrew a cast-iron frying pan. Weapon in hand, he crept closer to Sid.

Without breathing, Tom ever so slowly raised the frying pan into the air behind Sid.

CLANK!

Sid crumpled to the floor without a sound. Perfect. He went down so fast, he didn't even know what hit him.

"Out like a light," Tom confirmed to himself, after making sure Sid was truly unconscious. "Sorry, Sid, but this here is one adventure I'm not letting you ruin."

Tom didn't particularly enjoy violence towards others, even to the annoying Sid, but he wasn't taking any chances. He had no intention of letting Sid wake up and tell Aunt Polly what happened. He'd surely be in for it then.

Deciding he needed to hide the crime, Tom dragged Sid back into his first floor bedroom, lowering him carefully back onto his bed. But last-minute doubts assailed Tom. He hadn't really hit Sid that hard, and he had no idea how long Sid would be out. What if Sid woke up and went to tell Aunt Polly? Or worse: What if he woke up and followed them?

Tom thought for a minute, then crept into the living room. He soon returned to the unconscious Sid with a skein of yarn he had borrowed from Aunt Polly's quilting basket. Yarn wasn't as strong as rope, but it would do. Working quickly in the dark, he carefully tied Sid to the bed. Deftly, Tom attached Sid's wrists to the bedpost corners. Then, he moved on to Sid's ankles and tied his feet together. Tom worked efficiently and was done in no time. He surveyed his mischievous handiwork one more time: Sid was completely immobilized.

Satisfied, Tom left the house, toting the picnic basket. Adventure awaited.

But before he headed down to the boat dock, he decided to play one more prank on Sid. Outside the house, Tom figured that he could get away quickly enough before Sid could wake up, figure out what had happened to him, and possibly escape from his bindings.

Tom filled a metal bucket with ice-cold water from a pump, went outside Sid's open bedroom window, and threw the water in the bucket through the window, onto where Sid was sleeping. Because Sid had been knocked out, the first wave of water only served to revive Sid, nothing more. Tom realized this and went back down to the pump to refill. Two minutes later, Tom returned and threw the second pail of water through the window also. This time, Tom heard a very high-pitched scream that definitely didn't sound anything like Sid!

Tom gasped softly in horror as he realized that the water had not landed on Sid but had actually hit Aunt Polly instead!

In that moment, Tom remembered that Aunt Polly was a very light sleeper. Tom figured that after he had thrown the first wave of water through the window, the sound of the water splashing loudly must have awakened her. Then, she had come downstairs, walked into Sid's room to see what the noise was, and had been directly hit by the second wave of water. Nervously, Tom peeked around the wooden shutters outside Sid's window to get a peek at the chaos he caused.

Sure enough, in the light of the moon, he could see his sopping-wet brother thrashing around, still tied to the bed. Aunt Polly, standing next to Sid, looking utterly confused, was also soaking wet! Not a single inch of her white nightgown had been spared the chilly, watery attack!

Hastily, Tom fled from the house before Aunt Polly could identify him as the troublemaker, because it wasn't going to take her long to do so.

When he got to the dock, he found his four friends, plus Amy's brother Andrew, waiting.

"What took you so long?" Andrew asked him.

"Sorry, I had to take care of Sid first," Tom explained casually.

"What did Sid do this time?" Amy asked.

"Long story," Tom deflected. "But let's just say that Aunt Polly was an accidental victim, unfortunately."

"Tom," Becky chided. "You're unbelievable. But don't ever change."

As they stood there talking, Tom came to the gradual realization that Becky and Amy looked completely different. Instead of a dress, Becky now stood clothed in a long pair of faded, blue overalls with a white shirt. Amy looked very similar, except she was wearing a green shirt.

"I never reckoned I'd see you two looking like us menfolk," Tom commented to the girls, rather surprised.

"Well, we thought we'd dress for the occasion," Becky and Amy explained. "There's no telling what wild adventures we'll get into, and dresses are such a bother."

"Didn't even think you girls owned any clothing like that," Huck remarked, concurring with Tom.

"We don't," Amy clarified. "Ben Rogers and Johnny Miller loaned us these clothes. They found it awfully strange we wanted to borrow their spare clothes. But when we mentioned you, Tom, they stopped asking questions and just gave us their clothes."

"Sounds like Ben and Johnny, alright," Tom affirmed, smiling at the generosity of two of his close friends. "I'm just glad they fit you alright."

"Okay, enough about clothes," Andrew interrupted. "We'd best be going. It'll only be dark for a few more hours."

"Right," Huck affirmed, leading everyone down to the end of the dock. "Time to set sail!"

Tom looked at the raft Andrew had built. "Whoa, that's a mighty good-looking piece of handiwork!" he complimented, as he gazed upon the magnificent vessel bobbing up and down in the calm waters of the Mississippi.

"I know," Andrew smiled. "It took me the whole three weeks to build, but I wanted to make sure it was fit for the Mississippi. Sorry we couldn't leave sooner, but it needed to be strong, and the shop's been busy."

"It's ok, Andrew," Tom assured gratefully. "We're just glad to have your help. Besides, a good raft takes time to build."

Andrew's raft had been very ingeniously designed. It consisted of eight large, thick pieces of hand-hewn pine wood nailed on top of a couple of rather large logs. Tom could tell, just by looking, that the raft would have amazing buoyancy. It looked to be a perfect square, 12 feet by 12 feet. Just big enough for its five passengers.

In the middle of the boat were two smaller pieces of flat pine, hinged together, folded up, and laid flat. The two pieces were designed to be unfolded to act as a makeshift rain shelter, a sun shelter, and a place for the girls to sleep at night should they so choose.

On each of the corners of the raft was the bottom half of an empty wooden barrel. These four barrels sections were secured to the middle of the vessel by short lengths of rope. Andrew explained that they would act like lifeboats if something happened to the raft. If the raft flipped, or was otherwise disabled, the four younger kids could each sit in a barrel half and float to safety while Andrew would swim to the shore. Granted, Andrew said, he hoped that it wouldn't come to that, but one could never be too prepared.

As Andrew explained to Tom how the life rafts worked, the others waited close by, on the dock. They were ready to go.

At first glance, the raft looked like a platform on logs, but it proved much more sophisticated than it seemed. After both boarded the craft, Andrew showed Tom a metal handle screwed onto the middle of the deck. When he pulled at the handle, a door raised up from the deck, revealing an empty space under the raft, which sat more than a foot above the water. A mesh net was strung between the walls of the hidden compartment, hanging slightly below the wooden deck, but still elevated out of the water.

"I figured we might need to store our supplies somewhere on board," Andrew explained, while taking the picnic basket from Tom's hands and storing it safely below. Then, he took off a burlap backpack from his own shoulders and added it into the compartment.

"What on earth did you bring, Andrew?" Tom asked inquisitively.

"Well, there ain't no telling what the weather will give us; so, I brought a nine-foot square sheet of canvas. As soon as we find us a couple of stout branches, we can make ourselves a nice canopy to shelter under," he explained.

Tom nodded his approval. "Anything else I ought to know?"

Andrew shrugged. "See for yourself."

Attached to the back part of the raft, a large, wooden paddle and handle mechanism dipped into the calm water and acted as the rudder for the craft. Finally, lying on the deck of the raft sat two beautiful, handcrafted oars. Each showed signs of expert craftsmanship.

As simple as the raft looked, it would need several hands to operate it: One person at each of the oars, and a third, in the back, to steer.

After making sure that they hadn't forgotten anything, the three remaining teenagers climbed on board. As soon as everyone had found their places, Andrew untied the rope that anchored them to shore. With a gallant push, they floated away from the dock. Tom and Huck each picked up an oar and started rowing. Andrew stood at the back, near the rudder, to guide the craft. In no time at all, the slow, gentle current of the great Mississippi took over. The raft picked up speed, and they were off. Their destination: Jackson's Island.

Not too long afterwards, both of the boys watched enviously as Becky and Amy unfolded the wooden rain shelter and crawled inside, where they soon fell asleep. The desire to sleep weighed heavily on their eyes, but there was to be no sleeping for them, or at least not for all of them, not while they were on the river.

"How do you want to do this?" Tom asked. "Take shifts?"

"Doesn't really matter too much to me," Andrew remarked, looking at Huck.

Huck quickly volunteered to steer the raft. "Andrew, you've gone and worked yourself silly building this raft. You and Tom can both rest; I'll take the first shift."

"You sure, Huck?" Tom asked.

Huck shrugged. "Yeah, I'm kinda used to sleeping whenever. But staying awake at night ain't too hard for me. I'll wake you in a little bit, Andrew, and then you can take over."

"Works for me. 'Night, Huck," Andrew called, just before laying down and dozing off.

"Good night, Huck." Tom responded, as he too reclined himself onto his back, looking up briefly at the abundant stars dancing in the sky before closing his eyes.

"Good night, Tom. Good night, Andrew," Huck returned, as he quietly crawled to the rear of the deck and sat down near the rudder. As he began his job, he casually looked over at Amy and smiled at her beautiful, sleeping form. "Good night, Amy," he whispered quietly.

With his hand on the rudder and a warmth in his heart, Huck expertly steered the raft downstream.

Another adventure had begun!

CHAPTER 17

THE JACKSON'S ISLAND TRESPASSERS!

At dawn, Becky and Amy woke up to find Andrew seated near the back of the raft. The sun had come up, but fog and mist covered the entire river, creating terrible visibility. Becky tiredly blinked her eyes open and tried to get her bearings. She hadn't gotten a good night's sleep: Andrew's snoring had kept her awake - her and everyone else, she suspected.

"Where are we, Andrew?" Becky asked, as she and Amy emerged from their wooden tent.

Andrew shrugged his shoulders. "Really wish I knew, Becky; I've only been awake for an hour, maybe two, after I took over from Huck. I'm trying to keep us level, but I can't even see where I'm going. I hope I haven't passed the island. I've rafted before, but I've never been downriver this far, and I've got no idea of what Jackson's Island even looks like. You'd be better off asking the boys where we are when they wake up."

Amy and Becky glanced over at Tom and Huck soundly sleeping. Becky thought their positions were perilously close to the edge of the raft. Just as she thought to say something to Amy, the raft twirled in the current and rolled both boys off the deck into the cold water of the Mississippi River!

It was not three seconds before two heads surfaced next to the raft, howling at the cold water. Clinging to the raft, they asked accusedly, "Who did that?!"

Both the girls laughed as they helped the boys climb back on board. "No one did anything," Becky snickered. "You got tossed into the river **by the river**!"

Chuckling, Amy broke in, "Going for a bath already, Huck?"

Huck shook his head back and forth like a dog, trying to get rid of the water in his hair. "Well, it's been a week; I reckon I may as well have one."

Everybody but Tom groaned at hearing of Huck's once-a-week bath regimen. Andrew spoke quickly, changing the subject. "Huck, we've got to be getting close to Jackson's Island by now. Is it possible we've passed it?"

Huck took in his surroundings, like an experienced captain of a ship. These waters were deeply familiar to him. "Well, the island stretches a few miles long by a quarter mile wide. It would be hard to miss, but, then again, you could miss anything in fog like this. Tom, mind giving me a boost?" he asked.

His best friend bent forward, allowing Huck to hop atop his back, and then straddle his neck. Once in place, Tom straightened up, giving Huck the advantage of an extra five feet of height. Huck craned his head, mapping their location.

"What's going on up there?" Becky inquired uneasily. "Where are we?"

Huck peered down at his friends. "Well, Andrew didn't take us too far. I always remember this area of forest because of the lightning tree," Huck explained. "The island lies only a few miles away from home, but the current of the river moves so slow that it takes a couple of hours to get down there."

"I'm sorry, lightning tree?" Becky asked.

"Yeah," Huck confirmed, pointing to his left, where a blackened, dead oak tree stood upright in the soil, its lifeless branches devoid of any vegetation. Its woody arms remained spread wide, as though waiting for an embrace it would never receive. Although barely visible through the fog, the others looked in the direction Huck was pointing. "That there tree is kinda my marker for getting down here; Tom knows about it too. A few years ago, lightning struck that tree and killed it. I see it whenever I raft down these parts; either way, we're pretty close."

"I find it kind of strange that it took us all this time to make it down here, Huck," Tom mentioned curiously. "It normally doesn't take four hours, does it?"

"Well, normally, it doesn't. But last night, when you all were asleep, I ran into some unexpected trouble," Huck confessed, as he climbed down from Tom's shoulders.

"Trouble?" Becky repeated uncomfortably. "What do you mean by that?"

"Well, I was just minding my business, steering the raft, when suddenly, I heard loud, bickering voices coming from somewhere behind me on the river. I didn't know who it was, but I thought it would be best to keep us all hidden. I steered the raft off of the main river stream into the cover of some trees. I waited a good while, and sure enough, a rowboat eventually paddled into view," Huck explained.

"A rowboat? Whose was it? I mean, who else travels the Mississippi by night?" Amy asked.

"I couldn't tell, Ames, but if I had to guess, it was probably someone who doesn't want to be seen, just like us," Huck joked. "In all seriousness, there were probably two men in the boat, and from what they were yelling about, I figured that they might be house burglars. One of them bragged about making off with somebody's good silver."

"This happened when we were all asleep?" Andrew questioned.

"Yep, and for all our sakes, I'm glad they were talking loudly, otherwise your snoring just might have gotten us all caught," Huck muttered.

"Sorry about that," Andrew apologized, embarrassed.

"Anyway, I kept us hidden for a couple hours, even after they were long gone down the river. I didn't want to risk exposing ourselves until I was sure there was no one else coming," Huck finished his story, as the raft continued its downstream journey.

Shortly afterwards, a dark growth of treetops appeared on the horizon, arising out of the mist. Soon, the trees came into view, planted firmly on the ground. And in front of the trees lay a nice, white, sandy beach.

"Is that it?" Becky asked Huck.

"Yep. That right there is Jackson's Island," he confirmed.

A loud cheer went up from the raft's passengers.

Suddenly, Amy stopped cheering. "Andrew, am I seeing things?" she asked. "Or is there someone on that island looking at us?"

CHAPTER 18

IN THE CROSSFIRE

At Amy's words, quiet descended over the raft.

"Amy, are you sure you can actually see someone?" Huck asked cautiously.

Amy nodded nervously. "I'm absolutely certain," she gravely affirmed.

Tom retreated to the stern of the raft and grabbed the oars off the deck. Tossing one to Huck, they worked together to bring the momentum of the raft to a stop. As the raft bobbed in the water, still a ways away from the island, they all began to talk quietly about the safest way to handle the situation.

Amy asked Andrew if he had brought anything with them that would allow them to get a closer look at the stranger on the beach. Andrew, in turn, pulled open the door of the deck compartment. Returning with his backpack, he produced an intricately designed, wooden telescope. Handing it to Amy, he set the backpack on the deck.

Bringing the spyglass to its full-length, Amy peered through its lens, but the mysterious stranger was no longer there. "I don't see him anymore," she reported to everyone.

Tom quickly stepped in and borrowed the telescope from

Amy to get a lay of the land, but he too lowered the eyepiece in disappointment. "Where could he have gone?" he asked.

"I don't know, but something about this doesn't feel right," Becky deduced. "Huck, who else knows about this island?"

Huck narrowed his eyes in suspicion. "Well, anybody with a map of Missouri, I reckon. But it ain't like anybody travels down here; there's too many trees, and there ain't no people or houses to steal from. Heck, when the river rises, it covers part of the island: No sense in building houses here. Joe Harper and Tom are the only ones I've stayed on the island with. Well, them and Jim," he acknowledged.

"Jim?" Amy, Becky, and Andrew repeated, unfamiliar with the name.

"Former friend of mine," he explained. "Not really important right now. The important thing is that somebody else we probably don't know is hiding out on our island, and I'd bet good money that it ain't Jim."

"You mean IF you had any money," Tom joked. "Judge Thatcher still thinks you're a fool for giving it all away to him."

Huck rolled his eyes. "You're bringing that up now, Tom? I think we've got more important things to discuss. Besides, we've been over this: If I had kept that money, my Pap probably would have taken it from me and drank it all away."

"Guys!" Becky interrupted. "We still need to find a way to get to the island without being spotted."

"Paddle around to the other side?" Tom suggested hopefully.

"We could, but it might take a while. Swimming there would be a little faster," Huck offered.

"All of us?" Becky squeaked out incredulously. "Paddling the raft to the shoreline has to be faster than swimming."

"No, no, no. That's not what I meant," Huck explained patiently. "I was trying to suggest that one of us swim ahead of the raft to scout out the island and make sure it's safe."

"I'll go first," Andrew proposed bravely.

"No, I'll go!" Tom decided. And with that, he jumped into the water and started swimming toward shore before anyone could protest.

Amy continued to peer through the telescope, watching Tom swim to the island. Bored after only a minute or two, she rotated the telescope around and looked at the various forest landscapes offered by the island, as well as the neighboring bodies of land. From what Huck had told her, she knew that the island was situated close to the Illinois border. The island was very pretty, she thought, filled with lots of big trees and other plants. Swinging the telescope back around, her gaze was caught by something. She moved the eyeglass again, toward the point where she had first seen the mysterious man, right at the water's edge.

There he was again! A rather fat man was frantically trying to scramble up a tree. As Amy focused the telescope, she could see him holding tightly onto a branch to keep from falling. Just as she found him in her sights, the branch broke, and he fell quite a distance, landing on his backside.

Then, to her consternation, someone in the tree above the fat man lobbed a rope down to him. That person was trying to help pull the other guy up the tree! As Amy watched, the husky man finally made it up the trunk. One moment later, the tree started swaying, and the branches parted, revealing two men hiding in the canopy of the tree. Amy recognized the one man, but she also saw a second, taller, skinnier man with him. By this time, even though the raft had floated close to the island, Amy could not quite make out what they were saying. A closer look at the mysterious men up in the tree showed that they both were now lying on their stomachs on a large, flat piece of wood. Were they in a tree fort? What was going on?

As Amy watched, the taller, skinnier man produced something long and skinny. It looked like a long tube or a long stick – but that was all she could see. Then, the figure put one end of the pole in his mouth. Suddenly Amy realized what it was! She was looking at a weapon! And not just any weapon. The deadly object the man was holding was a blowgun! They were all in danger!

"Becky! I think you ought to look at this! Hurry!" Amy whispered fearfully.

Amy passed the telescope to Becky, who hastily peered through it. Becky also saw what Amy had seen. A blowgun!

Suddenly, the figure in the tree aimed the blowgun right at the raft!

CHAPTER 19

A DANGEROUS WELCOME

Becky quickly told Huck and Andrew what she and Amy had seen. For a moment, no one could move. They had experienced frightening times before, but this was something else. They were sitting ducks on the raft, and there was nowhere to hide!

As Becky watched through the telescope, the second, shorter, fatter figure suddenly grabbed the barrel of the weapon in both his hands and pulled it away.

What was going on?

By now, the raft had all but run aground on the island. Only 100 feet away from the shore, they were within reach of the blowgun. But, plain for all of them to see, the two men started fighting! As the squabble continued, their voices grew louder.

"Phillip! Let go right now! Give it to me!"

"But Boss, you could really hurt someone with that stick!"

"It's called a blowgun, Phillip, and that is exactly what I'm trying to do! Didn't nobody tell you what weapons are for?"

"But Boss..."

"No buts about it! NOW, GET DOWN FROM THIS TREE AND TAKE YOUR FILTHY HANDS OFF THE BLOWGUN BEFORE I DECIDE TO SHOOT <u>YOU</u> WITH IT!"

With that, the taller of the two men yanked the blowgun out of the shorter, fatter person's hands and gave him a hard shove, causing him to roll off the platform and fall out of the tree fort. Then, the man in the tree lifted the tube once more to his mouth!

Amy reacted immediately. Quickly, she ran to the corner of the raft and grabbed one of the half-barrel life-rafts. Turning it on its side, like a shield, she motioned for Andrew, Huck, and Becky to crouch in line behind her. She didn't know what kind of dart was in the blowgun, but she assumed that it wouldn't be able to easily penetrate the wood of the barrel. No sooner had the others taken their position behind Amy when, suddenly, the barrel Amy was holding gave a shudder! The point of a sharp metal dart had punctured the wooden bottom of the barrel, about a foot away from Amy's face! But its momentum had been stopped before it could go all the way through!

The wood of the barrel was thick enough to protect them! Amy had been correct.

A viscous liquid slowly dripped from the tip of the projectile; poison, Amy presumed. She risked peeking over the shield in time to see the shooter having an angry fit at the miss. He raised the weapon once more to his lips. Just as he took a breath in, the other man on the ground threw a rock at him. Startled, the man with the blowgun dropped the weapon into the water below him.

Jumping to the ground, the man who had lost the blowgun angrily charged the other. Trading blows, the two figures ended up chasing each other away from the edge of the sand, deeper into the forest of Jackson's Island.

Standing up on the raft, Huck burst out, "Hey, wait a minute.

SEBASTIAN JOE

I thought that those voices sounded familiar: Those were the two men that passed us on the river last night!"

"Are you sure, Huck?" Amy asked worriedly.

For a moment, staring deep into the forest, Huck said nothing. After a while, he turned to his friends. Soberly, he declared, "Without a doubt. Those are the men from last night."

CHAPTER 20

OLD WOUNDS AND PAYBACK

"What are we gonna do, Huck?" Becky asked, frightened.

"Well, we can't paddle back up the river against the current. We need to get off the raft and onto the island, first. Then, we've got to find Tom and get hidden real quick!" Huck ordered.

Grounded on a shallow sand bar, only yards from the shore, the raft seemed to be safely parked. Still, Huck and Andrew pulled the raft further aground, out of reach of the current, and tied the anchoring rope line around the trunk of a tree. After securing the raft, each stretched out a hand to the girls to help them off the raft. Scrambling up the riverbank, they found Tom waiting for them, completely unaware of the commotion that had just taken place.

"Woah! Woah! Guys, what's the hurry?!" Tom asked, as the others ran up to him, pulling frantically at his arms.

"Tom, Amy was right," Becky explained fearfully. "There are other people on this island with us!"

"What?"

"Didn't you hear them? Or see them shoot the blowgun at us?"

"A blowgun? What are you talking about?" Tom asked incredulously.

"Tom, it's true. There are two men on the island. They're the same men Huck saw last night," Andrew vouched. "And they really don't want us here." At that point, he showed Tom the poisonous projectile he had pulled out of the barrel half and brought with him.

"That what I think it is, Andrew?"

"Yep, a poison dart," he confirmed.

Tom was still trying to understand what had happened while he was in the river. He looked to Becky to explain.

"Tom, the two men Huck saw in the rowboat late last night are here on the island, and they're really scary. One of them shot this dart at us. We're pretty sure it's poisonous. If I had to guess, I'd say he might have possibly used hemlock, or some other poisonous plant. But that's not important, Tom," Becky said. "What matters is that one of the men fired this at us with a blowgun."

Tom raised his eyebrow and looked closer at the dart. "A blowgun? Kinda an outdated weapon. Why would he attack us with that?"

Andrew looked bizarrely at Tom, who seemed to be missing the point. "Well, as far as medium range weapons go, a blowgun ain't a bad option if you've got some skill and you don't want to attract attention…"

"It doesn't matter why," Huck broke in, keeping a careful eye on their surroundings. "Someone wants us dead; if that ain't dangerous, I don't know what is. We need a plan."

"We could and should leave, but we don't even know who those men were. I think we should get a closer look at them, so we can describe them to the sheriff," Amy reasoned. "He can take over for us."

No sooner had they finished talking when, suddenly, they heard the two voices approaching! All five of the friends ran for the tree line at once. Together, they shimmied up the boughs of a willow tree. Concealed by a veil of willow vine branches, they waited fearfully as the quiet island came alive again with the sound of angry arguing.

"One of these days, I'm really gonna have to teach you about respecting your leader, Phillip! Now, get back to the edge of the water! We need to know who those people were and what they were doing here! If they catch me, I'm done for. Do you understand?!"

"Of course, Boss. Hey, look, they left their raft here!"

"That means they're on the island. They can't have gotten very far. Keep a sharp eye out for them. Can you do that?" the taller man asked, his low expectations as clear as glass.

Together, the two men determinedly set off to inspect the raft. Above them, five pairs of eyes peered curiously through the willow fronds.

"Look," Huck whispered to the others in the tree. He very gently parted the vines and pointed at the two men down at the edge of the water. "That guy on the left, that's Dead Eye Dan. I've seen him before; he and my father worked together."

Dead Eye Dan. If the rumors were right, there were many healthy reasons to fear the man. He stood about six feet tall and appeared strong. He even LOOKED dangerous.

Wearing brown trousers and a faded, red work shirt, he

resembled the type of man who might join a criminal gang and hold up trains for money, though Huck had heard Dead Eye Dan usually worked alone. Holstered onto a belt strapped to Dead Eye Dan's waist were two matching "Smith and Wesson" revolvers. He also carried a Bowie knife in a sheath, tied to his left thigh. Those who had seen their friends challenge Dead Eye Dan in a duel or a fight had known him to be a crack shot. Dan was also known to possess excellent knife throwing skills. A worn, brown fedora hat provided ample shade for his intense, shifty eyes as they scoped out the peripheral environment like a hawk.

As they watched, the man they thought was Dead Eye Dan slowly stroked his jaw, which was covered by the greyish-brown stubble of a beard. Taking a cigarette out of his pocket, he lit it and took a long drag, then handed the cigarette to the other man – Phillip? – who was rambling on about something. The two men were too far away and currently talking too quietly for the kids to hear.

Speaking in a whisper, Tom said to Huck, "You never told me your father worked with Dan."

"For a while he did," Huck acknowledged. "I only slightly remember him. I was just a little kid. That's why his name terrifies me."

"But who's that other man?" Becky asked Huck.

"Well, that right there looks like Phillip Morse, the village's telegraph operator," Huck replied.

The four others stared in shock. Sure enough, it was Phillip Morse!

Phillip Morse outweighed Dan by about 100 pounds, and wore a stressed, blue pair of overalls, with a white cotton shirt underneath. He didn't look anywhere near as intimidating as Dan did; frankly, a circus clown might frighten someone more than Phillip Morse. But he did wear a holstered six shooter on his right hip. Of course, that weapon wouldn't do much for him; Phillip was not particularly known in town for being a good shot or possessing the gift of basic intelligence. The half-wit would probably end up shooting himself before shooting anyone else.

"What on earth would inspire Dan to work with him of all people? I done thought Dan worked by himself," Huck wondered.

The argument then continued between the two men, who were oblivious to the curious teenagers spying on them from the branches of the tree.

"I reckon I could have dealt with them if you hadn't been so careless! Why in the world did you throw a rock at me, Phillip? I had a perfect shot!"

"Boss, I was afraid that you were going to hurt them with that stick of yours!"

Dead Eye Dan rubbed the bridge of his nose in frustration. "For the last time, it's called a blowgun, Phillip! And hurting them was my intention, you moron!"

After taking a couple of deep breaths, Dan stared coldly at the man beside him. "You were supposed to be holding the floor plans to the bank, Phillip. Where are they?" Dan asked, his voice icy. "Where are the floor plans to the bank?"

"What bank?"

Dan thought he might shoot Phillip Morse right there on

the spot for his immense idiocy. He had killed others for far less. "Phillip, if I were to put a bullet in your skull right now, would that be murder or charity?"

Unbelievably, Phillip actually took time to ponder the rhetorical question for a moment before Dan rolled his eyes and continued his rant.

"You imbecile!" Dan yelled again. "The Thatcher Bank! What do you think we're doing?!"

"Dan, I plumb forgot about the bank. But I put those plans down on the ground in the hideout. I can't exactly hold anything in my hands when I'm gonna be climbing a tree, can I? I can't carry the floor plans in my pockets, either; they're too big to fold up. And I barely had enough room in the hideout cause of those empty sacks you asked me to bring, Boss. By the way, what do we need those sacks for, anyway?"

"Phillip, you are growing treacherously close to useless. Those sacks are part of your job; you're supposed to kidnap that two-faced Thatcher brat!"

"Becky Thatcher? She's a nice kid. What did she do, Boss?"

"Not her. I've got a fight to settle with her father!"

"Well, what did he do?"

"The wretch had me locked up for 10 years for a robbery at the general store - the only time I got caught in all my criminal history. I've been plotting against him since they put me in jail. Now that I'm free, I'll get my revenge! I'm gonna kidnap Rebecca and hold her for ransom. Judge Thatcher is going to pay through the nose, Phillip."

"Well, what if he don't pay, Dan? What are you going to do then?"

"Well, if he won't pay, he'll never see his daughter again. I'll just dispose of her."

"Dispose of her? You mean you're gonna throw her in a trash can?"

"It's an expression, Phillip! It means I'm going to kill her! You are such a simpleton. I did not hire a fool to act stupid and mess up all of my plans! Do not disappoint me, Phillip."

And with that, Dan gave Phillip a sharp slap across the face, turned, and disappeared into the forest, leaving Phillip to follow closely behind.

Still perched in the tree on the river's edge, the five kids looked at each other in horror. None could believe what they had just heard. Rob the bank?! Kidnap Becky?! They had to get off the island now, but they were almost too stunned to move. After a few long minutes, they began to make their way, one by one, down the trunk of the willow. No one spoke.

Huck was the last to make his way down. As he sought a foothold with his foot, the branch he was holding onto snapped! With a loud crack, the branch gave way, and Huck was left hanging by the thinnest of willow vines!

Tom reached out his arms to grab his best friend, but he was too late. The thin vine broke in Huck's hands, and he plunged ten feet to the ground below!

CHAPTER 21

THE GROUP SPLITS UP

Landing hard, Huck's head slammed against a rock at the base of the trunk. For a second, he seemed okay, appearing only dazed. But a moment later, he soundlessly slumped to the ground, unconscious.

Frightened, the rest of them scrambled down to him as quickly as they could. Becky got down on her knees and placed two fingers at the side of Huck's neck, feeling the arteries for a pulse. "He's alive," she called to the others. "But he's out cold. Could be a couple of hours. He hit his head pretty hard."

Amy gently stroked the hair off of Huck's forehead, careful not to hurt him. She was on the brink of tears. Andrew sat next to her and then looked at the others.

"So, what should we do now?" he asked. "Do we head back to town?"

"We should," Tom admitted. "But it would be very hard to go back without help from a steamboat. We could wait for one, but Dan might see us trying to leave. He would definitely try to stop us. No, I don't think we should go back to town, at least not yet. I want to find out more about what Dan wants with Becky," he decided determinedly, taking Becky's hand in his. "We're going to follow Phillip and Dan, see what we can learn, and maybe get a closer look at their hideout. Also, I'm still mighty curious as to why the map sent us to search Jackson's Island for Red Beard's treasure."

Becky gave him a slightly exasperated look: Tom's priorities were off. But she too wanted to find out what secrets the island held. "We may have time to do both," she reasoned. "Huck's unconscious; we're not going to be able to leave until he wakes up. Right now, he's just dead weight." Turning to Amy and Andrew, she said, "Take Huck away from the riverbank, but not too far. Find a hiding spot until we get back. You've got to keep Huck safe. In his condition, if Dan and Phillip return, he'd be helpless."

"Oh no, no way," Andrew muttered, shaking his head. "Ain't no way that we're leaving you to get caught by Dan alone."

"But you've got to protect Huck until he comes to," Becky argued. "Besides, Dan's after me, not you. I don't want him hurting the rest of you. I couldn't live with that on my conscience."

After arguing for a short while, Andrew and Amy lost the fight and agreed to hide Huck away somewhere while Becky and Tom explored.

"But where on earth can we take him? It's not like we can haul him back up a tree," Amy surmised.

"Well, Huck's told me about all of his travels. One time, he and Jim hid in a cave right here on the island. See if you can find it, and take Huck there," Tom offered.

"You know where it is?" Andrew asked.

"Not really, no," Tom admitted. "Huck could find it better than me. He did tell me that it wasn't too far from the shore, around the middle of the island, and he said he had to climb a rock ridge to get to it. But he did say that the cave was pretty big; about the size of three rooms was the way he described it."

"Ok, shouldn't be impossible to find," Andrew declared resolutely. "Amy, I should be able to manage Huck. You can come with me to help. Tom and Becky, you two go on. Try to stay out of trouble!"

Tom nodded at Andrew and grabbed Becky's hand, pulling her along toward the forest. Looking back over his shoulder, he called to Amy and Andrew, "I'm Tom Sawyer, trouble always seems to find **ME**!"

Amy and Andrew chuckled softly as they watched the pair depart: There was much truth to Tom's statement. Bending over Huck, Andrew gathered the still-unconscious teen into his arms, and, with help from Amy, pulled him over one shoulder. Straightening up, Andrew set a course for the center of the island, and the two of them took off. Eventually, they were able to find the cave that Tom had described.

Exhausted, and grateful to be wearing sturdy shoes – the path up to the cave was littered with sharp shards of rock – they gently laid Huck down on the floor of the cave and sat down next to him. The cave had high ceilings; both of them could stand fully upright. Like Tom had explained, it was at least as big as three normal-sized rooms.

"The cave's pretty big, all right; we could all set up camp here for a short time," Andrew said, partly to himself.

"Don't we have to worry about Dead Eye Dan finding us, Andrew?" his sister asked.

Andrew shrugged his shoulders. "I'm not sure. But we'll lessen the chances of that happening if we don't make too much noise. As far as we know, Dan knows that there are people on the island, but not specifically who we are. I'd like to think we don't have much to worry about. Course, now that I think about it, we didn't think to bring our supplies with us; they're still on board the raft."

"So, we're basically just sheltering here for a few hours or so?"

"Yep, 'til Huck wakes up, or Tom and Becky return, whichever happens first. Either way, we'll need to get off the island and back to Missouri. We need to warn the sheriff about Dead Eye Dan's plot to kidnap Becky and tell him where Dan is hiding. As far as I'm concerned, this expedition is over till Dan is no longer a threat. I ain't gonna risk the safety of any of you."

Amy nodded, and then turned her attention back to the still form of Huckleberry Finn. Tracing her hand over Huck's cheek, Amy started to wonder if coming down here was such a good decision. In no time, tears were streaming down her cheeks. Andrew quickly sat down on the floor to comfort her.

In the dim light of the cave, they hadn't noticed that Huck's eyes had opened. With Andrew bent over Amy, his arm around her side, and Amy hugging him back, neither saw Huck stir and slowly sit up. Gingerly feeling the back of his head, Huck felt a huge bump that was sore as the dickens.

"Ow," Huck muttered loudly. "That ain't gonna heal for days."

Startled by the voice, Amy whipped around, wiping the tears from her face. "Huck! You're awake!" she exclaimed. Crawling over, she very gently touched his head. "How do you feel? You hit the ground really hard."

Huck nodded. "Well, apart from a mighty headache, I think I'm fine." At that point, he stretched out his arms and legs. Nothing too painful. "I think I was lucky," he said. "Nothing's broken, except maybe my head a little bit."

Reassured, Amy and Andrew quickly explained their current predicament to Huck, as he had been unaware for most of it.

"So, Becky and Tom didn't come with you guys?" Huck repeated, unable to believe their bravery.

"Nope, they seem to think that spying on Dan is a better idea. I swear, Tom's made Becky more and more reckless every day," Amy muttered.

Huck climbed to his feet and walked to the edge of the cave. Looking out across the entrance, to the sky above, he noted the dark clouds on the horizon. "Well, wherever they are, they'd better get what they need and meet us here; sky's about to open up," he warned.

"How bad are we talking?" Andrew asked, concerned.

"It looks like it's gonna be bad. I was here a few years back during a big storm. If the rain's heavy enough, we might even have a—"

"A what, Huck?" Amy asked, looking outside as well.

"I forget the word. I know I've heard the term; it's used by pilots on the river...they call it a flash...flash..."

Andrew's eyes narrowed. "A flash flood?"

"Yep, that's it alright," Huck gravely confirmed.

Just then, Amy began sniffing the air in the cave. After

inhaling, she scrunched up her face in a grimace and pinched her nose. "Is it just me, or am I picking up a horrible smell?"

Andrew and Huck broke off their conversation. Amy was right: What on earth was that smell?

CHAPTER 22

BLOWN COVER

On the other side of the island, Tom and Becky stealthily crept through the underbrush, checking for anything unusual. They needed to find Dan, Phillip, or something to help them solve the mystery of the treasure map and Red Beard, but they kept running into dead ends.

"I sure hope that Huck is doing ok," Tom fretted, worried about his best friend.

"Don't worry, Tom. That injury was very superficial. He's probably awake now, and after a few days, he'll be right back to his good ol' self," Becky assured him.

Tom listened intently to his girlfriend. "You never cease to amaze me, Becky. How do you know so much about medicine, anyhow?"

"Well, that's easy, Tom. I've always found medicine fascinating and even studied its basic principles and functions in my spare time. I've always thought that one day I might be a nurse, or possibly even a doctor if I work hard enough. A couple of years ago, I asked Mr. Dobbins to teach me all that he knows after school. He's long been interested in being a doctor too, you know.

He's got several books on the subject that he's loaned to me over the years."

Tom didn't know what to say or where to begin. A doctor? His Becky wanted to be a doctor? And studying outside of school? With Mr. Dobbins? "What? But why, Becky? Why would you want to spend a single extra minute of your life with that man? He's awful!"

"Tom, he's not the villain you make him out to be; he's actually quite approachable if you just show an interest in academics."

"Well, that's the problem right there. I ain't got no interest in academics."

Becky rolled her eyes. "Sometimes, I wonder why I fell for you, Tom Sawyer. Anyway, do you remember a few years back when I went reading through his anatomy book and accidentally tore one of the pages straight down the center when you startled me?"

Tom smiled, remembering the incident. "That happened after lunch, didn't it? By golly, the teacher sure got mad about it. Course, I wasn't about to let you take the blame, Becky. The whooping he gave me when I confessed to the deed was worth it, though; I mean, I'd do just about anything for you."

Becky blushed, and then said, "It's awful funny that here we are, running around the woods, looking for treasure and some nut who wants to kidnap me, and **THAT'S** what we're talking about! Anyway, just so you know, I did confess to Mr. Dobbins that I was the one that had torn his book."

Tom's eyes went wide out of shock. "What? Why?"

"Don't really know. Had a guilty feeling to get off my chest, I suppose."

"Well, golly, what did he do to you?"

"Nothing, Tom. It had been a few years since it had happened. However, he was impressed with my honesty, and he even commended you."

"Now that's too far of a stretch, even for my imagination. What did he say about me?"

"He told me that a guy like you must really have cared something awful about my well-being to intervene the way that you did."

Tom smiled and took Becky's hand in his, squeezing it warmly, as he cast a sideways glance into Becky's beautiful eyes. "Well, he ain't wrong about that."

Tom suddenly stopped walking and put his hand in front of Becky to stop her. He could hear voices loudly arguing up ahead. It was Dead Eye Dan and Phillip!

Tom hurriedly looked for a place to hide. Scanning the trees, his eyes came to rest upon a large, dark green, leafy bush growing nearby. With a finger at his lips, Tom motioned silently to Becky and pointed toward the bush, which was large enough to shelter them both. They had no other options: They were going to have to wait out Dan and Phillip and hope the hiding place protected them. Both Becky and Tom had just enough time to crouch down inside the bush and take cover before Dan and Phillip suddenly marched into view from around the corner, bickering angrily like a long-married couple.

"And I'm saying, don't count your chickens till they hatch, Phillip! We don't even have Judge Thatcher's money in our possession; talking about dividing up the spoils before we even have the spoils will put a jinx on the whole darn thing."

"But Boss, there's so much money in the bank, I could buy everything I ever wanted," Phillip whined. "I want to know how much of the money I'm going to get so I can start planning what I'm going to spend it on."

Dan sighed. "All right, Phil, you wanna talk about splitting up the loot from the robbery? I'll tell you how we're gonna split up the loot from the robbery. Watch this."

Dead Eye Dan broke off a stick from a branch of a nearby tree and marched to the sandy edge of the water. Then, using the stick, he proceeded to draw a pie-chart in the sand, in an attempt to better educate Phillip's underdeveloped mind. "Take a gander, Phillip. I'm gonna get about 90% of the money because I'm the smart, intelligent brain of this operation, and you're gonna get about 20% of the money because you're...how do I say it? You're intellectually broken beyond hope of any repair, and you've messed up this whole plan so far. That there equals 100% exactly."

Phillip looked at the pie chart for a couple of minutes and then snatched the stick out of Dan's hand. Dragging his foot across Dan's drawing, Phillip erased the pie chart and began drawing a new chart himself. "Boss, Boss, you did your math wrong. The correct amount each is 50% for me, and 40% for you. That equals 100% exactly." Phillip clearly did not know much more about math than Dan.

Inside the bush, Tom and Becky were clutching their sides, trying ever so hard not to laugh or make a peep; it was very difficult, mind you. Never before had they heard such complete and utter nonsense. Even Tom couldn't help but cringe at their terrible understanding of mathematics.

Somehow, Becky got the scary impression that, as silent as they were, they had already given away their position to their enemies! She put a finger over her mouth, signaling to Tom to pipe down.

Too late! Phillip suddenly turned in their direction. He was looking directly at them. "Boss, I could be crazy, but I swear I just heard a noise coming from that bush!"

Drawing the pistol out of his holster, Phillip approached Tom and Becky's hiding spot! Armed with a loaded weapon, Phillip seemed much less of a fool and more like the threat he really was. Aiming his weapon at the bush, he shouted, "Alright, come out with your hands up!"

CHAPTER 23

THE HEIST IS FURTHER REVEALED

Under the cover of their bush, Tom and Becky froze with fear. Slowly, Phillip moved closer to the bush, cocked the gun, and steadied his aim. "Come out now," he yelled, "or I'll start shooting!"

Just as he spoke, a grey squirrel sprinted from behind the bush to the trunk of a nearby tree. From Dead Eye Dan's viewpoint, the squirrel appeared to have come directly out of the bush. He shook his head in disgust: There was no one in the bush - Phillip had pulled his gun on a squirrel!

He angrily ran up to Phillip and grabbed the revolver out of his hand. "Are you crazy?!" he shouted. "Don't be such a coward! You about gave away our position for a lousy squirrel!" Dan seized hold of Phillip's lapel, glowering at his buffoon of a partner, who stood there, cowering, expecting the worst. "You know," Dan mused. "You remind me of how cowardly Judge Thatcher acted when he arrested me, harassing an innocent man who was just trying to make a living for himself."

Phillip slowly opened one eye. Once he realized that Dan wasn't going to attack him, Phillip realized that what he really needed was a distraction. So, Phillip piped up weakly, "Hey Boss, now that you're talking about the judge, can you tell me the plans for robbing the bank again?"

Dan sighed, and roughly released his grip on Phillip's shirt. "Oh, I reckon once more couldn't hurt. We'll be perpetrating this robbery and kidnapping the girl a week or so from now, on July 4th, which, by the way, is a holiday named um…um…"

The words stuck in Dan's throat; how come he couldn't remember the name of the holiday? Annoyed at himself, he snapped his fingers together, trying to bring the answer around.

"Independence Day?" Phillip gleefully suggested. Then, he asked, "Hey, Boss, while we're there, can we visit the festival they have and watch the fireworks?"

Dan slapped one hand over his face in disgust. With the other, he pushed Phillip hard on his chest. "Really, Phillip? Is that a real question? 'Can we visit the festival and watch the fireworks BEFORE OR AFTER we rob the bank and kidnap the girl?'"

With disbelief, Dan once again watched Phillip's face go serious as he actually considered answering the question. "No, Phillip, you idiot, we will not go to the festival or watch the fireworks!"

Under the bush, Tom and Becky were incredulous. How could anyone be so stupid? Nevertheless, they were paying critical attention to the plan that was being laid out in front of them.

"Anyway," Dan continued. "The important thing to remember is that the entire village will be out having fun, and the adults probably ain't gonna be completely sober. While everyone celebrates, I will break into the judge's bank and steal as much loot as I can carry without being caught, and you will snatch

Rebecca and carry her to our hideout. If, after two weeks, no one sends the required $50,000 ransom money to gain her release, I shall execute her."

"But Boss," Phillip reasoned. "No one but Judge Thatcher has that much money. And how do you expect him to pay you the ransom if you take all the money he has?" Phillip looked confused.

"That's the brilliant part, Phillip," Dan laughed coldly. "It's a wicked form of payback, isn't it? But who cares? We'll be rich, and I'll have finally settled the score with Judge Thatcher. After we kill the girl, we disappear. We'll stowaway on a ship, maybe head to Europe. The United States is starting to become too dangerous of a place for me to hang around in."

"But Boss, killing an innocent girl? That just doesn't sit right." Only now did Phillip become aware of just how dangerous the man was with whom he had allied himself.

"Phillip, you clearly weren't born for a life of crime, and normally, because you know my plans in abundance, it would make so much sense to bury you six feet under," Dan growled, slowly approaching Phillip until they were almost standing chest-to-chest. Jabbing the point of his Bowie knife into his lackey's throat, Dan was clearly torn. The fool was beyond stupid, but he needed the help.

Phillip trembled in fear, too scared to move. Dan's indecision was clear.

"P...p...please, Boss," Phillip begged weakly. He stared into Dan's black eyes and waited for the thrust of the knife.

But it never came. Instead, Dan placed the Bowie knife back

in the sheath at his thigh and gave Phillip's revolver back to him. "Get a hold of yourself, Phillip. You'll find that revenge is a powerful thing. Don't talk to me again about the girl. I will take Judge Thatcher for everything he has, and then I swear I will silence that Thatcher brat if it's the last thing I ever do!"

CHAPTER 24

LOST IN THE MIDST OF THE STORM

Hearing this threat firsthand proved too much for Becky to bear. She uttered a high-pitch wail and passed out, leaving Tom to frantically worry about their position being uncovered. Both Dan and Phillip perked up at the disturbance that had been caused, but both men appeared very startled, rather than curious. For the first time since arriving on the island, Tom witnessed Dan's complexion turn white with fear.

"Phillip, get out of here!" Dan yelled, sprinting away. "I think this here island's possessed with evil spirits. Run!"

"Ghosts!" Phillip gasped, taking off after Dan in a clumsy crisscross pattern.

After Dan and Phillip had disappeared from sight, Tom poked his head out of the bush, checking in all directions. Satisfied, he stood up and picked up Becky in his arms, holding her securely, determined, more than ever, to not let any harm come to her. Quickly, he carried her off towards the small beach and set her down on the sand, flat on her back. Using the cold water of the Mississippi River, he gently wiped her face as he tried to revive her.

"Come on, Becky. Come on. Wake up," Tom called to her.

When she opened her eyes and stirred, he cracked a gentle smile. "I thought for sure that when you screamed, it would be the end of us. But I guess your scream scared both of 'em away. Now they both think that Jackson's Island is haunted."

Trying to remember what had happened before she fainted, Becky wasn't sure at first what Tom was saying. "So, they're superstitious?"

"I'd reckon so; or they're just fearful of evil spirits."

Becky pushed herself up into a sitting position. Seeing that she was fine, Tom asked, "So, what do you think we should do now?"

Becky thought about it for a minute. Coming to a decision, she said, "Well, I think we should find Huck, Amy, and Andrew. Then, I say we try to get off this island and go back to somewhere safe. Not sure where to head to, though; I'm sure they already know where I live."

"We can worry about where to go later; let's just find the others and abandon this place before Dan discovers us," Tom agreed, nodding his head. Standing up, he reached his hand down to help Becky to her feet. The two began walking toward the center of the island, hoping their friends had made it to the cave.

Overhead, the bright, warm sun began to dim. Ominous looking storm clouds gathered overhead. The weather was beginning to alarm Tom, but they had more pressing concerns. "Didn't we pass by this tree five minutes ago?" he asked Becky.

Becky stopped cold. "Yes, you're right. I do believe we have," she remarked. "Don't you know where you're going? I've just been following you."

"I hate to admit it, but I think we might be lost."

"Lost on an island? Really, Tom? McDougal's Cave was one thing, but we're out in the open now! You can't honestly tell me that you've lost your way." Becky's voice grew higher and higher the more anxious she got.

"Becky, the island is a few miles long; I don't think I've ever seen the whole area before!"

Their argument went back and forth, like a game of tennis, until both grew tired from the griping and decided to put their heads together.

"Well," Becky commented. "Things can't get any worse, that's for sure."

The moment the words were out of her mouth, thunder crashed around them, and branches of bright, white lightning split the sky. The heavens opened as heavy rain poured down upon them. Becky wasn't sure if she had the worst timing ever, or if the elements just personally wanted to punish her for some random reason.

"Apparently, things can get worse," Becky corrected herself, as she raised her hands above her in a futile attempt to avoid getting pelted by the downpour.

"Well, we're easy targets for the weather out here," Tom chuckled, taking Becky's hand, and leading her into the torrent. "C'mon! Let's go find the others!"

CHAPTER 25

INDIANA BONES AND THE PLAN OF ESCAPE

Back in the cave, Amy stood wrinkling her nose at the faint, stinging odor assaulting her senses. The others began to sniff around as well: Both recoiled at the stench. Something definitely smelled off. Slowly, they each began to pace around the cave, trying to locate the source of the smell.

"Huck," Amy called out. "When was the last time that you had a bath again?"

"Can't be me," Huck retorted, feigning offense. "Had myself a dreadfully unwelcome bath just this morning in the waters of the Mississippi."

"Amy, that's not the smell of unkempt hygiene; that's the smell of decay," Andrew spoke seriously, not really getting their humor.

"How do you reckon?" she called back.

"Been to a few funerals, and the smell ain't one of the highlights." he answered, his voice trailing off. "I guess what I'm saying is don't be surprised if..."

"HOLY MOLY!" Huck gasped.

CRACK! Just as Huck spoke, an enormous flash of lightning exploded just outside the cave's entrance, followed by a clap of thunder as loud as 100 cannons. For just a moment, the lightning chased away the shrouding darkness and illuminated the entire inside area of the hideout. It only lasted a couple of seconds, but the flash of light was enough for Huck to realize they weren't alone in the cave.

"Guys, there's someone over there!" Huck shouted, pointing his finger shakily at the far wall.

Amy and Andrew whipped around. They too saw what Huck was pointing at: There, braced against the edge of the inside wall of the cave, was a figure, but it didn't move at all.

The three approached with caution, taking slow, small steps. Another flash of lightning cast a frightening mixture of shadow and light on the figure. It was a dead man. The figure was a human body, but there wasn't much left of it.

"Hang on, we need some light, guys," Huck spoke up, reaching into his overall pocket for his flint and steel. At the same time, Andrew handed him a crumpled, torn piece of paper out of his own pocket.

"Huck, here," Andrew offered. "You'll need this; whatever else is in your pocket has to have been soaked by the river."

One quick strike of the flint and steel together created a cascade of sparks, which landed on the wall of the cave. Huck pressed the small sheet of paper against the sparks, causing the paper to quickly burst into flame. In a few seconds, the small blaze lit up the cave. Looking closely, they could tell that the man had died wearing overalls and a white shirt. The figure still had quite a bit of skin, but the entire body was in the late stages of decay. What was left of the man's mouth hung open in an expression of sadness and final resignation. The corpse leaned against the wall of the cave. Several short, thick, wooden logs lay in a neat pile next to him.

"I guess he was gettin' cold," Huck said solemnly.

"Yeah," Amy agreed, "But who was he?"

"Look at the dirt stains on his clothes; I'd guess he was a farmer," Huck ventured. "But I'd like to know how he died; he can't be older than 40."

"If I had to guess," Andrew deduced, pointing to the dead man's bare foot, upon which could be seen two identical puncture wounds, "I'd say those bite marks had something to do with it."

"Snake bite?" Amy volunteered.

"Probably, or maybe a rabid rat for all we know," Andrew answered.

"But why would he come here, of all places?" Huck asked.

"Your guess is as good as mine, Huck," Andrew spoke quietly. "It sure would be nice to know."

Death had made him a bit fearful. Maybe it was time to move on.

Meanwhile, deep in the forest, Tom and Becky were charging through the rain and dodging from tree to tree, seeking shelter under the branches. They were still lost. By now, the sunlight had vanished from the sky, making finding their way to the cave almost impossible.

"Becky, we can't keep running around; we've got to find some shelter!"

"Tom, right now, we have to find the others. Focus. We need to find that cave."

"Huck told me that it was in the center of the island; but it's too dark to see much of anything. We'd need a miracle to find it."

As though their prayers had been heard, another flash of lightning lit up the sky, bathing the island in the strobing light for a second!

"Tom, there's a bluff over there. Huck said you had to climb a ridge to get to the cave. Let's try it!"

"You certain, Becky?"

"As certain as I'm ready to get out of this rain! Follow me!"

Full of certainty, Becky forged ahead. As they ascended the ridge, Tom began calling out loudly, trying to make his voice heard above the overwhelming noise of the weather. "Huck! Amy! Andrew! Are you guys up here?!"

For a while, there was no answer. Then, without warning, Andrew appeared before them! Gesturing to the cave's dark entrance, he led the two waterlogged individuals inside for some much-needed relief from the elements. "Yell any louder than that, and you might just get us all killed," Andrew scolded Tom.

"Frankly, I don't reckon Dan could hear anything above the noise of this storm," Tom snarked, sitting down on the floor with Becky, who had settled next to Amy. "And besides, Dan can't kill us if we drown from all the water coming down out there."

"You two look like a sight for sore eyes," Huck muttered, walking over.

Tom jumped up and hugged his best friend, overjoyed that Huck had recovered from the fall. "How's your head treatin' you, Huck?"

Huck shrugged his shoulders. "Still hurts a little, but I reckon a night of sleep and some food will work wonders on fixing it."

In the very dim light of the cave, Huck observed that Becky and Tom were shivering, trying to return some heat to their bodies that had been snatched away by the cold and unforgiving winds and rain.

"Gotta say, though, you guys look a lot colder than I do," he remarked. "Here, let me get a fire going to warm you two up."

Though cold, Tom's curiosity got the better of him at the mention of a fire. "You brought in some firewood before the storm? That's great!"

"Not quite," Huck admitted, as he pulled out his trusty flint and steel again. "But I've got something that'll burn just as good."

He struck his flint and steel together once again, causing sparks to fly. Quickly, he pulled off his straw hat and placed it against the wall, where the sparks had fallen. Then, he struck the flint again, over the hat.

"Aw, no, Huck, that's your favorite hat," Becky moaned compassionately. She was shocked; Huck always had that hat on.

"It'll be alright, Becky; it's just a hat. I'll get another one next chance I can. But right now, it's more important to me that the two of you warm yourselves up," he declared.

In no time at all, the straw began to burn. Quickly, Huck set his hat down on the floor of the cave. Becky and Tom crowded in gratefully around the small fire.

"You know, as sweet as that gesture is, your hat ain't gonna burn for very long, Huck," Andrew advised.

"Well, then go get me some of those logs from Sir Bone Voyage over there," Huck sarcastically suggested.

"Huh?" asked Tom.

"I'm sorry, Huck, what?" Becky asked. "Who's Sir Bone Voyage?"

"The dead guy in the corner of the room," Huck answered, not even batting an eyelid.

Becky's eyes swept to the far corner of the cave, and she slightly recoiled.

Tom's eyes, however, lit up with curiosity. They were sharing the cave with a dead man? That was awesome!

Andrew brought over a few of the logs and placed them around Huck's burning hat. With the straw acting as kindling, the large, dry logs easily caught flame. The fire grew in size and began to put off enough heat for them all.

Andrew waited till Tom and Becky had a bit of time to recover, and then he said, "I think we all know that we're not completely safe staying on this island, guys."

"We know, Andrew," Becky nodded in acknowledgement. "Tom and I discovered that Dan plans on robbing my father's bank and kidnapping me on July 4th."

"And seeing that those are Dan's intentions, I had originally intended for all of us to return to Missouri, where we could be safe," Andrew finalized.

"Originally? You've changed your mind," Tom asked, trying to clarify.

Amy jumped in. "You mean until the weather took a turn for the worse?" she said, motioning towards the entrance of the cave, where the rain continued to brutally pound down upon everything outside.

"Exactly," Andrew confirmed. "Huck and I talked, and he thinks the island is currently being hit by a historic storm."

"What do you mean by 'historic'?" Tom inquired.

"Remember the thunderstorm we faced on this island a few years ago, Tom?" Huck asked.

"Yeah?"

"Well, this storm is much worse and much more powerful than the one we sat through; I'm afraid we might even see some serious flooding. Also, with all that extra water coming down, the river will be extra dangerous. A big rain like this always brings down trees from the banks."

Tom gulped but said nothing.

"So, what are our options, then?" Becky asked, keeping a level head.

"Well, we could stay here for the night, maybe longer," Andrew proposed. "The problem with that idea is that we left our food supplies on the raft, and if we try and get them during the day tomorrow, Dan might see us and try to kill us again."

"That's our only choice?" Tom asked, frustrated. "Why don't we try to ride the raft back to Missouri when the storm lets up? There might be some late-night steamboats coming upstream."

"Not a chance, Tom. We have no way of knowing if and when a steamboat would come. And on our own, I wouldn't count on us being able to get anywhere near home," Becky cautioned.

"Besides, who says that the storm **WILL** let up? I've lived through my share of mighty thunderstorms. Even if it does temporarily let up, a storm as big as this one is bound to come back and hit us again. If we're on the river when that happens, we might just end up dead, Tom."

"What about floating downstream a bit into Illinois?" Huck asked. "It'd be dangerous, but we'd be traveling with the current."

"I'm not so sure," Andrew voiced. "Seems risky. What if the storm comes back and we get hit by lightning on the river, or we get overturned by a tree?"

"That is all true," Tom pointed out. "But so it this: Sooner or later, Dan will find this cave, and when he does, we'll all be goners."

Andrew stopped to think.

"Look," Tom spoke, taking charge. "Here's the plan. Once the storm calms down, we'll leave under cover of night. We'll go through the forest, where it will be impossible to track us. Once we get to the riverbank, we'll untie the raft and push off toward Illinois. The Illinois shore is much closer than the Missouri shore, and the current should carry us in the right direction. If we need to, we'll use the oars to maintain our heading."

Andrew thought hard, trying to determine the best course of action. Finally, he nodded in resolution. "Very well, we'll try it your way, Tom. I may not like it, but we don't have any better alternatives. Let's bide our time and just pray that we get out of this alive."

CHAPTER 26

THE EYE OF THE HURRICANE

A couple of hours later, the wild winds finally settled down, and the pounding rain lessened to a tolerable level. A quick check outside the cave told them that the time had come to act.

"Well, the weather's with us," Huck announced hopefully. "It's now or never, I reckon."

Andrew quickly placed his hand in front of Huck, effectively halting his advance. "What gives, Andrew?" Huck queried, confused.

"I just want to make sure we're all on the same page here," Andrew explained. "With the weather finally calming down, our best chance to leave is now. That being said, Dan could be having similar thoughts. When we're running through the woods of this island, the trees and darkness should hide us well enough. But near the edge of the island, we'll be out in the open, with nothing to hide us from Dan. I suggest that we run to the raft in smaller groups: All five of us would be too easy to spot."

"Okay, that makes sense. How should we split up?" Becky asked.

Andrew gently grasped onto Amy's hand and squeezed it. "I'll take Amy with me to the raft first; you both escort Becky, since Dan wants to go after her."

Becky had no objection to this setup and nodded to Andrew.

Taking one final look around outside, Andrew carefully began climbing down the slope of the hill, so as not to make too much noise and attract unwanted attention. Amy followed closely after him. Tom led the second procession, holding Becky by the hand to guide her, while Huck made up the rear of the parade.

Their guarded sprint through the forest of Jackson's Island proved somewhat difficult; the rain had turned the once solid dirt into slippery mud. Somehow, they all managed to stay on their feet.

Exhilarated, they reached the north-western edge of the island in no time at all. The raft was still there! The ties to the tree had held. Looking quickly at the raft for evidence of sabotage, they found none. Then, all five friends scanned the expanse of the forest to their rear, checking to make sure that nobody was lurking behind them. It was now or never. A good 200 feet of open space stood between them and the edge of the raft.

"This is where we split up," Andrew whispered to the others, who nodded in agreement. He spared a glance at his younger sister, who shivered a little as she tried to hide the fear growing inside her.

"It's okay, Amy," Andrew spoke gently. "We're going to be fine. I'm going to be with you the whole time; I won't let you out of my sight, understand?"

Amy slowly nodded her head. "Let's go," she confidently responded.

Andrew and Amy crossed the open space fairly quickly and caused almost no commotion while doing so. In no time at all, they had made it to the raft. Andrew did a more thorough investigation: Nothing had been damaged by the rain. Motioning to Amy to stay down, he turned back towards the woods and scanned the tree line for any other signs of life. Nothing. Once satisfied, he motioned for the three others to join them.

Looking left and right, Becky, Tom, and Huck sprinted as fast as they could to reach the safety of the raft. They were almost at water's edge when they heard Phillip bellow, "BOSS! BOSS! Those guys are getting away!"

Their immediate fear was that Dan would hear the alarm and come running, weapon in hand, to personally kill them all. However, only Phillip Morse emerged from the forest. He was all by himself. Awkwardly, he started running toward them!

Frantically, Tom began working on untying the knots that secured the raft to the tree. But, soaked from the rain, the knots had swollen, and nothing Tom did could loosen them. With each lumbering step, Phillip came closer and closer. In an instant, Tom knew what he needed. He reached into his front overall pocket and drew forth a short folding knife. Popping open the blade, he started sawing frantically at the rope, trying to beat Phillip's awkward pace.

A quick glance upward confirmed his fears: He wasn't going to make it.

Twenty yards away, Phillip began laughing in triumph. "Just wait till the boss takes care of all of you!" And then, abruptly, as he reached the raft, he stopped laughing. "Well, I'll be darned; it's you kids from the village," Phillip remarked, as he slowly scanned the familiar faces in front of him. He drew in his breath sharply, and his eyes dilated dangerously when they settled upon Becky. "Wait a second! You're Thatcher's kid! Just wait till the boss hears about this…"

CRACK!

Holding his head and letting out a small moan, Phillip slid silently onto the beach, at the edge of the water, unconscious. Without a word, Huck walked up to his friends, clutching a thick branch. He had saved them all, for now.

"That was too close, Huck!" Tom muttered, as he finally sawed through the rope, freed the raft, and then jumped aboard.

Huck just smiled at Tom as he boarded, taking an oar from Andrew and dipping it into the water. Tom grabbed the other oar, and the two of them began to guide the raft into open water, leaving the island behind them.

"Shouldn't be but ten minutes to the Illinois shore!" Tom called back to Andrew, who was stationed at the rudder.

"Better row quickly before the weather picks up!" Andrew yelled in return, motioning to the growing thunderheads in the sky.

The weather looked ominous, but at least they were off the island.

Back on Jackson's Island, Phillip Morse lay unconscious at the edge of the water. He woke up about three minutes later to someone slapping him on the face. Blinking his eyes, he awoke to find Dan yelling his name repeatedly, his hand continually slapping Phillip's cheek in a violent attempt to revive him. Quickly, Phillip grabbed Dan's rough hand to stop the onslaught of attacks. "Boss! Boss! I kept a lookout like you told me to, and I tried to stop them from leaving!"

"Phillip, what in the world were you thinking?! You're out of your mind trying to fight more than one enemy at a time!"

"I know, Boss, those kids fought back harder than I thought they would!"

"Huh?" Dan shook his head to clear his ears. With astonishment, he asked, "Phillip, did you say...**KIDS**?!"

"Yeah, Boss, that's right, there were five kids altogether; and one of 'em was Thatcher's daughter!"

Dan's eyes widened, and his mouth dropped open, unable to believe his bad luck. "Becky Thatcher? Are you absolutely certain it was her?"

"Pretty sure, Boss! But one of them hit me on the head with something pretty hard."

Dan took a moment to examine Phillip's swollen head for any injuries that could be life threatening. When he found none, he began to nervously pace the riverbank, his mood darkening. Muttering to himself, he growled, "Shoot. Did they hear our plans? They'll surely sell me out to the sheriff!"

Phillip noticed his superior having a verbal fit with himself and spoke up. "Maybe we should go after 'em, Boss! Let's just get to the boat, and then we'll..."

"No, Phillip," Dan declared resolutely. "I'm pretty sure that this storm ain't over yet, and as long as that's the case, we're incredibly vulnerable on the river. If those kids are heading back to Missouri, I wouldn't bet two cents they make it. They're more likely to die on the river, if anything. If we're lucky, they'll drown."

"So, what's our plan then, Boss?"

"Well, it's too dangerous to return to town. We'll have to hide out until things calm down. But for now, head back to that hollowed out tree that we hid inside; the storm's winding back up, Phillip."

With one last dark look at the roiling surface of the river, he growled under his breath, "I sure hope the storm comes for you, Rebecca Thatcher. Better the river take you than me!"

CHAPTER 27

AN UPROOTED SHELTER

The kids only made it halfway to the Illinois shoreline before the weather reared its ugly head once more. Powerful winds created endless rows of large, choppy waves that threatened to crush the raft into splinters. A heavy rain once again pelted the weary travelers. And though Tom and Huck rowed valiantly, they weren't making very much progress. It seemed the mighty river had completely turned against them.

Amy and Becky tried to assist Andrew as much as they could, throwing their weight against the rudder, trying to keep them on track, but to little avail. The raft continued to be sucked into the vortex of the raging center current. Every pounding wave threw them all around like a beach ball. Soon it would only be a matter of minutes before the violent river claimed all of their lives.

Though caught in the midst of a life-threatening crisis, Tom felt the fear that had gripped him on the island blow away with the winds. This was his kind of adventure! They really were like pirates, and he was their captain! Overwhelmed by the excitement, he loudly called out orders to the others as the mighty wind charged again and again through his wet, disheveled hair.

"Steady yourselves, mates! Batten down the cannons! Up

the mast, ye scallywags, and unfurl the sails!" Caught up in the power and energy of the moment, Tom was at his dramatic best.

Understandably, Andrew had had enough of Tom's role-playing shenanigans. Frustrated, he started yelling back, "Tom, first of all, no one could steady themselves on a vessel this size in this weather! Second, this raft doesn't have any kind of cannons! And third, there ain't no mast on this raft, and certainly not a sail..."

Midsentence, Andrew's voice cut off. Tom's silly mention of sails had given Andrew a sudden burst of inspiration. "Or maybe there is," he said to himself exuberantly.

As quickly as he could, Andrew staggered midship and opened the center cargo hold. Reaching inside, he withdrew his backpack and pulled out the nine-foot square sheet of canvas. "Becky! Huck! Tom! Amy! Take a corner!"

With each of the four fiercely holding onto a corner, the thick material soon ballooned out into a makeshift sail. Retreating to the unmanned rudder, Andrew grabbed its wooden handle and threw his weight onto it, angling the raft towards the shore. Luckily for them all, the wind was coming from the west, blowing their rig straight towards the Illinois border. With Andrew braced at the rudder, and the other four braced against the wind, holding their new sail, it took but ten more exhausting minutes to reach the Illinois bank. To the weather-ravaged treasure seekers, the time seemed like hours.

Eventually, they steered the raft into a tiny lagoon, where they could tie up. Hastily, Andrew hopped off and secured the remaining tow rope to a nearby tree, taking care to make sure he

didn't tie the knots as tightly as he had done them last time. Becky, Huck, and Tom collapsed the canvas sail into a more manageable size. Amy opened up the cargo hatch and withdrew Tom's now very damp picnic basket, ensuring that none of them would go hungry tomorrow. Then, they all disembarked quickly and joined Andrew on land.

"We need to find some shelter!" Tom shouted, trying to make himself heard over the wind, which continued to roar like a wildcat.

"Little bit difficult to find shelter in the middle of a storm, Tom!" Becky yelled back.

And indeed, finding refuge in the dim light of the moon was tricky. The unrelenting weather continued to accost them as they began to explore the area, eager for some way out of the torrent.

"Hey, everyone! I think I've found something!" Huck called out loudly from on top of a short hill he had climbed.

The others hustled up the hill and found themselves amazed at his incredible luck. Huck had stumbled upon the remains of a huge, old oak tree that appeared to have been uprooted, possibly from some other violent storm. Laying on its side, the trunk had been half hollowed out, possibly from wood rot. But the empty space that remained was more than large enough to shelter the five of them. Recognizing the bounty offered by the tree, they hurriedly crawled inside the dry, hollow trunk.

They quickly fit themselves inside, two-by-two, side-by-side, to save space. Tom and Huck lay next to each other, while Amy and Becky paired up. Andrew entered last, hiding underneath with the others, as he gathered the picnic basket and canvas next to himself.

The tree was more than they could have hoped for. First of all, the shelter was situated on top of a hill, which meant that the rain would drain away from them. Second, the waterproof exterior of the tree ensured a calm, dry night's sleep. Third, sleeping this close together would keep them warm, and maybe even allow them to dry off a bit. Last, even though the weather outside the tree continued to roar, it was comparatively quiet inside the hollow trunk.

Soon, semi-dry and warm, the five teenagers slipped off into the land of dreamers, exhausted from their harrowing first day of adventure.

CHAPTER 28

UNEXPECTED NEIGHBORS

At dawn the next morning, first one set of eyes and then another began to open. Snug and mostly dry, each had slept through the whole night. Now, stretching off their slumber, they emerged from their shelter and found themselves surprised to discover that, aside from an excess of muddy water, the violent storm had left little damage. Almost no trees had been uprooted or destroyed, and the top of their hill was sunny and peaceful. It was as if the storm had never happened. That being said, all of them could only wonder if Jackson's Island had been left as untouched by the weather.

"How's everyone holding up?" Andrew asked, getting a look at each of their tired faces.

"I'm awfully cold," Amy spoke, shivering.

"I'm hungry," Tom confessed. "I say that we should eat something before we travel anywhere else."

Andrew looked over the edge of their short hill, towards the location of the tranquil lagoon. There, still tied to the tree, was their raft. He was glad to see it floating there, unharmed.

"Tom's definitely onto something," Huck said. "How are the supplies holding up?"

Becky quickly checked the contents of the picnic basket that had shared the space underneath the tree with them. "Everything's still there," she noted. "Quite a bit wet on the outside of the basket, but the food is mostly dry. Honestly, it could have been a lot worse. That cargo space you built under the raft really did its job, Andrew."

"Thank you kindly, Becky; I built that space to withstand basic moisture contamination from the river, but I couldn't have predicted that we were due for a storm like that," Andrew admitted. "In any case, I agree with Tom and Huck; I'm definitely in the mood for some breakfast and maybe making ourselves a nice, toasty fire to warm up."

"Great, so let's get a fire going," Amy suggested helpfully.

"That's going to be a challenge, Amy. Everything around here is wet." Tom told her, shaking his head. "We can't just light big branches on fire; we need to find some dried leaves and twigs to use as kindling. And I'd do just about anything to get ahold of some kerosene."

"Tom's right, but we may find some drier branches if we keep moving inland to the forest over there," Andrew proposed, pointing to a large growth of tall trees in the distance.

"As long as we can make a fire and have breakfast, I don't care where we go," Amy conceded, as she grabbed the picnic basket in both hands once again.

After walking through the vast, lush forest for only about ten minutes, the five came upon an open area of the woods. Most of the trees out here had clearly been cut down for some purpose. That was curious. And there seemed to be a walking path leading from the clearing back into the forest on the far edge. That was even more strange. They were in the middle of nowhere, Illinois. Who cut down the trees? Who made the path? They all looked a bit nervous, but nevertheless, they continued on their pathway, which eventually approached the edge of a small drop off.

Carefully navigating their way down the side of the cliff, they discovered a small camp at the bottom. Two very basic canvas tents had been set up with poles and rope, just big enough for one person to sleep inside each one. Though initially unnerved at seeing the handles of rifles protruding from each shelter, their worry quickly turned to joy at the marvelous sight in front of the tents: A big, blazing campfire!

Over the middle of the fire stood a metal tripod, with a rusty iron pot hanging down into the fire from the tripod's metal legs. Better yet, there was something cooking in the pot, and it smelled delicious! Forgetting the presence of the rifles, and rivetted by the food – in fact, ignoring all the danger signs around them – they peeked inside the pot and found a wooden spoon dipped in what looked like some sort of chili.

Just for the fun of it, and because she was really hungry, Amy loaded the end of the spoon with chili and dropped a bite in her mouth. "That sure tastes amazing," she proclaimed.

"Well, I reckon it should; I've made it that way for most of my life," came a low, grizzled voice from behind them!

CHAPTER 29

THE TIES THAT BIND

Startled, they all whipped around to see a brown-haired figure emerging from the far side of the forest. His clothes were obviously worn and patched. His thick, unkempt beard crawled down over his jaw and chin. He was far older than they: His skin was wrinkled, and his hair showed a few random patches of grey. They should have been terrified, but he was smiling and didn't appear to want to do them harm.

"Don't worry, I ain't gonna hurt you," he assured them peacefully, putting his hands in the air. "But I would like to know what brings you here."

"Well, sir, it's quite the story," Andrew admitted.

The man shrugged. "I've got plenty of time. By the way, my name's Gregory...Gregory Scrubbs. I've actually lived here for most of my life," he said, holding out his hand cordially.

After exchanging handshakes, Andrew briefly recounted their extraordinary day yesterday, though he didn't go into too much detail.

"That's quite a story," Gregory remarked. "Is this your first time braving a storm as wild as the one last night?"

Tom nodded his head. "We get quite a few thunderstorms in

Missouri, but it's safe to say this one was much worse than any of those."

"Yes, it was a powerful one," Gregory empathized. "We're incredibly fortunate that our little camp is situated here. Up against the bluff, we didn't get the wind that surely blew down on the river. Otherwise, we'd have been in really big trouble."

All of them looked up at the bluff they had climbed down. They could tell that it would have effectively protected Gregory's camp from the harsh winds, as well as some of the rain.

"I'm sorry," Andrew apologized suspiciously. "You said **WE'D** have been in big trouble. Who else lives out here with you?"

Gregory held up his hand. "Forgive me, I do agree that proper introductions are due. I don't live here alone; sometimes my good friend, Dr. Wesley, stays out here with me."

"That's right," came a friendly sounding voice from nearby.

Sure enough, a man in his late forties soon materialized from the concealment of the tree line and kept walking towards them. He was carrying a basket full of supplies in the crook of his elbow. Dr. Wesley had reddish-brown hair, hazel green eyes, and strong muscles on his arms and legs. He stood tall, at six feet, and wore dark-green, dusty knickerbockers, black stockings, boots, and a crisp, white linen, long-sleeve shirt. He also wore a black waistcoat.

"Dr. Wesley Goldman, M.D. It's a pleasure to meet you," he introduced himself.

Amy and Becky both giggled and sighed romantically to each other. Dr. Goldman was a bit dreamy.

As if reading their thoughts, he walked up and gave them

each a friendly kiss on the hand to greet them. Both girls blushed deeply. Huck and Tom, meanwhile, pretended to be nauseous and jokingly gagged at the girls' flirtatious reactions.

Wesley finished greeting the other visitors and then gently set down his basket in the dirt next to the campfire.

"Well, if I had to guess, I would say that you're all feeling mighty hungry," Wesley commented. "What say we get our visitors something to eat, Gregory?"

"I believe we could arrange that," his older companion contentedly agreed.

In order to add extra substance to the chili that Gregory had prepared, Andrew and Wesley worked quickly with knives to chop up the smoked ham that Tom had brought. In the picnic basket, Tom had also brought some jars of seasoning, as well as a few delectable onions, and several cloves of garlic. By inserting the ham, dicing up and including the vegetables, and adding just enough seasoning, the additional ingredients turned the already delicious smelling food into an almost irresistible dish. As they waited for the food to continue slowly cooking over the fire, the friends couldn't help but bombard Gregory with questions.

"So, you and Wesley really live out here by yourselves?" Andrew asked.

Gregory nodded, as he sat down on a hollow log near the campfire. "Well, I live out here most of the time, but Wesley runs a medical practice in town. He still makes time to come out here for a few days at the end of every week, though."

Wesley nodded and seamlessly took over the conversation. "Town's actually less than a mile away from this here camp. Makes it ideal for refreshing supplies when they run out," he finished, lifting up the basket he had brought with him.

"But aside from Wesley, nobody really bothers coming out to these here parts. Can't honestly say that the solitude bothers me, though; life in town's just too tiresome for these aging bones of mine," Gregory sighed contentedly.

As Gregory and Wesley continued talking, Tom found his thoughts turning back to Red Beard's treasure. Sure, Gregory and Wesley were great, but he didn't want his friends to get too comfortable. They still had treasure to find!

With a gentle hand, he pulled out the piece of the treasure map he had found in the ground in Aunt Polly's garden. His face contorted in frustration as he pondered the mysteries of the parchment. Quietly, he motioned for Huck to come join him a few steps away from the campfire as he laid out the paper on the ground in front of them.

"What's going on, Tom?" Huck asked.

"I just can't shake the feeling that we didn't need to go to Jackson's Island at all, Huck. We didn't find nothing except a wanted criminal and his cotton-headed sidekick. There's something that we're missing. I need you to think harder," said Tom.

Huck nodded.

Out of the corner of his eye, Gregory noticed that Tom and Huck had become otherwise preoccupied. Gently, he picked himself up off the log and walked over to see what was absorbing the two young men. His countenance changed noticeably when he realized what they were examining.

"Gentlemen, is that there what I think it is?" he questioned.

"Yep, it's part of a map to Red Beard's treasure, sir," Huck answered.

Gregory stared at Huck for the longest time. Eventually, he put his hand to his chin and remarked in amazement, "Well, I'll be darned. I ain't seen one of Red Beard's maps in ages."

In unison, all five heads turned in Gregory's direction. His statement made them immediately cautious and confused.

"You used to hunt for his treasure, Gregory?" Becky asked nervously.

Gregory put up his hands in a gesture of innocence. "Oh, heavens no. Never went on a treasure hunt, and I'm sure as heck too old to be doing it now. You just never mentioned that it was Red Beard's treasure in particular you were after."

"Must have slipped our minds," Amy offered, uneasy with all of Gregory's questioning.

"Well, far be it from me to get in your way," Gregory spoke. "But if you'll accept my help, I bet I could get you all a few steps closer."

Gregory's statement was greeted with noticeable silence. The teenagers looked at one another, unsure what to say.

It was Huck who broke the silence first. "What do you mean by a few steps closer?" he asked curiously.

Gregory didn't respond. He just got on his hands and knees and crawled into his tent. Seconds later, he emerged with a piece of rolled up paper clutched between his teeth. After making his way over to Tom and Huck, he unfurled it and set it down beside the other piece.

Side by side, the two pieces of paper were roughly the same size. They were also the same aged, yellow color. Huck could see that each piece bore rough, bumpy outer edges.

What was he seeing?

No one moved. But all were thinking the same thing.

Huck's gaze was fixated on the two pieces of paper. Eventually, with a quick look at Tom, he reached down and picked up their section of the treasure map, laying it down next to Gregory's piece of parchment. With shaking hands, he tried aligning the two pieces up together.

The jagged edges of the papers aligned in a perfect match! Gregory had another section of their treasure map!

"So, youngsters, how did you get a hold of Red Beard's map?" Gregory asked, unsurprised at the match.

Suddenly, every one of the kids started talking at once. "How come **YOU** have a piece of the map?" "Where did you get that?" "Who are you?"

Gregory smiled at the five. "Well, those are easy questions to answer. You see, I used to be Red Beard's cabin boy."

Once again, silence reigned. Tom, Huck, Amy, Andrew, and Becky had all been struck dumb with amazement.

Finally, they found their voices. "You have to tell us about that," they begged.

"Of course," Gregory promised. "But it smells like breakfast is almost ready."

After Wesley had passed out spoons and bowls, filled with

the hearty chili, to the new visitors, he ladled two more bowls for himself and Gregory and sat down in front of the kids, next to Gregory. All of the treasure seekers were breathless with anticipation.

"So, you want to know about Red Beard?" Gregory began quietly, "Well, it's a long story that began many years ago, far, far from here . . ."

CHAPTER 30

SHANGHAIED!

I may be old, but I can still remember most of my childhood memories. My parents raised me in a small house, close to the sea, down near the southern edge of Mississippi. I didn't have any siblings or any relatives that I knew of, but surprisingly, life was never very lonely for me. For a few years, I grew up like most children and got a basic education. However, my parents weren't the richest people in town, so, at the age of 12, I dropped out and started working as an assistant to my father, who worked as a fisherman in the Gulf of Mexico.

"Have you all heard of the Gulf of Mexico?" Gregory asked his audience.

All nodded yes.

To please my father, and to further his good reputation in the village as a man of the sea, I worked very hard. One time, we were fishing together, and I caught a huge fish – it must have been as big as a shark, which is a huge fish with enormous teeth!

Its tremendous weight began to sink our fishing boat! Then, suddenly, without warning, the monster turned and swam away, swiftly towing us behind it! I surely would have lost the fishing pole if my father hadn't helped me hold on to it. The creature dragged us along at tremendous speed for a great distance. Finally, my father decided that enough was enough. He pulled out his knife and cut my fishing line.

The moment the line was cut, and the great fish was loosed, I was thrown back into the boat. After our boat had stopped violently rocking, my father and I enjoyed a hearty laugh over the incident. Unfortunately, we didn't catch anything else that day.

However, my next adventure would change my life forever.

On my 21st birthday, my parents organized a family trip to the beach. The sun was shining quite brightly that day, I remember. I thought for sure that nothing could spoil our plans. Little did I know how wrong I was.

When we arrived, I immediately ran to the water and jumped right in. While I was swimming, my mom started to unpack our picnic. It was then that she realized that she had forgotten to pack the sandwiches for lunch! So, I patiently waited on the shore while my parents walked a couple blocks to the local corner store to retrieve some provisions.

What came next was the greatest shock of my young life. You see, the beach we lived near was situated very close to a number of huge piers. Trade ships from all over the world would dock at those piers. It was quite easy to watch the ships come in: Doing so was one of my favorite pastimes.

That afternoon, while I waited for my parents, the largest ship

I had ever seen began to pull into port. Our picnic spot was so close that I could read the enormous black letters that decorated the side of the vessel: THE DARK MYSTERY. Although the name should have meant something to me, at the time, I thought nothing of it. I was too distracted by the spectacle.

A ship docking, especially a big ship like that one, is something incredible to behold. The crew on board began tossing ropes over the side to help anchor the craft in the harbor. Then, as I watched, as many as 100 of the toughest, meanest looking men, brandishing lit torches, disembarked from the vessel. They all were dangerous looking and had cutlasses strapped to their belts.

Well, you know, I was beginning to get a bad feeling about this ship.

Suddenly, I noticed the huge, black flag flying from the central mast: The flag bore the emblem of the Jolly Roger - a skull and two crossbones. I had been watching a pirate ship make port in our harbor!

At once, I put together all those scary looking men, armed to the teeth with their cutlasses, and I realized their intention: This was a raid!

Suddenly, the pirates all began running and shouting into town. As I watched, they set fire to a number of the town's biggest buildings with their torches! I began to worry for the safety of my parents: They still hadn't returned! In an instant, I made up my mind to go find them before something terrible happened. Quickly, I left the peaceful and safe confines of the beachfront and found my way back into town.

Nothing could have prepared me for the immense horror that awaited me. It was truly awful.

The once pleasant, amiable town, which had been full of shops and stores, was ablaze! Where once many people had walked and gone about their business, there now lay dozens of bleeding, motionless corpses! I encountered only a few pitiful souls still alive, frightened, and running to escape the chaos. It was too much for me to take in, all of that death and destruction.

Somehow, in time – it couldn't have been too long – I pulled myself together and went in search of my parents.

Their destination, the corner store, had been set on fire by the crew of the ship. But rather than just setting fire to the outside of the building, it looked to me as though someone had poured a lot of oil inside the store and then set the place ablaze, to ensure the fire did far more damage! The thick smoke and wild flames inside clouded my ability to see into the store, but I could see the remains of a few unlucky individuals who hadn't escaped the flames.

Terrified by the sight, I swiftly turned around, only to find myself confronted by an enormous pirate! He was every bit as scary as my worst nightmare. He had an eye patch over one eye, and his teeth were yellow and crooked. He grinned an evil grin and raised his long sword, pointing it at me. I did the only thing I could think of: I humbly got on my knees and raised my hands in clear surrender.

The huge pirate in front of me just laughed. Then, he grasped his sword in two hands, and raising it high, brought down the hilt of the sword upon my head.

And that was the last thing I remembered.

I awoke later that day, my mind swimming, and my head pounding. We were at sea, and I was kneeling upon the deck of a ship. My hands and feet were bound tightly together behind me with sturdy rope. I was completely hogtied. Looking behind me, I realized that they had also bound me with ropes to one of the masts of the ship! Several crewmen walked by me without saying a word. However, once they realized I was awake, they glared hatefully in my direction.

I knew I had to escape soon, though I had no idea how. Although I pulled against my restraints with all my might, I couldn't budge an inch: It was obvious to me that they had tied the ropes together well. Nevertheless, I kept trying.

Then, at the dead center of my back, I felt a huge knot of ropes. If I could loosen that knot, I'd be free. Trying to get my hands on the knot without gathering any attention was hard, but I managed to find an end of the rope. And then, I realized that some fool had carelessly finished tying me up with a bow!

"*What idiots,*" I thought to myself. "*This will be the easiest escape ever.*"

Sure enough, after shimmying a bit, I was able to fully grasp both ends of the rope. I gave a huge tug, and the rope loosened and came off my wrists and ankles like thread. Then, with my arms and legs free, I was able to squirm my way out of the rest of the rope binding me to the mast. Because the ship wasn't far out to sea, I made up my mind to jump off the vessel and try to swim for shore.

I would try to make it home. Hopefully, it hadn't been burnt to the ground. I couldn't let myself think about my parents. It was just too painful. I quickly ran to the ship's rail. Yes! The shoreline was still in view, but I was too late. Before my hands could grasp the rail, I felt the sharp edge of a sword at my neck! Slowly, I turned my head to see who it was. But it was not the same pirate! Even though I had never seen him before, I could recognize the captain of a ship any day.

This man stood much taller than I. He had a graying head of red hair, but a muscular build, and weathered skin that had seen many a sea voyage. His pirate hat was of an elegance only befitting the highest officer on the ship, and his moustache and beard were colored a bright hue of rust.

I knew in an instant who this was. "Red Beard?" I asked fearfully.

You see, when I was much younger, I had read stories about his unforgettable adventures; supposedly, he had never once been caught. My parents told me the stories were just legends, but I always believed otherwise.

The man now standing in front of me nodded and gave me a glare. Then, between gritted teeth, he warned, "Don't be gettin' any wild ideas about leaving my ship, clever boy, or it will cost you your life."

He spoke with the slightest remnant of an Irish accent. I gulped nervously and nodded obediently. For some reason, the captain seemed to realize that I had learned my lesson. He sheathed his sword and looked down at me. "Now that proper introductions are out of the way, I must say I am most impressed. Not many prisoners get out of their bindings as quickly as you did."

"Wait a minute," I interrupted him foolishly. "You actually wanted me to escape?"

He laughed heartily at my question. "Why of course, lad. Learning many kinds of knots is a pirate's most important skill. You don't honestly believe that, out of all the knots I learned to tie as a pirate, I would normally choose a simple bow to restrain a prisoner like yourself, do you?"

"No, sir."

"Sonny, what's your name?" he inquired.

"Gr...Gr...Gregory," I answered, still completely frightened. Just because he acted kindly for a moment or two didn't mean that he wasn't about to kill me.

"Well, Gregory, you are hereby now a member of my crew. As such, my ship is yours to explore. However, you will do what I say, and you will do so immediately. Understand?"

I wasn't sure what else to say, so I respectfully nodded and answered, "Yes, sir!"

"Good," he approved. "Come with me."

"What for?" I asked.

And for a moment, he just looked at me, as if he were going to laugh. "What for? Do you know what happened to the last man who questioned me? Now, no more questions. Follow me," he ordered. "If you're going to live on my ship, you will need your own sleeping quarters."

I gingerly followed him across the deck, through a wooden door with shutter-like planks covering the frame, down a flight of stairs, and across a long, empty hallway to another door on my left. The captain pulled a ring of dark, metal keys from his pocket and flipped through them until he found the particular key he sought. He inserted the key into the lock and gave it a quarter turn to the left. The lock gave a click, and the door opened easily.

There it was. My room. It was small, but there was a slightly cracked, white pitcher and wash basin, a cloth hammock suspended from two wooden rafters on the ceiling, an old, wooden bookcase without any books, and a cushioned armchair.

"Tomorrow, Gregory, you will begin your job, starting at the crack of dawn."

"What job?" I asked, feeling quite confused.

"Gregory," he began, and I swear he was laughing. "Has anyone ever told you that nothing is free?"

"Ummm, yes sir?"

"To pay for your life, you will be serving as my cabin boy. You will clean the rooms, swab the deck, and anything else I think of."

"You mean I'm not a prisoner, or a hostage of some sort?"

"Well, I'd be lying if I told you that you were a free man. You're not. But you will be given greater freedom than most prisoners are granted. In any case, however, the best option for you is to make the best of the situation."

"No way am I doing this! I'd sooner jump off this ship to freedom!" I protested defiantly.

"And just where would you go? As I recall, I burnt your pitiful village to the ground. There is nothing left for you to go back to. And in any case, it's too late; we've long since set sail." And with that, he began to walk away. But then, he turned back. "Oh," he added. "There's one more rather important reason why you can't leave: You would never get off the ship with your head attached."

Only then did I realize that he held all the power. And he was right: I was trapped. I knew I couldn't live on board that ship for the rest of my life, but for now, I would have to submit to his orders, at least until the time was right for escaping.

He must have thought I was thinking through my options, because he simply raised an eyebrow at me. It was terrifying.

Cringing, I quickly said, "All right, sir. I'll do my best."

"Good lad," he replied, patting my head like I was his pet spaniel. He started to turn around to leave, but at the last minute, he removed the ring of keys from the lock on my door and tossed them to me. Apparently, he really did want me to explore the ship.

"Get yourself a good night's sleep, Gregory!" he called out mightily. "Welcome to the pirate's life!"

CHAPTER 31

WRONG PLACE AT THE WRONG TIME

"Wait a minute!" Tom interjected, eagerly interrupting the storyteller. He could hardly believe Gregory's thrilling testimony. "Weren't you at all excited to join Red Beard's actual pirate crew? I would have given just about anything to live your life, Gregory!"

Gregory smiled at Tom's question, but there was a noticeable sadness in Gregory's eyes when he replied. "In time, Tom, I did feel the excitement of sailing with Red Beard. You and I aren't that different: Before I understood all that it entailed, meeting Red Beard and sailing on the open seas used to be something of a fantasy of mine. But I eventually found that living life as a pirate wasn't all that it was cracked up to be. We rarely set foot on land, I got really homesick, and I missed my parents all the time. On top of that, the other pirates never really became my friends; and just about everyone else in the world wanted only to see me and the rest of the crew hanging from the end of a rope."

Tom gulped grimly, and his face fell at the mention of all the terrible stress and anguish that came with being a nautical misfit. His understanding of a pirate's life was limited to just seeking fame and fortune and living with no rules. He couldn't imagine a world where he had no one to call a true friend, or where everyone hated him enough to want him dead. Yes, most adults thought him a nuisance, but none wanted him dead. In any case, Gregory had given him quite a bit to think about.

"So, when did you get Red Beard's map, then?" Huck asked eagerly.

Gregory raised a hand to Huck as if to say, 'patience.' "Don't worry, Huck. We'll get there, eventually. Now, where was I?"

<hr />

Despite my forced position of servitude, I tried my hardest to get to know the rest of the crew while performing my duties. But because I was a newcomer, and because, as a cabin boy, I was totally unimportant, almost no one befriended me. I suppose it can be hard to make friends as a pirate when the constant warfare with naval ships often meant the death of your companions. About the only person who came to regard me as a friend was the cook's son, Aaron MacCarthy. He may have been a pirate longer than I had, but he treated me like a brother. From his red hair, you might guess that he was Red Beard's kin or something, but there was no relationship.

Every day, I made sure that I visited the kitchen a few times, so that he and I could talk together. Course, I had to make sure to keep busy, so as not to get yelled at for slacking off.

After I had been on board for about three weeks, I had almost completely gotten used to swabbing up the ship. Didn't think I could handle waking up early every day, but sure enough, my body adjusted. Additionally, the continuous, hard labor began to turn my small muscles into larger, tougher ones, more befitting a pirate. One day, I was mopping the floor of the captain's living quarters. I believe the captain was on deck at the time. In any case, I had almost finished cleaning around his desk. That's where he kept his charts and maps.

In a moment of unfortunate weakness, I found my attention helplessly captured by one map unrolled on the top of the desk. I set down my mop back in the bucket so I could get a closer look.

The map I saw didn't seem to be complete; rather, it appeared that perhaps the captain was still drawing the location and clues to one of the burial places for his treasure. I could only imagine just how much wealth that a seasoned veteran like Red Beard could have amassed in all his time on the seas. The total collection of his treasure would have been enormous!

Anyway, I think the map hypnotized me; I must have stared at it for a solid 30 minutes. Not until a very angry shout brought me out of the trance did I turn away from that map.

"Oi! What do ya think ye be doin', ya scurvy dog?! Only the captain be worthy of them there maps!"

I looked up to find a very large, very angry pirate named Erickson staring daggers at me from across the room. Among all the pirates I had come to know, Erikson was the only one who spoke like a true pirate - or at least like how I **THOUGHT** a pirate should speak. I think he had been a pirate the longest, even before Red Beard became captain. Anyway, he was mad - really mad. My situation was pretty dire. If Erickson ratted me out to the captain, I was doomed.

I put my head down and hurried over to my mop and bucket, grabbed my supplies, and tried to rush past him. But Erickson grabbed my arm fiercely. "Well, we'll just be seeing how the captain feels about ye plotting to steal his treasure!"

"But I wasn't..."

He slapped me hard across the cheek and told me to shut my mouth. Then, he hauled me along with him, down to the main deck, below where the captain was still shouting orders at the men sailing the ship above us.

"Tighten those sails, Jones! And for the last time, Davy, port is left, and starboard is right!"

"Oi! Captain!" Erickson yelled. "Ye better come down and take care of a problem before it stabs ye in the back!"

The captain spared a glance at both of us and immediately looked confused when he saw me held captive by one of his crew. He came down the stairwell to the deck, where he asked, "Erickson, what are you doing keeping my cabin boy from doing his duties?"

"Beggin' ye pardon, Captain, but I found this little maggot with his eye on your treasure maps! The little parasite likely planned on stealin' your treasure, I'd wager."

The captain's eyes came alive with a fiery anger. I wanted to curl up and disappear.

"Gregory, is what he says true? Are you after my loot?"

Humbly, I told him the truth. "Sir, I did look at your map, but that was all I did. I would never try to steal from you, sir!"

Erickson pointed his finger angrily at me. "LIAR! Sir, ye gave the lad too much freedom, and now he'll surely be ye downfall if you don't..."

"ERICKSON!" the captain thundered, instantly silencing his

subordinate. "Gregory, I'm going to take you at your word. But so help me, if you have plotted mutiny against me..."

The captain abruptly cut himself off. "Indeed, perhaps it would teach you a lesson to see how I do deal with those who dare to rebel against me."

I didn't know what he was talking about, but something told me I didn't want to know.

Red Beard looked up and spoke to Erickson, "Go to the brig and fetch me my two youngest mutineers. I'm in the mood for a double hanging!"

CHAPTER 32

A DARING RESCUE

Nothing could have prepared my young mind for what happened next. Erickson quickly returned, hauling two young boys across the deck. Both boys had their hands tied behind their backs. Erickson marched them to the center of the deck, gripping their necks in his huge, meaty fists. They both appeared to be around my own age. One boy had sandy-blonde hair and a freckled face, and the other boy had reddish-chestnut colored hair. Both looked fearful at what was to come.

I risked Red Beard's anger. "Who are they, Red Beard?"

He glared down at me and ground out each word he spoke like pepper upon a tasty dish of food. "You would do well to call me Captain, Gregory! Both used to belong to my crew. Blondie was my last cabin boy, and the other boy was my crows' nest sentry. They were part of my crew...until I discovered them stockpiling gunpowder in a poor attempt to blow up this ship and escape. I would have killed them when I caught them in the act, but something told me to hold off until a more appropriate time."

A good number of the crew were on deck, listening. As one, they moved toward an area of the ship directly underneath the sails. I knew this area because I came here to chop wood for the kitchen every day. The sharp, double-sided axe I used still lay against the wall, near the logs that needed to be cut. If only I could reach it, then I and the two boys might stand a chance. Sure, I may not have known who they were, but anyone brave enough to defy Red Beard was good enough to call an ally in my books. But Red Beard kept a tight hand on my shoulder to keep me from intervening; he wanted me to witness their deaths. I caught my breath. It was my fault they were going to die. I held on tightly to my mop and bucket and waited for the right opportunity to act.

Both of the boys were forced by the crew to stand up on a couple of large, empty rum barrels. Other crewmen fashioned nooses out of some old ropes lying around the ship. Once the nooses were tied, the crew threw them over an arm of the mast and hooked them around the prisoners' necks. Then, they wound the other ends of the ropes around a couple of strong, metal cleats mounted to the wall. After the ropes were pulled taut, everyone stepped back to wait for one or both of the prisoners to lose their balance on the precarious footholds and slowly suffocate to death.

Panicking, I couldn't watch the execution; but I couldn't turn away either.

As the ship tossed in the waves, both boys wobbled treacherously on their stands, unable to use their arms for balance. Both came very close to falling off!

Something suddenly snapped in me. I may belong to a pirate crew, but I wasn't about to let them kill two kids my own age if I had anything to say about it. Still grasping my big, wooden mop bucket by the handle, I tore myself out of Red Beard's firm grasp and rushed towards the two helpless prisoners. Anticipating my move, two of the pirates quickly broke away from the group to intercept me.

In an instant, I swung my bucket in an arc, pouring out all the liquid inside over the deck of the ship. The soapy, slippery water slickened up the wood, and both of the pirates pursuing me lost their balance and fell over backwards. Seeing my opportunity, I grabbed the firewood axe near the wood pile and hacked through the hanging ropes holding up both teenagers. Though their hands were restrained, both were able to jump down and run over to me. I removed their nooses, but the rest of the crew had begun to advance on us.

Though the pirates may have been stronger and more familiar with the layout of the ship, the three of us had speed and agility on our side. Fleeing into the interior of the ship, we managed to get into the office of the navigator. Once we were inside, I locked the door with my keys, and we quickly sought concealment underneath a wooden table with a long tablecloth draped over the edges. We were just in time!

From under the table, we could hear an alarm bell being rung, alerting the rest of the crew. Over the bell, we could hear the captain. "We've got ourselves three young traitors hiding somewhere on board the ship! Find them! The man who brings all three to me will get a treasure portion twice as big as usual at the next port we raid. But be aware: I want them taken alive!"

CHAPTER 33

DISTRACTING THE CAPTAIN

I realized that, even on a ship as big as ours, sooner or later they would find us. Quickly, I turned to the two teens under the table and began untying the ropes binding their hands. "Hey, kid?" I spoke to the blonde-haired one. "We've got to get off this ship somehow; any ideas?"

He responded rather quickly. "Listen, my name's not kid: It's Cody. And that right there is my brother, Wesley," he finished, nodding his head at the other boy.

Here, Huck interrupted Gregory to ask Dr. Wesley a question. "So, Gregory really rescued you from Red Beard?"

"Yes, he really saved me," Dr. Wesley affirmed. "I owe him my life - and my freedom as well."

"How did you and Cody join Red Beard's crew anyway?" Amy asked.

The doctor nodded as Amy spoke. "My brother and I were incredibly reckless. One day, Red Beard made port in our town. But rather than a raid, he stopped just to gather supplies. One thing led to another, and pretty soon, we had each dared each other to sneak onto his ship undetected."

"You stowed away?" Becky quizzed.

"Essentially, yes. And we meant to leave shortly after, but we both were awfully tired, and it was so hot that day, that we settled down for a quick nap in the supply room."

"You didn't!" Tom gasped.

"We did, and we only woke up when the crew kicked us awake and took us to the captain. We didn't even get a chance to try to escape. By then, the ship had left the harbor, and we had very few options. The captain appeared rather impressed with our gumption and offered to let us live if we pledged our allegiance to him for life. So, we did. Eventually, though, we got tired of the pirate's life, and we wanted to escape. And, well, you know what happened to us."

Gregory allowed Wesley to finish his part of the conversation before he continued his own unreal story.

So, anyway, Cody, Wesley, and I were hiding underneath the table, trying to figure out the best course of action. We had to get off the ship immediately, because if they found us, we were doomed, and only Heaven could have helped us then. In almost no time at all, we heard loud footsteps coming down the hall. My heart was beating incredibly quickly. Two of the pirates had come looking for us, and they were shouting.

"Maybe they're inside the office; take a gander!" one yelled.

I could hear them jiggling the doorknob, attempting to break in. The deadbolt held, but I knew that it probably wouldn't stall the pirates for very long.

Frustrated, the other pirate called out, "It's locked, but I can't see anyone inside through the window! Let's try another room!"

"You blundering buffoon! Gregory's the blasted cabin boy; he'd have the keys in his possession! Break down the door!"

"What? I'm not doing anything of the sort! It's a perfectly good door. The captain will have my head if we break the door down. Besides, it wouldn't make sense for all three of them to hide together. It would be like shooting fish in a barrel!"

"Fine. But if I were them, I'd be looking for a way off this ship! Stand guard over the lifeboats, and don't let any of them get into one!"

Under the table, I breathed a quiet sigh of relief. With the danger temporarily removed, I told the others, "We all need to get off this ship right now; it's too dangerous here. They're going to find us."

"And just how do you plan on doing that, Gregory?" Cody stopped me. "The jump overboard might not kill us, but we're too far from any port to swim, and there are sea monsters in these waters as well."

Huh. Well, Cody certainly wasn't offering any brilliant solutions. Nevertheless, an ingenious idea was beginning to form in my mind. Addressing Cody, the naysayer, I said, "I know that, Cody! We'll have to use a lifeboat to escape."

"But that's impossible, Gregory," Wesley jumped in. "You heard the men; they're standing guard over the lifeboats!"

"I know, Wesley, but I wasn't planning on using the lifeboats meant for the crew."

Cody and Wesley eyed me bizarrely, confused at what I was saying. "Look, I've learned a lot about this ship in the few weeks that I've been here. The captain will most likely have a few men watching over the lifeboats at the sides of the ship; but the captain has his own personal lifeboat, built to hold just himself and a few of his closest crew members. His boat is stationed at the very stern of the ship, which means it's very secluded. They're unlikely to see us there. I can lower you two into the ocean before anyone realizes that you've jumped ship."

"Wait a second, Gregory. What do you mean, LOWER US? You aren't coming with us?" Wesley asked me, sounding very concerned.

"No, Wesley, I will come with you, but the boat will have to be lowered by someone standing on the ship. His particular boat isn't rigged to be lowered by someone sitting in it. But I promise, after I lower you safely, I'll jump into the water and join both of you."

Wesley looked worried. After a minute, he spoke again. "One more question, Gregory: What if the crew's keeping watch over the captain's lifeboat? What then?" he asked.

"Well, seeing as how our options are limited, we'll just have to take that risk and be very careful," I responded.

We waited for the right moment, and after a short while, we stole swiftly and quietly away from the office. Thankfully, the crew had given up their search and were gathered midship to report their failures. The captain, needless to say, was not happy, and was throwing a huge fit.

With everyone's attention focused on the captain, we silently crept to the rear of the ship, occasionally ducking behind supply barrels to catch our breath and check our rear.

It took only minutes, though it seemed like hours, but we finally reached the stern, where the captain's lifeboat was hung from the wooden deck supports. From our vantage point, the boat looked tiny: It would barely fit four people. Luckily, it came stocked with a basket full of hardtack, some salt pork, and a few canteens - filled with what I assumed was fresh water. "Looks like we'll have ourselves food for a week if we ration it correctly," I observed.

"Well, given that we made port in Havana, Cuba yesterday, we can't be too far from the U.S. border. We can find Cuba and then row our way back to a port in North America," Cody suggested helpfully. "Wherever that is."

"Well, North America's better than the wide-open ocean," Wesley admitted. "At least we'd be safe and at home in our own country."

The boat was secured by a sturdy rope laced through the front and back of the vessel. I gently swung the craft off the edge of the deck, where it hung in midair, awaiting its passengers.

"Alright then, get on board," I said quietly, but firmly.

Wesley and Cody scrambled aboard. The small boat swung a bit with the extra weight. Slowly, I began to lower the boat with its two passengers down the side of the ship, toward the water, careful to not let them fall too suddenly.

Just as I was about to lower them the final stretch, I spied two pirates through the glass of a window of the room we were in front of, as they made their rounds on the ship. Problem was, they spied me too! The pirates ran from the room and sprinted in our direction, and I had to make a hasty decision.

Leaning over the edge, where I could still see Cody and Wesley patiently waiting in midair as the boat descended, I yelled, "Guys, I don't think I'm gonna be able to go with you! Start rowing! Now!"

"What?! What are you talking about?" they called frantically up to me.

"If you don't start rowing away right now, then all three of us will die! Now brace yourselves!"

"What? Why?"

I let the rope go, and the boat fell the remaining ten feet into the ocean. They were safe. The loss of the boat meant the pirates had also lost any chance of getting their hands on Cody or Wesley.

It also meant that I was soon to die.

After making sure that both Cody and Wesley were safe, I ran toward the pirates in a deliberate attempt to distract them. They quickly caught me, though, and viciously hauled me towards the center deck, muttering threats in my ear about my future. In no time at all, I was standing below the deck of the helm, facing the captain, who glared down at me.

"Well done, Dickson! Where did you find the scoundrel?!" he questioned the pirate on my right.

"At the back of the ship, sir. He was trying to sneak overboard in your private lifeboat, but I grabbed him!"

"Well done, but I tasked you with bringing all three escapees into your custody. Where are the others?"

Dickson had nothing to say, so the captain turned his gaze to me. "How about it, Gregory? Where are the others?"

I looked away, darned if I would sell Cody and Wesley out to this pathetic excuse of a man. Dickson, however, was feeling in a particularly violent mood, and twisted my arm painfully upward. "OK! OK! I'll tell you everything!" I yelled out.

The captain smirked at the ease with which he gained my surrender. "Well, well, you've got less of a spine than I imagined, boy! Don't think that this will change how I deal with you, though. Well, out with it; where did they go?!"

I looked up at the captain, already regretting how easily I had caved. But I was also smirking deviously at the 'choice words' I had decided to unload on the captain: "They've gone to that shameful place where your mother makes a living at night! I think she was offering a two for one special!"

Taken aback by my crude answer, the captain's smirk disappeared instantly. Most of the crew were silent, and a few even backed away. Only a couple of brave souls let out a chuckle at my audacity.

The captain's moment of stunned disbelief dissipated, replaced by anger. Blasting me with his eyes, he drew his sword, raising it high into the air. "Boy, you've been a pain in my side long enough! I gave you a chance to become one of us, but it's clear to me that you and I are of two different cloths. You have no place among us anymore! Men, to the starboard side! Today, this scallywag walks the plank!"

CHAPTER 34

LOSING A GOOD FRIEND

I was roughly seized by the other pirates. There would be no escape this time. I was dragged forcefully over to the starboard side of the ship, where the captain often coerced prisoners to walk the plank. I knew that the fall off the ship probably wouldn't kill me, and I would swim as if my life depended on it – for it did. But my mind was also filled with visions of the horrible sea creatures waiting to devour my body. At least I would know that I finally had escaped Red Beard's tyranny. That provided some comfort.

"Wait! Captain, stop!" I heard a voice call out loudly, interrupting my vision of being eaten by sharks.

Everyone stopped what they were doing and turned around. Who was such a fool as to interrupt the captain? The fearsome group of men parted, and out of the line of pirates stepped Aaron. It remained clear to me that Aaron was frightened at speaking up directly to the captain, but he didn't let his face show it too much.

"Please, Captain. Gregory and I have become good friends. It would break my heart to see him killed. I'll do anything to save his life, please!"

The captain stood lost in thought for a minute, contemplating a course of action. At long last, an evil smirk spread over his face.

"All right, Aaron. I will spare him for now, but in exchange for his life, you will jump overboard in his place! Both of you will learn, sooner or later, that I do not allow crimes aboard this ship to go unpunished."

Aaron appeared frightened at the captain's demands, and understandably so. "That's the only other choice?" he questioned the captain.

"Well, either that, or I could have the boatswain flog you endlessly until the entire deck is painted red with your blood. That is my only other offer, Aaron; I suggest you make your decision soon!" The captain pointed his sword in Aaron's direction to emphasize his point, and we all waited to find out how this dastardly situation would unfold.

Amazingly, the prospect of the captain sparing my life seemed to satisfy Aaron, for without hesitation, he began to walk towards the edge of the ship! I couldn't believe it! He was willing to give his life to save me – someone he had only known for three weeks. It was all happening so fast, too fast. I couldn't stop the tears from pouring down my cheeks.

"Wait, Aaron!" I cried desperately, as I watched him step up onto the wooden board that led straight to his demise. "Why would you do this for me?"

He stopped walking just as he had almost reached the edge of the plank. Quietly, with a benevolent smile on his face, he turned back to face me. "You're my best friend, Gregory; I'm honored to do this for you. Don't forget that!"

And those were the last words he spoke that day before he sprang off the plank and dove headfirst, like a knife, into the water. Desperately, I ran to the railing and peered over, looking for some sign that he was ok, but I wasn't so fortunate. The ripples in the water caused by his entrance were still present, but other than that, he had completely disappeared, like a ghost. No air bubbles, no clothing articles, not even a sign of his distinctive red hair was visible in the ocean below.

I took a moment to realize how truly alone I was at that moment. My closest friend on the ship was as good as dead, and the only two other people I could call allies were hopefully rowing their way to safety. I was stuck and alone, doomed to be a slave for the rest of my days. I turned bitterly to face the captain; I couldn't bear to watch the surface of the murky sea any longer for signs that Aaron had lived.

Inside, I seethed, hating the captain for what he'd done to Aaron. In truth, I had half of a mind to push **HIM** over the edge of the ship. Of course, I had not the strength, nor would I be given the opportunity to do so.

But the captain was far from finished with damaging my morale. "Ah, don't cry right now, sonny; you'll still be needing some water to finish making my ship shine! Back to work! And not a peep out of you!" he ridiculed, and laughed heartily, as the rest of the crew returned to their duties.

CHAPTER 35

A GIFT AND A TRIP TO DAVY JONES' LOCKER

Compared to that soul-shattering incident, the rest of the day remained uneventful. But when the day drew to an end, and darkness covered the sky, I had a premonition that we all were about to face a terrible downfall. That night, the ship ran into the most powerful storm I had ever seen. It could have been a monsoon or even a hurricane for all I knew. Maybe the good Lord had had just about enough of Red Beard's endless tyranny on the high seas.

The powerful waves stole control of our ship from us. Though we tried our best to fight the storm, The Dark Mystery was spun so violently that, with an enormous crash, we went aground on the rocks! The impact left in its wake an unfixable hole in the wood of the hull. In no time, immense waves of seawater flooded in, bogging down the vessel. Though the crew worked their hardest to bail out the water, their valiant efforts eventually proved for naught. The ship was going down.

Though the men were as tough as nails, deep inside, they knew when it was best to retreat and live to fight another day. If we stayed on the ship, we would be taken down with it. The cold, wild wind whipped aggressively through my hair as my body was battered by the fearsome downpour of rain. The untamable lightning seemed bent on tearing the heavens apart.

At this point, the First Mate was instructing the crew to board the lifeboats. I assisted in this task, making sure that the boats still tied to the ship were fully packed with crew members, before the stronger men inside the boats lowered everyone down to the dangerous waters below.

As I checked around, I realized that the captain had not yet boarded. In fact, come to think of it, I wasn't sure how the captain could get off, considering Cody and Wesley had stolen his private boat. Nevertheless, I shouted loudly to the others, trying to make my concern heard above the noise of the storm. But none of the crew could hear my cries.

Worrying about the captain was probably the dumbest thing I could be doing right then – why would I have even an ounce of sympathy for the man? Nevertheless, I knew it was the right thing to do. So, I ran up the water-slicked, wooden stairs to his chambers.

Inside the thick, wooden walls of the cabin, the rain and violent weather were silenced. I found the captain lying in his bed, coughing, and sputtering hoarsely. He looked like he had aged 40 years since this morning! He looked like an old man! "Captain! Captain! The ship's sinking! We need to get going!" I urgently called to him.

He shook his head. "No…No…boy," he croaked weakly. "My days are near finished; I couldn't stand up if I tried."

I rushed over to his side to examine him further. His body appeared to be cramping every so often, and his skin appeared looser than I had ever seen it. "Captain, what's happening to you?"

"I believe it's cholera, my boy. I've weathered the dastardly illness many times before, but this time, it's so much worse."

I was beyond shocked at the captain's condition. Despite the cruel ways he had abused me, I felt a deep pity. "C'mon, Captain, put your arm over my neck, and I'll help you down to the boats! You're Red Beard! Surely you won't be stopped by a simple illness, will you?"

The captain seemed to detect my underlying compassion, and so he asked me, "Boy, now you've got me good and confused. Why would you care so much about an old sea dog like me, especially after how I've treated you?"

Respectfully, I answered, "Because I think that your life has been filled with much more turmoil than mine."

"Well, my boy, you're right," he replied. Then, in the midst of the storm, knowing that the ship was foundered and destined to sink, the captain told me a story.

He told me that he had grown up in a house with parents who relentlessly argued with each other, probably almost to the point of divorce. In addition, his younger sister was killed in a horse carriage accident.

He also told me of how his life at school brought him many friends, but he fell deeply in love with a girl named Lydia, whose father was a manager in one of the Lowell factories. Then, he told me how, when he was old enough, he wanted to marry her. Her father, however, saw him as incompetent, unfit to marry his daughter, and wanted her to have nothing to do with him. So, he married her off to some affluent swell named Richard, who cared nothing about her.

The loss of Lydia tore Red Beard apart; he couldn't bear life without her. So, at the age of 18, he ran away from his parents and stowed away on <u>The Dark Mystery</u>. He didn't know at the time that <u>The Dark Mystery</u> was home to pirates. He wasn't thinking; he just wanted to get away. The desire to escape from his pain must have kept him from realizing it was a pirate ship. Once he was onboard, most of the crew saw him as an intruder, who should have been dealt with by fatal means. But instead, the captain treated him almost like a son. He was given all that he asked for and eventually rose to the rank of First Mate. All the crew eventually came to regard him with respect. And when at last the former captain's days on the ship were over, Red Beard was promoted to captain.

But I had to know: How did a man who had been so deeply loved by the captain change into the ruthless, cutthroat, and bloodthirsty legend of the seas? So, I asked.

Red Beard claimed that he was once a happy man, plundering and hiding treasure just for thrills. But all of that changed when he took a hiatus from fortune seeking. He claimed that once, during a stay in the United States, he courted and even got married for a few years, but the constant need for adventure just kept getting in the way. Sadly, for him, the call of endless adventure was just too alluring, and he ended up choosing the wide-open seas over the woman he married. From there, his morale plummeted, and he lost the will to live his life in any kind of decent manner.

I stood in awe at the captain's story. And he smiled, glad to have unburdened himself. But he didn't seem any better. In fact, by the time the captain had finished his story, he looked even more ill than when I had first entered his cabin. It was then that I knew that Red Beard's time as 'The Terror of the Seas' was truly coming to an end. I wanted to tell him something to reassure him, but he cut me off.

"Here, Gregory," he coughed. "I want you to have something." Reaching into his shirt pocket, he removed a worn piece of paper. It was probably decades old. "If I can't bring this with me into death, maybe you could make some use of it."

I examined and ran my fingers over the faded parchment. "Captain, what are you talking about? What is this?"

He leaned up a little in his bed, motioning to the document I held in my hands. "That, my boy, is part of the map to my biggest treasure hideout. I pillaged a great many ships in my day. So great is my treasure that I had to hide most of it. I can't bring back your parents, boy, and for that, I'm sorry; but maybe I can give you this as a small consolation."

The fact that the captain would entrust me with the ownership of his treasure map, and quite possibly his treasure, was more than my mind could take in. Upon opening it, I found that it was indeed a genuine treasure map! But I could tell, just from the appearance, that the map was incomplete and would probably need two or three other pieces to lead me to the treasure. If I was to be entrusted with the captain's wealth, I needed the missing pieces to the map.

SEBASTIAN JOE

"Sir. The other pieces? Where can I find the other pieces?" I asked urgently.

The captain heard me and struggled to sit up. "Boy, I...um... buried one of the pieces, and...um...oh yes, I sent one to a friend of mine. We used to be pirates together."

"Wait, how come you..."

But I was too late. The captain's last breath had slipped silently from his body.

Suffice it to say, even at my age, and even after seeing things that no boy my age should have seen, I still felt a sobering respect for the finality of death. That being said, I knew there wasn't much I could do.

After a moment of silence, I gave the captain one final salute, tucked his map into my pants, and dashed outside, looking for a way off the ship.

The force of the gale violently attacked me as soon as I came out onto the now slanted deck of the ship. The captain's cabin, the upper deck, and the sails were the only sections of the ship still above water! I was safe, but not for much longer.

The other lifeboats had left without me!

I was stranded!

CHAPTER 36

FRIENDS WHO ROW THE DISTANCE

The rest of the pirate crew had literally jumped ship without a second thought about the captain or me. I was left alone for myself until the ship sank, and I eventually drowned. I had few options: I had no boat. I could try to swim, but where? And besides, I was hundreds of miles from land.

So, I made a firm decision. If I couldn't get to safety, I would have no choice but to go down with the ship and Red Beard. Surrendering myself to the inevitable was never my first choice. Nevertheless, I decided to ignore the turbulent, frothy water and just get on with it.

Gingerly, I kneeled down upon the deck and leaned against the railing, letting the unrelenting rain pound down on me.

Gradually, my young mind began to drift from reality. The terrifying claps of thunder and the cold chill of the battering rain eventually faded away into nothingness. I became enveloped in a feeling of warmth as my short life flashed before my eyes. I remembered the cozy house I lived in, my wonderful parents, whom I loved very much, and the last time that I saw them on that day before fate brought Red Beard to my beach. The final memory to occupy my mind was from the night before that memorable day, right after they had tucked me into bed for the last time.

"Goodnight! I love you!" I called out to them, as they left to go to bed.

They both smiled benevolently, and then dad said to me, "We love you too, son. Good night, Gregory...Gregory...Gregory..."

The vision was ending. The comforting images of my parents were eventually funneled away into darkness.

Stil, strangely, my dad continued to call out to me. "Gregory... Gregory...Gregory... GREGORY! GREGORY! GREGORY!"

Suddenly, the strong, soothing voice of my father had turned shrill and desperate. And it didn't stop. For some reason, it sounded as if he were very close by. Or was my mind playing games with me?

"GREGORY! GREGORY! GREGORY!"

There it was again. This time, I opened my eyes quickly in confusion. The wind, thunder, lightning, and the pouring rain once again assaulted my senses. But I really could hear someone calling out my name!

"GREGORY! JUMP! HURRY!"

As the lightning lit up the dark ocean, I forced myself to focus. Looking out to sea, I saw the faint silhouette of what looked like a small, wooden rowboat rowing valiantly against the towering waves of the ocean in a brave attempt to reach me!

Was it the pirates? Did they come back for me?

Suddenly, I knew where I had heard that young voice before! "WESLEY?!" I screamed out.

"YES! YOU HAVE TO JUMP, GREGORY! HURRY!"

How hard they must have rowed to reach me, I'll never know. But I didn't wait a second longer. Jumping from my small platform, I felt the cold air whisk wildly against my face moments before my body plunged deep into the frigid ocean. Thrashing through the black waters to the surface, I swam hard in the direction I had last seen the lifeboat, desperately hoping I could make it. Seeing it materialize in front of me, I reached out my hand, which was quickly grabbed. Treading water, trying to see through the tossing waves, I managed to help haul myself over the side of the small lifeboat. Climbing in, and falling shakily into the bottom of the boat, I saw both Wesley and his brother Cody sitting at the front of the craft, each manning an oar, heroically rowing. I was confused. If they were rowing, then who had helped me into the boat? Turning to my right, I saw that Cody and Wesley had taken on another passenger!

"Aaron! You're alive! You're here!"

I was so grateful that I almost forgot to breathe. He had lived. My friend had lived.

While Cody and Wesley rowed the craft toward land, they hoped, Aaron and I talked while we bailed the ocean and rain out of the small, waterlogged vessel. Upon questioning him, I learned that when Aaron had dove into the water, he had actually swum all the way underneath the ship, starboard to portside, to mislead the pirates and the captain. Then, he swam to the back of the ship and hitched himself to the rudder, just floating along until he could devise the next step in his escape. After a short time, he saw Cody and Wesley's lifeboat quietly making its way towards him. They had helped him in and were delighted to find that Aaron was

my friend. It was Aaron who convinced them to row the boat through the storm to find me.

Not long after I had boarded the little boat, and over the boisterous noise of the weather, I heard a loud, creaking noise. Quickly, I looked behind me to see The Dark Mystery finally relinquish its hold on the rocks and slip beneath the surface, down into the briny depths of the ocean. The vessel that had been my home for a very long three weeks had at last completed its final voyage.

I gave the ship a final, solemn salute, said a quick goodbye to Red Beard, and then turned my attention back to the task of surviving another day.

We rowed as hard as we could, for hours on end, trying to use the strong current of the ocean to our advantage. By early morning, the mighty storm had begun to let up, and the early morning sunrise provided us direction. Since we were still some ways away from land, we worked meticulously to carefully ration our food and water supplies. When the sun went down the next night, Aaron helped us find our way by means of the stars; he actually possessed great skill in that regard, having learned much from the pirates on board The Dark Mystery. We rowed for five more days until, at last, we arrived back at the shores of Mississippi, relieved to return to familiar land. From there, Wesley and I kept trekking north until, eventually, we arrived here, at the great state of Illinois, where we continue living to this day.

The five friends sat in awe at Gregory's story. But within a matter of minutes, they began to ask questions.

"So, what happened to Cody and Aaron?" Tom inquired.

Gregory nodded, pausing to remember. "Eventually, they parted ways with us. We've never seen them again, but I reckon that they formed a pirate gang of their own."

"Your brother just let you go, like that?" Huck queried disbelievingly, directing his response towards Dr. Wesley.

Wesley gave his shoulders a small shrug and looked pensive. "We cared a great deal for each other, but by that time, we were both young men with our own lives to live. I hope very much that he's safe and happy somewhere. I still miss him and think of him often."

"You didn't want to go with them?" Becky asked Gregory. "I thought Aaron was your best friend."

"He still is," Gregory affirmed, laughing, while Dr. Wesley looked at him, pretending to be offended. "But no, I wanted to stay put on dry land. And I had had enough adventure to last a lifetime! Aaron, on the other hand, had only been on land a few times in his life and was eager to explore as far as his legs would carry him. I encouraged Wesley to go with them, but he was adamant about staying by my side. So, Wesley and I put the Mississippi River on our left and headed north. We made it this far and decided we liked it. Eventually, Wesley went to medical school, graduated, and began working in the town, but I've pretty much stayed here the entire time. I thought about possibly looking for Red Beard's treasure, but the clues he had given me about the locations of the remaining pieces of his map were so vague that I basically gave up. So, anyway, that's how I came to acquire part of Red Beard's map."

"And you've stayed out here, in the middle of nowhere, for most of your life?" Tom questioned incredulously.

"That's pretty much how it went. Red Beard was right when he suspected that my folks were probably dead. When we returned to the United States, we made for my hometown. Though I asked around, I never encountered my parents again, and no one had seen them since Red Beard's violent raid. I trekked with Wesley to this small, secluded stretch of land and have camped out here ever since."

"And how long ago did this all happen to you, Gregory?" Andrew probed.

Gregory leaned his head back to look into the sky, mentally trying to recall his past. "It's been a good 30 years since we made it back to the mainland; and honestly, to me, it still feels like it only happened yesterday."

"Wow!" Huck marveled. "That was probably one of the best stories I have ever had the pleasure to hear."

Gregory uttered a low chuckle. "I'm glad that you enjoyed it. You're the first ones that got to hear it. I'm just curious myself, though; where do you all plan on going now that you have my piece of the map?"

"Well, I'm still on the run for my life, sir," Becky uncomfortably reminded them all. "I was figuring on returning to Missouri as soon as possible."

"But after that, we're not completely sure," Tom admitted on behalf of the group, as he examined the two paper fragments currently in his possession. "Neither of these pieces have any sort of X marking the location of Red Beard's treasure. We'd still need to find the final piece to get anywhere."

"Well, I don't see any reason why you need to be leaving as soon as you got here; why don't you stay with us for a day?" Wesley generously offered.

"Well, I guess one day couldn't hurt anything," Andrew figured. "Not like Dan would think to find us out here."

"Then it's settled," Gregory declared, clapping his hands together in a gesture of welcome. "Our home is your home. Please acquaint yourself and make camp wherever you see fit!"

CHAPTER 37

BRIGHT STARS AND LOVE SPARKS

It didn't take long for Andrew to unfold the nine-foot sheet of canvas they had brought with them. From there, Gregory helped to skillfully arrange the material over a few strong tree branches, ensuring a comfortable shelter for their protection that night. Gregory made sure that the shelter sat close enough to his and Wesley's tents and was still within range of the campfire's heat, to keep everybody warm and comfortable. The remainder of the day was spent by everybody telling their life stories and discussing their ambitions.

Late that night, after another hearty meal of chili, the seven campers were ready to turn in for the night. They had spent a good two hours telling tall tales and myths, which usually revolved around somebody dead or famous - sometimes both. After the fire was banked, everyone cozily settled in for the night, stretching their feet towards the fire's embers. The wild weather of the night before had vanished without a trace. Instead, the sky above them now twinkled with thousands of bright stars. Wesley and Gregory softly described some of the various constellations, telling the others how to locate them in the sky at night. At this moment, Gregory had just finished pointing out the location of Ursa Minor, also known as the Little Dipper.

Tom groaned quietly, but noticeably, underneath the shelter of the canvas. "You remind me a lot of my schoolteacher," he complained, feeling rather annoyed. "How about teaching us something interesting and useful?"

Becky, lying beside him, nudged him with her elbow as a nonverbal scolding for his rudeness. She might have said something additionally as chastisement, but Wesley spoke up first.

"Actually, Tom, constellations are more useful than you may realize. Before the invention of the calendar, farmers used constellations as a mark for knowing when to plant their crops. Also, look at the Little Dipper. Do you see where the tip of the handle would be? Right there? The bright star on the end? That there's called the North Star. Even though the other stars may be in different places every night, the North Star always stays still. This makes it ideal for finding your way when you get lost at sea or on land, even if you don't have a compass or can't find any moss on a tree."

"Oh, I see it!" Tom said, quite in awe, and feeling mildly humbled. "Wait, how do you know all that?"

Wesley smiled. "I was a pirate for a bit of my life, Tom; I had to learn the skill at some point."

When the talking ended, one by one, they each surrendered to sleep's gentle call – all except Tom. He had learned more about himself and the world in the past couple of days than he thought possible. And his mind wouldn't shut down. It kept wandering back and forth, preventing sleep from reaching his body, tired though he was.

He tried for a whole hour to fall asleep, but his mind was still racing with tough questions he had yet to find the answers for.

Restless and wide awake, he stood up quietly and walked away from camp, up to a ledge overlooking the bank of the river, close to where they had anchored their raft. The moon was out, and visibility wasn't a problem. Shucks, he snuck out at night on a regular basis; he could navigate in the dark almost as well as a cat. Finding an oak tree, with many strong, low-hanging branches, he shimmied up and took a seat on the rough wood.

There, at last, he found himself alone with his thoughts, the quiet flowing sound of the river, and the gentle chirping of hundreds of crickets. He couldn't figure out why, but he was WORRIED about his friends. He was worried about all of them. And he didn't know why he was suddenly caring SO much. Worrying about others was unlike him, but there he was, up a tree, worried.

As he swung his feet back and forth over the branch, he heard the sound of a stick snapping on the path behind him. He whipped his head around to face what his mind told him was a sudden danger. What he saw, however, was only Becky, standing a few feet away from his perch in the tree.

"Don't worry, Tom, it's just me," she quickly reassured him.

"Well, I guess it doesn't hurt to be too cautious, does it?" he figured, turning back to face the lagoon.

"What are you doing up this late, Tom?" she questioned.

"I'm Tom Sawyer; I always stay up late. You oughta know that by now," he chuckled, trying to make a joke, but not succeeding.

At least Becky didn't buy it. "Tom, it's past midnight, and you're up a tree, alone, rather than asleep with the rest of us. What's wrong?" Becky pushed, concerned at the unfamiliar behavior.

She ducked underneath the tree branch that Tom was sitting on in order to stand in front of him. Still, Tom wouldn't look at her.

"*Well,*" she thought to herself. "*if he won't come DOWN to talk . . .*" Smiling to herself, she placed her hands on the tree branch and quickly hoisted herself up to Tom's level. With a little adjusting, she settled herself close to him on the branch.

Tom was astonished by the ease with which she accomplished this. "Well, gosh, Becky, that's a skill I don't think I ever taught you; when did you learn to climb trees?"

"I've got some big trees in my backyard, Tom. I've actually used them for hiding whenever my dad tries to bug me about attending local women's gatherings and other nonsense like that."

"So, you can climb trees, and you're also a doctor? You just keep loving to surprise me, don't you?" Tom asked.

Becky smiled faintly. "Tom, seriously, is something going on with you? You've seemed different ever since we embarked on this expedition."

Tom faced away from her, looking towards the raft, which was still floating silently in the lagoon.

"Tom, it's okay. You can tell me anything. I won't tell anyone else."

His resistance gradually withered under her gentle, nurturing approach. He still didn't face her, but he gave in a bit. "It's just... when we started on this expedition, I thought it would just be five friends going on a harmless adventure. I had absolutely no idea that our lives would be in so much peril, or that we would find out that some fiend wants nothing more than to take your life, Becky."

"Tom, there is no way you could have predicted we'd run into that outlaw or that he wanted to hurt me. We couldn't even predict the weather," Becky reasoned.

But Tom wasn't finished. "And another thing: Remember how Gregory talked about how treasure seeking and the life of a pirate ain't nearly as exciting as he thought?"

"Tom Sawyer, are you losing interest in being a fortune seeker?"

"Oh no, far from it. Perish that thought, Becky. I just want to know what's wrong with me. Why am I so worried about you all? Because I am, you know."

Becky stared directly at the young man sitting next to her. Tom's face was serious in the moonlight. Turning his head to face her, he looked to her for an answer.

"Tom, I figure we're all growing up - even you," she said softly.

Tom's eyes went wide when he heard her say those two words. "I'm sorry...growing up?" He repeated the words uneasily, almost fearfully.

"Yeah, Tom. It happens to everybody. For some, it might happen a little later, but it will happen."

Her kind answer sent Tom into a small panic. Stressing over the implications, he pinched the bridge of his nose and then cradled his head in his hands. "But I ain't ready to grow up," he fretted.

Becky smiled again. "Tom, growing up, getting a bit of wisdom, and becoming a bit more mature...well, it's a good thing. I rather like it."

"Huh? Really? You like it? Aren't you worried you're gonna change or something?"

"Tom, growing up doesn't mean your personality disappears – it just grows up with you. I mean, it's your personality that makes all the kids in the village idolize you. You're never going to lose that - it's who you are."

Tom turned to face her once more. "So, you'll still like me when I'm all grown up?"

Becky stared hard at Tom to see if he was joking. She decided he wasn't. "Yes, Tom, even when you're all grown up. I mean, I'm glad you'll always be my mischievous, school-hating Tom. If you became a different person entirely, I don't know what I would do."

"Court someone with more money than me?" he teased.

Becky smacked her hand to her forehead. "You got lucky, Tom. That's all I will say: You got lucky! But even if you were poor like Huck, I'd still love you. Money has nothing to do with my feelings for you," she finished, scooching closer, squeezing his hand affectionately, and laying her head on his shoulder.

"Gee, Becky," Tom spoke. "That means a lot coming from you. And I guess I understand: Growing up makes you care more about your friends."

"Now you're getting it, Tom. Glad I could help you," she returned. And she was. Becky was about to push herself off the branch to walk back to camp, but she stopped. There was one more thing to say. "Tom?" she asked.

He turned to look at her again. "Yeah, Becky?"

Even in the gentle light of the moon, Tom could see a soft blush pinken her cheeks as she nervously bit her lip in a timid smile.

"You'll always be my swashbuckling hero. Don't ever change that," she said.

She then leaned in and pressed her warm lips to Tom's cheek in a sweet, gentle kiss.

As she pulled herself away, she watched Tom's eyes widen. A bit pleased with herself, Becky pushed herself off the branch, back onto level ground, and made her way back to the others.

Tom sat on his branch without moving, frozen by the affection shown him. He looked up to the sky, as though trying to see God's face in the heavens, and spoke. "Lord, please make her mine someday," he petitioned quietly.

Then, he hopped off the branch and walked back to camp, his mind now free of the burden that had been weighing on him. Tomorrow, the adventure would begin again, like it or not. But now, he felt ready to face anything they came across!

CHAPTER 38

JUST INN TIME

The next morning, renewed by a refreshingly good night of sleep, Amy, Becky, Huck, Tom, and Andrew packed up their supplies and said goodbye to Wesley and Gregory. Though the latter two were anxious to have them stay – they were great company – the five friends had to respectfully decline. They had a serious purpose: They had to get to Missouri and find the sheriff.

In single file, the explorers hiked back down to the lagoon and boarded the raft. Getting back to St. Petersburg, Missouri would be a difficult task, for it meant rowing against the strong current of the Mississippi. Luckily, they sighted a steamboat chugging slowly up the river, whose pilot was more than willing to throw them a rope and tow them back to town. With the tow line in place, there was little for them to do but gently guide the rudder. Together, they chattered about the next steps to ensure Becky's safety.

"Becky, it just ain't safe for you to stay at home: You'd be too vulnerable," Tom argued.

"I'm sure I'll be safe in the village, in my own house, Tom. The sheriff will see to it that I'm protected," Becky protested.

"Becky, the sheriff can't just stay in your house every day and hour until July 4th. He's got other people to watch out for and other responsibilities," Huck jumped in on Tom's side. "Andrew, what do you think?"

Andrew drew his glance away from the quiet shoreline to look at Huck. "This sounds like something that shouldn't be decided quickly. I'll tell you what: When we get back to the village, we can continue this discussion in my shop," he cordially offered.

"Won't you have customers to help, though?" Tom asked.

"Not really, Tom," Amy assured him. "When we left for the trip, Andrew locked the door and put out a sign telling the public we were closed until further notice. There shouldn't be anyone coming to the shop."

"Hope that doesn't cost you too much business or money, Andrew," Becky spoke, in some semblance of an apology.

"Becky, Amy and I are fine as far as money goes; I just want to make sure that you are kept safe," Andrew promised. "Now, let's focus on getting back to the village."

In what seemed to be no time, they approached the quiet edge of the St. Petersburg wharf. Docking the raft and securing it to the pier, they waved goodbye to the steamboat captain. Satisfied that the raft wasn't going anywhere, the five quickly walked up the quiet main street of the village to Andrew's carpentry and woodworking shop.

Looking around, they could see that the small Missouri town had been spared the greatest wrath of the weather. Sure, the street was a bit muddy, and there were tree branches lying in a lot of people's yards, but the houses and buildings were mostly untouched. Several dedicated grown-ups were already working to collect the branches and the roof shingles that had blown down. They would set the village right in no time.

Andrew pulled a small, brass key from the pocket of his trousers and unlocked the front door to his shop. Looking back and forth to make sure that nobody was watching them, they quickly disappeared inside and shut the door, making sure to lock the deadbolt after them.

Inside, the front room was crowded with numerous, wooden items in various stages of completion. There were chairs and tables, a rocking horse, a clothing cabinet, and a rowboat and some oars. One of the walls was lined with various hammers, saws, chisels, and other tools a carpenter might need.

"The shop looks bigger than the last time I stopped by," Huck remarked, looking around.

"I've gotten a lot more requests for fixing leaky roofs since the April showers began, so we've been blessed with more money, and with it, the ability to increase the size of the building," Andrew explained. "Now do me a favor and close the curtains; I'm not comfortable with exposing ourselves more than we need to."

Tom and Amy ran to the glass windows and drew the thin cotton curtains across the glass. No one would be able to see them from the street. Luckily, the curtains blocked the gaze of curious individuals, but not really the sunlight, so adequate light remained in the shop. Becky, Amy, and Andrew took a seat in the chairs Andrew had been building, while Tom and Huck sat on the floor, beside each other, against the wall.

"Now then," Andrew began solemnly. "We need to discuss our plans for the next week, leading up to the village's celebration of Independence Day. If the sheriff can't watch Becky all day long, would she still be safe in the village?"

Tom shook his head, deep in thought. "From the way Dan described it, his greatest desire is to punish Becky's father by physically hurting Becky – he said he was going to kill her. That being said, Phillip discovered us on Jackson's Island and may have told Dan about us after he regained consciousness. If Becky stays here in the village, she may be at risk of Dan possibly kidnapping her early or even deviating from his plan in some way."

"How do you reckon, Tom?" Amy probed, curious to Tom's logic.

"Becky and I talked about this before. If Dan's grudge against Judge Thatcher is as personal as he claims, there could be a chance that he knows where Becky and her father live. And, having lived and worked in our village for a while, Phillip knows a little about each of us. All Phillip would need to do is ask around, and he would learn where we all live; then, he would eventually tell Dan this information. I wouldn't even put it past Dan to hurt any of the rest of us for getting in the way of his plans."

Becky applauded him. "Now where is that smart mind when school is taking place, I wonder?"

"Probably on extended summer vacation, I reckon," Tom suggested sarcastically.

"Tom may be right, in any case," Becky figured. "We can't stay at home until Dead Eye Dan has been brought to justice. We'll need to stay someplace where he will never find us."

"I'm used to sleeping anywhere; count me in for wherever you want to go," Huck voiced cheerfully. "However, I might suggest sleeping indoors this time. If that storm was anything to go on, I'd reckon there'll be more rainfall this summer."

"A valid point, but where could the five of us go where we'd be able to sleep inside?" Andrew asked the group. "Amy and I have got a couple of relatives up north a ways, but I'd bet they wouldn't be too happy with five people showing up at their house. Not to mention it would probably take us a couple days travel by wagon to get there."

Silence fell as each pondered their options. Surely they could come up with something reasonable?

Tom was next to suggest an idea. "We may not have to bother relatives at all, Andrew. I've got us a plan: A few miles south of this village, there's a fellow by the name of Horace, and he owns a large house on Paradise Road. From what I've heard from the other adults, he rents out the rooms of his house to travelers, kind of like an inn. I bet he could be persuaded to let us all stay for a while. Nobody from the village would know exactly where we've gone. We could be cared for until all the tension dies down or the sheriff catches Dead Eye Dan. It's the perfect solution."

"But getting room and board would cost quite a bit of money, Tom…" Becky began, but cut herself off when she realized how small of an obstacle this would be for Tom to overcome.

"For the safety of us all, I'll gladly pay for us to stay the week," Tom offered generously. "Probably wouldn't cost that much anyway."

"The question is, would they have enough vacancy to take us all?" Huck asked. "Five people might be a lot for him to accommodate on such short notice."

"We may just have to walk down there and ask him ourselves," Amy admitted. "Can't imagine that he will have many travelers two days after that storm, though. The roads will be unpassable with mud. Won't be able to ride a wagon through those parts for a day or two."

"Alright then, does anybody have any other objections to this idea?" Andrew inquired.

There were none.

"Perhaps, though, Tom and I should let our parents know of our well-being before we go," Becky suggested thoughtfully.

"You can't seriously be considering talking to them, telling them we're ok, and that we'll be gone again, Becky," Tom protested adamantly. "They would put an end to the plan before we could leave."

"I meant we could leave a note, Tom," she calmly explained. "We wouldn't even have to tell them where we were going."

Tom's argument ended as quickly as it began. Becky could always be counted on to quell Tom's impulsiveness with a healthy dose of sensibility. "Well, I suppose it wouldn't hurt anyone to leave a note. Wouldn't want to have the whole village thinking that we were dead again," Tom conceded, remembering what happened in the town a few years ago when he, Joe Harper, and Huck were presumed to have drowned in the river, and the whole village had mistakenly held a funeral service for them.

"Then do what needs to be done and come back quickly," Andrew ordered. "Amy and I will wait here for you."

"What about me?" Huck asked. "What should I do?"

Becky considered his question and pulled a silver dollar from her pocket, handing it to Huck. "Go down to the clothing store and buy yourself a nice, new straw hat, Huck. It's the least I can do for you since you gave up your hat to make a fire for us," Becky offered congenially.

"Much obliged, Becky," Huck thanked her, as he stood up and hurried out.

Tom stood up to follow his best friend out the door, but he paused when considering his next course of action. "Becky, is your dad working in the bank today? I'm gonna need to withdraw some cash for our trip, and I'd hate to have him pester me as to your whereabouts," he explained.

"It's Thursday, Tom; he usually takes the day off and leaves the business in the care of the other bankers," Becky replied nonchalantly, as she prepared to walk outside. "He'll probably be out playing cards with a few of his gentlemen friends; you shouldn't have any trouble from him."

"Good to know," Tom acknowledged, checking the streets outside before leaving the shop.

About 30 minutes later, Huck returned from the clothing store with a new straw hat: Same color, but in better condition than his first one.

"Looking sharp there, partner," Amy complimented him with an exaggerated Western accent.

"Frankly, there were too many choices, Amy," Huck admitted. "A hat's just a hat; I had to flip a coin to make a decision."

Soon afterwards, Becky and Tom returned within moments of each other. Tom returned carrying about $200 worth of dollar bills, which he hoped would suffice for their expenses. Both had reported leaving notes for their kinfolk, and Tom had also taken the time to return the borrowed picnic basket.

Becky shared that whilst Tom had been busy withdrawing cash from his enormous account, she had left a note for the sheriff describing Dead Eye Dan's last location, as well as briefly detailing Dan's plans for July 4th. Hopefully, that would be the end of their troubles.

With their preparations now out of the way, they all began the long walk to the inn. The actual distance to their choice of lodging proved to be about five miles, but time was on their side, and they didn't really care. It was a beautiful day for a walk.

The inn was actually rather isolated. Though it could be seen from the roadway, along with a couple of rundown outbuildings, few other homes could be seen. The area was mostly uninhabited. Tom knew that this place would keep them concealed. All he had to worry about now was being able to secure lodging for them all.

No one had bothered to bring luggage or even a change of clothes with them. This was because they hadn't wanted the extra weight slowing them down. After dusting themselves off, they all took a moment to admire their potential new home for the week.

The house had probably been built in the late 1700's but had been renovated quite recently. It bore a modern-day architectural design and was three stories high, with many elegant touches, such as red brick walls and fancy wooden molding – and that was just the outside of the house. Additionally, hidden behind the inn

was an enormous, magical garden that captivated Becky and Amy. Standing here reminded Tom of an inn he had stayed in once when he was very young.

A double, wooden front door opened up into a comfortably spacious breezeway. Wiping their feet on the ragged front door mat, they entered the establishment and gently closed the door behind them. Inside the three-story building, the house appeared to be well taken care of. The home was quiet. A wooden hat and coat rack stood at attention proudly in the corner, its branches devoid of hats or coats. Huck handed over his own hat into the care of the rack as he took in his surroundings. A number of open windows circulated a cool breeze around the open space of a quiet living room. From the corner of the room, an older man in his sixties motioned for them to approach. In their group of five, they walked over to a wooden desk, where he welcomed them from the comfort of a large armchair.

"Hello, and welcome to the Riverfront Inn," the jovial fellow greeted them cordially. "My name is Horace McPherson; how can I help you good folks today?"

"Thank you kindly, sir. We need lodging for all five of us," Tom politely responded. "We're sorry not to have sent a letter or something in advance, but we've just been through a lot lately. We'll gladly pay you double your asking price if you can get rooms for all of us under this roof," Tom finished his plea, drawing forth a small pinch of his money to emphasize his point.

Horace eyed Tom's money but shook his head and held up his hand. "My boy, there's no need for any extra payment here. Truth is, you all happen to be in luck; the entire house is unoccupied at the moment."

The kids all looked at each other for a moment in astonishment before Huck spoke up. "Well, ain't that some good news to hear. But why, sir?"

"Well, the house has actually been unoccupied for about a week now, but after what happened yesterday, I don't think anybody from these parts is in the mood for a vacation. Probably too worried about the weather to travel and too busy repairing any damage from the storm."

"We were hoping that might be the case," Becky admitted.

"Glad to hear it," Horace acknowledged. "Now then, down to business; how long would you be interested in staying?"

"A week is all we really need, sir," Andrew replied confidently.

"Excellent, that should work out splendidly," Horace spoke amiably. "Though, there is one issue I should bring to your attention: At the moment, I am in the process of renovating some of the rooms, so unfortunately, a few of you will be in different rooms on different floors. Is that okay?"

"Yes, of course," Everyone assured him, just grateful to be together.

"Very well, then," Horace continued. "There are three available beds in the attic and two on the second floor. Wherever each of you wish to sleep is entirely your choice. For the week, the cost of living here will be 80 dollars."

Tom quickly produced the requested money and deposited it into Horace's waiting hands. After a quick count to verify the amount, Horace gently urged them to make themselves at home.

"Supper will be ready at around 5:00. Be ready for a feast," Horace called to them, as they filed out of the room.

"Thank you, Horace!" Amy called back, as they went up the stairs.

There were about five guestrooms on the second floor, with only two displaying open doors. Becky and Amy were quick to assess that the closed doors were the rooms being worked upon, just as Horace had described. A third door stood open, revealing a homey looking bathroom, complete with a copper tub and a wooden washstand, which the five of them would probably have to share between them. Becky and Amy selected the two bedrooms and walked around inside to inspect. Both rooms had twin sized beds, a small nightstand with candles close by, and a set of dark curtains on either side of a glass window overlooking the garden.

Tom, Huck, and Andrew continued past the second floor, up a lowered, wooden ladder, to the third floor in the attic. Though already massive looking from the outside, the inside of the attic was equally and impressively huge. The wooden roof climbed about five feet higher above the heads of everyone standing, allowing plenty of room to walk around. There were two, twin-sized beds tucked under a small alcove, and a third, larger bed sat next to one of many, nearby, large glass windows they could open for fresh air. Andrew selected the larger mattress as his own, leaving Tom and Huck with the twin beds. They were hoping that the attic wouldn't be too cold. But then they remembered that it was summer, and they could see thick flannel blankets draped across the beds, which promised to provide a warm sleep at night.

With a big breath of relief, all of them looked at each other. They had done it. Becky was safe. That was all that mattered, and they had really done it.

With a last look around the attic, they fell onto their comfortable beds for a quick afternoon nap.

CHAPTER 39

A SHOT IN THE DARK

For six days, all was well. Tom, Becky, Amy, Andrew, and Huck lived peacefully in the deep redoubt of the country, out of the reach of Dead Eye Dan. Horace allowed them to roam around the premises as much as they liked and provided them with three delicious meals every day. They even got a snack or two. And across the road from the house sat a small pond, just big enough for the occasional swim when it got really hot outside. Granted, the isolation caused Tom to feel a little bit homesick, but at least Becky and his closest friends were with him.

On the seventh night, however, their vacation took a turn for the worse.

That night was the evening of July 3rd, the eve of Independence Day. It was also the night before Dead Eye Dan and his paunchy henchman were to go looking for Becky. They just needed to remain vigilant – and isolated – for one more day. Then, they all could return to their normal lives. And if they had to skip the celebration in their village to keep Becky safe, well, that's just what they would do.

So, that night, they all gathered in the cozy living room of the inn to read books. Horace reported that he needed to leave the inn and travel into town to pick up some groceries for the morning. He assured them he would be back in time to make breakfast for everyone and promised it would be a special treat. They said goodbye as he walked out the front door and hailed the carriage he had arranged to take him into town.

Horace had left a warm fire blazing in the fireplace and a brass canister, full of tea leaves, on the coffee table. He had also set out some ornate teacups for them all to use. Intending to brew a pot of tea for them all, Becky hung a copper kettle, filled with water, over the flames. There were a number of comfortably cushioned couches in the room and a bunch of thick, wool afghans folded nearby to keep them all warm.

Contentedly seating themselves on the couches, with the blankets wrapped snugly around them, and warm tea in hand, the five friends settled in for the evening. Andrew selected an old copy of Shakespeare's <u>Romeo and Juliet</u> from a nearby bookshelf and began to read from the worn pages. Tom and Huck pretended to gag over this 'romance,' but no one much listened.

"*But soft, what light through yonder window breaks? It is the east, and Juliet is the sun. Arise, fair sun, and kill the envious moon, who is already sick and pale with grief. That thou, her maid, art far more fair than she,*" Andrew read aloud to everyone in the room.

Becky and Amy were infatuated with the classic story, but Tom and Huck squinted their eyes in confusion, put down their tea, shook their heads, and grabbed their ears, as if they were in pain. "Hey Andrew, why don't you try reading another book or something? I'm losing my sanity," Tom pleaded, burying his head in his hands.

Genuinely concerned, Andrew closed the book for a brief moment to respond to Tom's complaint. "Any particular reason why you want me to switch books?"

"Well, for one, the dialogue ain't realistic. If I courted Amy with such a statement, she'd probably laugh and think me drunk or something," Huck volunteered. Amy chuckled into her hand, as she slightly nodded to validate Huck's point.

"Yeah, and for another, this Romeo guy doesn't sound like he believes what he's saying at all," Tom added rather emphatically. "I know it's just a play, but he sounds extremely fake to me."

"Oh, Tom, it's all about the pure intent of the love shown between Romeo and Juliet," Becky explained, unable to believe her boyfriend could really be so dense. "When you grow up a little more, you'll probably come to appreciate it better."

"Becky, let it go," Amy urged. "It's really only something that a girl would understand. I also think it's a little bit kooky myself if you ask me."

BLAAAAM! BLAAAAM!

Two loud gunshots erupted in the distance. Everyone set aside their blankets and tea and hurried to the window at the far end of the room. Looking outside, they could see a bright light shining through the walls of a house a fair distance away - the inn's only neighbor.

"Oh dear, what do you suppose is going on over there?" Amy asked solemnly.

"I believe a gun may have been fired," Andrew deduced, sounding like a lackwit.

"That's there's a pretty good guess, Andrew," Tom sarcastically responded, rolling his eyes. "Shouldn't we go check and find out what happened, though? What if someone was injured, or worse?"

Andrew shook his head adamantly. "Too risky, Tom. There's no telling who's over there. On top of that, we'd be going out in the dark. As good as your point is, I'd really prefer to wait till daylight."

Becky disagreed. "Well, I think we need to check. If someone was shot by accident, they might be dead by the time morning arrives."

"Becky..." Andrew cautioned.

"Andrew, would you rather sit here, continue to read this play, and tell Tom and Huck the depressing truth of how the story ends?" she asked pointedly.

Andrew stared hard at Becky, but then relented. "All right, Becky; we'll go. But I want everyone to stay close together," he instructed, as he moved towards the front door.

"Wait, what happens at the end of the book?" Tom warily prodded her, as he opened the front door, gazing out into the darkness.

"You'll just have to read the book and find out yourself," Becky taunted, as they left the security of the building. Maybe it would have been smarter not to get involved, but they all had visions of someone lying hurt in that house.

Their trip was not long, but they had to cross a small field to get to the house - about 500 feet of open space.

The light across the field was still shining when they reached the house. Actually, the "house" was much bigger than they initially thought; "mansion" would have been closer to the right descriptive word. But the abode, no matter its grand size, was falling apart. A bright light continued to glow through the cracked, wooden wall of one of the lower rooms, and moonlight added to the brightness of the evening. As such, they did not have a hard time finding their way around. However, there was no easy way to tell what was going on inside.

At once, they heard muffled shouting coming from the inside of the house. Unable to see anything from outside, they began to search the perimeter. Taking the front stairs up one level to the main porch, which was raised off the ground, they discovered the front door hanging mysteriously open; the lower hinge appeared to be permanently broken. They took this as good fortune and went inside. But the moonlight did not follow them inside, which was completely dark. Without any light, they stumbled around the very large main parlor. Apart from some dusty furniture, it was empty. With a bit of trepidation, they slowly climbed the sweeping main staircase in the middle of the room. At the top, they advanced down a dark hallway toward the sounds. As they walked, gradually, their eyes adjusted slightly to the dark. But the closer they got to the noise, the clearer it became that the shouts were coming from beneath them!

In the lead, Becky turned a corner and let out a sharp gasp. Tom, Huck, Andrew, and Amy surrounded her, squinting into the darkness, trying to locate the danger. What they saw was a shadowy, motionless figure with no eyes and a face that could have frozen even time. It was a gargoyle.

Andrew had seen enough of them in old book illustrations

to know what they were and how they were used. People in the medieval and renaissance periods usually stationed them near the edges of church roofs to drain water away when it rained. For some reason, the owner of this house had one inside!

Their hearts racing, but otherwise safe, the five brave explorers continued on. The hallway was lined with more than 20 stone gargoyles, all posed like demons. Tom, noticing Becky's distress, put his arm around her waist protectively to prevent her from having a full-blown panic attack.

"What kind of person would keep a bunch of creepy, old statues in their hallway?" Huck asked out loud.

"Possibly a follower of the macabre," Amy guessed, startled that Becky's voluminous vats of knowledge were apparently rubbing off on her.

Along the length of the long hallway, they found themselves faced with a difficult choice, as there were a great many closed doors to choose from. Deciding to go through the door at the very end of the hall, they found themselves in what appeared to be a gentleman's office. They decided to quickly check it out. The moon, shining brightly through a glass window at the far end, provided some visibility. Glancing around the room, they came to a fast conclusion: Whoever lived here wasn't very tidy. There were old chicken bones tossed everywhere; dirty clothes were piled on top of a wooden desk; and everything was dusty, cluttered, and reeked. Though there was a window, it seemed no one had bothered to clean it. They stepped around the mess and decided to split up and look throughout the office for clues. As they paced around the room, Amy's foot stepped onto something that sounded hard and metallic. Perking up at the noise, the others quickly gathered around.

"That what I think it is, Ames?" Huck questioned.

"If you were going to guess a trap door, I'd say you're pretty good at this game," she responded.

Sure enough, it was a secret panel.

They were one step closer to finding those voices, whose shouting could still be heard loudly beneath them!

CHAPTER 40

IN THE LIONS' DEN

At once, Amy stepped off of the hidden entrance. The others quickly searched for a way to open the panel. Motioning the others away from the light streaming through the window, Becky was able to see the metal handle located on the panel. But there was also a deadbolt lying next to the handle, though the latch wasn't engaged. With a little help from Tom, Becky lifted the metal door off the floor. Sure enough, beneath the panel was a hidden staircase, leading down to a level beneath the office.

The staircase took them into a narrow passageway, barely wide enough for two people to walk through. Eventually, the path veered sharply to the left, leading them to a final staircase, which took them even lower into the house, and down into a brightly lit room.

Peering below them from the heights of the staircase, what they saw wasn't exactly an underground room, though the floor of this room was dirt; they were close to the ground floor. The light in the chamber came from two oil lamps settled into the dirt. The area at the bottom of the staircase sat on slightly higher ground than the rest of the room, creating a small slope leaning down into the room. Once they had reached the bottom of the stairs, Tom and Huck could see that the downward slope of the room led off into many smaller dirt pit areas midway down the hill, like the trunk and branch structure of a tree. The smaller pit areas sat amongst a few strong beams of wood holding up different points of the floor above them. But there were no walls or anything else to impede one's view of the whole area. It looked as though when this part of the house had been built, the workers had intentionally designed this room to rest on top of the natural downward incline of the land - a most architecturally unstable move to make.

"Who would leave a room as big as this completely unfinished?" Becky whispered to Tom.

"Probably the same genius who never cleans up the office he eats in," Tom joked back at an equally quiet whisper.

At that point, Huck motioned for Tom and Becky to shush: The voices were back. And this time, they were much, much louder.

"AND DON'T YOU BE CARELESS WITH THOSE RIFLES AGAIN! DO YOU UNDERSTAND ME?"

Frightened, Andrew, Tom, Huck, Amy, and Becky crouched down and hid behind the railing of the stairway.

Dead Eye Dan and Phillip Morse were there, in the same house! They were working together once again. Phillip was busy sorting all sorts of weapons into various piles, while Dan spat out directions and, occasionally, a few nasty curse words.

Making themselves as quiet and as small as possible, the five finished descending the staircase and pressed against each other as they hid behind the wooden structure.

Handling a rifle, Phillip raised it up and peered down the barrel at the open end. "Boss, what kind of rifle is this?" he excitedly asked Dan.

Dan had about had enough of Phillip. But as much as he would have relished pulling the trigger, he still needed Phillip's strength and manpower. Angrily, he yanked the gun away from Phillip's grasp. "That would be a loaded rifle, Phillip."

Phillip stood where he was, arms folded, and pouted at Dan, "Boss, why do we gotta do this now? What's wrong with waiting till tomorrow? I'm tired."

Dan whirled around, faster than ever before, and shot his hands forward, grabbing Phillip by the collar of his shirt and slamming him into the wall!

Phillip gasped with fright. This was the Dan he needed to avoid.

But Dan wasn't finished with Phillip. "YOU JUST DON'T GET IT DO YOU, PHILLIP? EVER SINCE BECKY AND HER FRIENDS RETURNED TO MISSOURI, THE SHERIFF HAS BEEN DOUBLING HIS EFFORTS IN TRACKING ME DOWN AND BRINGING ME TO JUSTICE! I CAN'T EVEN GO INTO TOWN ANYMORE WITHOUT RISKING MY LIFE! IF THE SHERIFF EVEN SUSPECTS THAT I'M LIVING HERE, HE'D BRING THE WHOLE DARN VILLAGE TO MY DOORSTEP AND HAVE ME EXECUTED! AND YOU'RE IN CAHOOTS WITH ME, WHICH MAKES YOU JUST AS GUILTY IN THE EYES OF THE LAW! DON'T YOU GET THAT?!"

Dan relinquished his grip on Phillip, who dropped to the floor.

"I've got no personal vendetta against you, Phillip Morse, and you'd best be thankful for that. But you'd better be careful with those rifles from now on. We're lucky that the inn is empty for right now; those gunshots could have brought the cavalry to our door! I'm not risking my life for another blunder on your part. I won't allow Judge Thatcher the satisfaction of seeing my body hanging from a rope! That's why we're preparing weapons at this ungodly hour of the night, Phillip," Dan finished, his temper having run out a bit. "If the sheriff does rally a search party for me, I won't go down without a fight. I'll take the whole darn village down with me!"

Andrew gasped quietly. Their well-intentioned quest was turning out to be a far deadlier situation than he could ever have predicted. "Guys, we need to leave right now," he whispered calmly, despite being desperately afraid.

Quietly, they hastily retraced their movements out of the room and stole back up the staircase. They almost made it, but going up, Andrew's right foot broke through a rotted stair! The timber cracked loudly!

They were caught!

Dan locked eyes with Andrew.

"Get them! Now!" Dan shouted to Phillip, who grabbed a rifle and began running in hot pursuit alongside his master.

"EVERYONE, RUN!" Andrew yelled, as he fought to dislodge his foot.

With Dan looming close behind them, they took off running.

Locking eyes with Becky, Dan went stiff with shock. Anger and hate filled him. He clenched his teeth and drew a revolver

SEBASTIAN JOE

from his side. Without aiming, he took three shots at the five escaping adventurers!

Blam! Blam! Blam!

With only the scant cover provided by the interspaced, wooden beams holding up the ceiling, they made it to the top of the staircase. Then, running to the end of the tunnel, they quickly ascended the final set of stairs.

Andrew had just escaped into the office, when suddenly, Dan reached the bottom of the final set of stairs!

"You're dead! All of you!" he shouted, as he began to climb the rickety stairs.

CLANK! Tom and Huck quickly slammed the metal door back into its place on the floor, which muffled Dan's angry threats and bought them precious time. They then both stood on top of the panel, trapping Dan in the stairwell beneath the office.

"Quick, Becky! The deadbolt!" Tom shouted.

"BECKY! YOU AND THE ENTIRE THATCHER FAMILY ARE AS GOOD AS DEAD!" Dan hollered, pounding on the floor panel.

Becky quickly locked the bar in place. Once done, all five sprinted out of the office and down the main staircase, but not before hearing Dead Eye Dan's last threat: "NO MATTER HOW FAST YOU RUN, NO MATTER WHERE YOU HIDE, I WILL FIND YOU AND KILL YOU ALL!"

Faster than a herd of animals escaping from the zoo, Andrew, Amy, Tom, Huck, and Becky fearfully dashed out of the mansion and sprinted across the field towards the inn.

Becky, the subject of Dan's words, was in a state. "Do you

think Dead Eye Dan knows where we are?" she asked aloud, as they ran through the front door and slammed it shut behind them. All of them were breathing quickly and raggedly.

"I don't know," came Andrew's response, as he locked up the front door. "I don't know."

"Do we need to head back to the village?" Amy queried.

After pondering a bit, Andrew said, "No way. Even in the moonlight, it's still five miles back in the dark. If Dan somehow does escape, he could ambush us. This inn is the safest place we could be right now. Let's take turns staying up, being on guard. I'll go first. The rest of you, get some rest if you can."

The girls ran to their rooms, shut the doors, and locked them tight, hoping that the deadbolts would keep Dead Eye Dan out if he somehow came looking for them. They quickly pulled the curtains shut, shed their outer clothes, and climbed into bed, pulling the covers up over their heads. They were almost too scared to sneak a peek out from beneath the blankets. Both were terrified, and rightly so.

Tom, Huck, and Andrew hurried up to the attic, pulling the ladder up behind them. From the viewpoint of his bed, out one of the large attic windows, Andrew could see anyone approaching the inn from the direction they had come from. The moon still shined in its full glory.

They were safe...for now.

CHAPTER 41

RUTHLESS NIGHTMARES AND JUMP SCARES

All night long, Tom found himself tossing and turning, unable to gain so much as an hour of sleep. His mind was racing with constant thoughts of the danger Becky was in. To top it all off, whenever Tom's mind allowed him a few moments of sleep, his dark premonitions came alive.

Unable to fight the disturbed sleep that came for him, Tom became trapped in the darkest labyrinths of his own mind...

———◦◦◦◦———

He was on the deck of a large pirate ship. Dressed in worn out clothes like the rest of the crew, Tom found himself the proud wearer of a magnificent, black pirate hat. There was also a razor-sharp cutlass strapped in a sheath to his left hip. He marched proudly forward as the crew began to chant his name.

"TOM! TOM! TOM! TOM!"

He couldn't believe it; the entire pirate crew knew him. They loved him!

He made his way to the main deck of the ship. There, lined up in a row, were 15 prisoners. Each captive had their arms restrained behind their backs by a thick, sturdy rope. All the prisoners sat quietly on their haunches, with burlap sacks over their heads.

A joyous, deafening celebration rang across the deck as the men rejoiced in their great victory. After a few minutes, and over the din, came a loud shout: The captain was coming! Everyone stopped what they were doing; it was time to pay respect to the man who had made their victory possible. Tom turned his head to see a tall, muscular man, dressed in slightly fancier clothes and a more lavish pirate hat, waiting for the commotion to calm down. Everything about this man, from the proud way he carried himself, to the telltale rough, auburn beard on his face, told Tom that he was standing in the presence of the great Red Beard himself.

Red Beard raised his hand in the air. After the noise had quieted down, he began to speak. "Mates! That was one of the fiercest battles that we have ever faced together, but The Dark Mystery came through as a mighty victor! Not only did we completely obliterate the enemy ship, but we also have taken prisoner 15 of their best fighters!"

The entire crew cheered loudly, falling under the spell of Red Beard's optimism, pride, and charisma. He allowed them a few seconds before he once again held up his hand, signaling them to quiet down. "Gents, there comes a time in every man's life when his short time on earth must end. And for those sitting among us, that day...is today!"

The crew cheered once more at the prospect of enjoying a pirate's privilege and right to shed blood.

"Therefore, take up your swords as we send these worthless scoundrels to the depths of Davy Jones' Locker!"

All the pirates cheered. A select few gathered behind each prisoner, drawing their blades and holding them near the necks of the condemned. Fourteen of the prisoners were accounted for by the other pirates. One lone prisoner sat unguarded, waiting for the inevitable to happen. Despite the captain's words and the clamor of the crew, this prisoner remained calm as they prepared for the doom which awaited them all.

"Thomas Sawyer!"

Tom looked up as he heard his name called by none other than Red Beard himself.

The captain walked over to him and placed his hand over Tom's shoulder, in a welcoming gesture, before he spoke. "Thomas, my boy, you have shown great improvement in the many years you have served as a pirate on my ship. Few are the men who have shown the confident tenacity that you have. That is why you are my First Mate."

"Thank you, my captain," Tom found himself saying, awash in the captain's approval.

"Therefore, this final prisoner's life will be yours to end; make the cut quick and clean, boy!" Red Beard commanded, as he pointed to the unattended detainee.

Astonished, Tom soon found himself pulling his cutlass from the sheath on his belt. Unsure of what to do next, he hesitated, the razor-sharp steel blade catching the glint of the sun as he considered his next course of action.

"Hurry up, boy, the other men are waiting!" Red Beard impatiently growled.

Tom looked up to see the 14 other pirates looking disdainfully at him, their cutlasses already out and placed at the necks of the other prisoners. Tom didn't think of himself as a murderer, but reluctantly, he too raised his weapon to the neck of his personal prisoner. As he gripped his hostage by the back of their shirt, he nodded confidently at his captain. The captain smiled proudly at the loyalty of his First Mate and raised his hand up in the air, like the lethal blade of a guillotine ready to drop. Three seconds later, Red Beard dropped his hand, signaling his men to commence with the execution.

One by one, each pirate quickly slid his blade through the neck of his prisoner.

Soon, it was Tom's turn to complete his rite of passage. So, with a deep breath, he swiftly ran his deadly blade across his prisoner's neck!

At once, his fantasy shapeshifted into the worst nightmare imaginable! His prisoner did not die, but rather, screamed in horrified pain! And his prisoner was not a man - it was a girl! Tom's inner world seemed to stop, and he felt the blood leaving his face. Horrified at his decision to participate in the murderous ritual, he rushed around to face his prisoner. With all the courage he could muster, he reached his trembling hand forward and removed the burlap sack from the prisoner's head.

"OH NO! NO! NO! NO! PLEASE NO! NOT BECKY, PLEASE!" Tom cried out loudly, as tears began to pour quickly from his eyes, and his throat became sore from his violent wailing.

His girlfriend fell flat onto her back, as blood continued to spill down the front of her neck! Her once vibrant, green eyes were frozen, just like her mouth, in an expression of pure shock, as the last of her life faded from her body. With a trembling hand, Tom reached out and closed her eyelids one final time, hiding her innocent eyes from his view.

"My, my, my, Tom," Red Beard chuckled. "If that's your reaction to seeing your girlfriend slaughtered, I'm afraid you'd better ready more of your pathetic tears at what else is in store for you. Men, remove the hoods!"

The remainder of the executioners pulled off the sacks of the now dead prisoners. The bodies that Tom had once believed to be random prisoners turned out to be his closest friends and family! Amy, Andrew, his best friend Huck, his brother Sid, his dear Aunt Polly, his friends Ben Rogers, Billy Fisher, Johnny Miller, and many more kids from the village!

He covered his mouth in horror and was close to ripping out his own hair at the sickening sight.

Red Beard gripped Tom tightly by the shoulder. "THIS IS THE LIFE YOU WANTED TO LIVE, TOM," Red Beard growled like a demon, his eyes coming alive with fire. "IF SOMEONE DOESN'T LIVE ON THIS SHIP, THEY ARE AN ENEMY TO OUR CAUSE! WE HAVE NO FRIENDS AND WE CALL NO PLACE HOME BUT THIS SHIP! SAY GOODBYE TO YOUR OLD LIFE, TOM SAWYER!"

Tom looked with gruesome disgust at the captain, who now appeared truly insane.

"YOU'RE WRONG, RED BEARD! I HAVE A PLACE I CALL HOME, A FAMILY, AND A VILLAGE FULL OF PEOPLE WHO LOVE ME! NO AMOUNT OF TREASURE WILL EVER CHANGE HOW MUCH I LOVE THEM!"

Wracked by tears of pain, Tom turned away. As far as he was concerned, his life was over. He looked to the rail of the ship, and without hesitation, ran toward it and jumped over, hoping to sink and drown in the dark, unforgiving depths of the sea...

With a start, Tom woke up screaming Becky's name. And then, someone was gripping his shoulder and gently shaking him. A voice called his name, and he struggled to focus his mind. As he attempted to control his erratic breathing, his eyes shifted and adjusted to the lack of light in the dimly lit room. It was Huck who was shaking him awake and saying his name.

"T...T...T...Tom? Are you ok? I came when I heard you screaming for Becky," he explained, putting a hand on Tom's arm to calm him down. "Was it one of your dreams?"

"Huck, it was so real. It was so terrible. Much worse than any other nightmare I've had before."

"Tom, I don't think I've ever heard you sounding more scared than you just did. What happened?"

Tom sighed deeply, as he focused his eyes on the roof of the attic. "Huck, in my dream, I was the first mate on The Dark Mystery, under the command of Red Beard himself."

Even in the dark, Huck could see that Tom's eyes were full of sadness. "That bad, huh?"

"Worse than bad, Huck; they made me kill Becky!"

Huck's eyes went wide, and he exhaled a breath of stunned disbelief. "What? Why did they make you kill Becky? Why didn't you stop yourself from doing it?"

"She had a burlap sack on over her face, and I thought she was a man," Tom explained.

Huck's face registered a look of absolute confusion. "Tom, I don't under...Wait, you know what? I don't even want to know how that happened. Just know that Becky is perfectly safe in her bed, one story below us."

"Yeah, I know that, Huck. But even if I unknowingly killed her, I still made a conscious choice to kill someone. What does that say about me?"

Huck couldn't believe the words he was hearing from his closest friend. "Tom, I want you to sit yourself up for a moment."

Reluctantly, Tom raised himself up on his mattress and sat himself up against the wooden headboard of his bed.

"Tom Sawyer, you're the greatest treasure seeker of all time, and a darn good friend on top of that. I'm your best friend, and if there's one thing I know, it's that you ain't a murderer. You've got too good of a heart to hurt anyone, much less kill someone."

"I hurt my brother Sid all the time," Tom objected.

"Nonsense, Tom. That's nothing more than sibling rivalry; it's completely normal," Huck assured him. "I want you to hear this: Red Beard's been dead for a good number of years now, but even if he were alive, and if you ever joined his crew, I know that you would gladly do anything it took to keep yourself from killing someone."

"You really believe that, Huck?"

Huck smiled warmly. "As much as I believe you're my best friend, Tom."

Tom drew a deep, solemn breath. "Thanks a bunch, Huck."

"No problem, Tom," Huck said. "Now, I'm going back to bed. Are you doing any better? Think you could sleep?"

"Immensely better," Tom promised him. "And I'm awful sorry if I woke you up with my screaming."

Huck dismissively waved his hands at Tom. "Not a problem,

Tom; I wasn't getting much sleep either. I just took over from Andrew a couple hours ago."

Both of them spared a look at Andrew, who lay sleeping soundly in his bed, confirmed by the loud snoring he expressed every ten seconds or so. They each chuckled.

Tom yawned and quietly lowered himself back down onto his mattress. As he tried to make himself comfortable, his eyes briefly settled upon one of the windows of the attic. What he saw caused powerful fear to take over his body. "Huck!" Tom hissed quietly.

"Yep? What is it, Tom?"

"Huck, I just saw someone's face at the window!"

"What? Whose?"

"Don't know, Huck; it's too dark, but I definitely saw someone looking in!"

"You're crazy! We're three stories up!"

"I'm telling you I saw someone!"

Right then, a scream came from outside the window, followed by the sound of a loud crash. Instinctively, both boys ran to the window. No one was at the window itself, but in the dim light of the moon, they could see what looked like a long, wooden ladder lying on the ground, facing away from the house.

"Still think I'm crazy, Huck?"

Huck shook his head. The whole night was beginning to seem like one big nightmare. "What should we do, Tom? We can't stay up here! We have to protect the girls!"

"Huck, I'll go to the girls! You wake Andrew up and let him know what's happened! The two of you check all the windows and doors, and then meet us in the girls' rooms! We'll stay there for the rest of the night! Together, we should be safe!"

"Right, I'm on it! See you in the girls' rooms as soon as we make sure everything's secure!" Huck shouted, as he ran over to warn Andrew.

Tom dashed past Huck and quickly headed down to the second floor in search of the girls, praying that nothing terrible had happened to them!

CHAPTER 42

DIVIDE AND CONQUER

The five friends spent the next several hours scared, but safe. After hearing from Huck about the would-be intruder on the ladder, Andrew checked all of the doors and windows around the house, while Huck stood guard. They then joined the other three in the girls' rooms, where they nervously waited for dawn to arrive. Andrew stayed with Amy, while Tom and Huck watched over Becky.

At the sound of someone entering the house around dawn, Huck and Andrew rushed downstairs, prepared to defend themselves and their friends. Horace, slightly startled by their sudden appearance in the kitchen, wished them a good morning and promised a feast within the hour. Relieved, Andrew and Huck hustled upstairs to let the others know it was safe.

An hour later, Huck, Amy, and Andrew came back down to the first floor and took a look around the premises. Their caretaker could no longer be found, but the evidence of his culinary handiwork remained to be seen at the kitchen table. That morning, Horace had taken the time to make them Scandinavian-style pancakes, complete with syrup, brown sugar, and an assortment of cold, juicy, fresh fruit! The children were amazed that Horace cared about them enough to spoil them with such a banquet of a feast. Eventually, Tom and Becky joined them in the kitchen as well, and they all took a seat around the cornucopia of sustenance.

"Wow, Horace made all this for us?" Becky marveled.

"Yep, he returned with the groceries early this morning and set to work cooking immediately," Andrew confirmed.

"So, where is he anyway?" Amy asked inquisitively, as she unfolded her napkin and laid it across her lap.

"Probably still in town, Amy. He left a note on the front door saying he had to go back to the village to deliver a couple of letters to the post office," Huck answered nonchalantly. "But he probably took a carriage, so I'm guessing he won't be gone for too long."

"Maybe he joined the festivities and met a nice girl in town," Tom brilliantly suggested.

Everyone laughed.

"It's the Fourth of July, Tom, and everyone in town is having a fun day. I know that's where I'd normally be," Andrew reasoned.

Everyone laughed at Andrew's sense of humor as they joined hands to say a quick morning prayer before breakfast began. Then, they loaded up their plates with the flapjacks and drizzled sticky maple syrup on top, before taking their first bites.

"Mmmm," Tom sighed contentedly. "These here are the best pancakes I've ever eaten. Why do they taste so delicious?"

"Well, Tom, I don't know if this is true at all, but I've heard that if you make food with love, it actually tastes better," Amy offered.

"Then Horace probably loves us a lot," Huck remarked, earning a laugh from all around the table.

Andrew waited till everyone was about halfway finished with their current plate of food before he spoke up. "Ok, everyone. If last night's events were anything to go from, then Dan is likely crazier than we think, and the sheriff needs to know where he's holing up right now. Frankly, I don't know if fighting a crazed gunman and his sidekick can be done by one man alone; for all we know, the sheriff might need to call in reinforcements."

"Makes sense," Becky remarked, popping in another bite. "I've got no problem leaving to return to St. Petersburg when we're all finished."

"Well, you may have to wait a while for us all to finish, Becky," Huck joked. "It seems that you were the hungriest of everyone here."

Becky looked down at her empty plate, devoid of all food, save for the last bite of pancake stuck to the end of her fork. Chuckling to herself, she raised the utensil to her mouth and proceeded to chew and swallow the last of the savory meal.

"Gee, Becky, how many pancakes did you eat anyway?" Tom asked.

"I believe my plate had four pancakes on it," she recounted.

The others looked at her in complete shock, unable to believe that such a skinny girl could hide such a huge breakfast in such a tiny body.

"And now, to finish my second plate," she announced, reaching for the spatula to serve herself seconds.

Tom's mouth dropped in stunned disbelief at his girlfriend's insatiable appetite.

"Naw, I'm just pulling your arm this time," Becky laughed, putting the spatula back on the serving plate. "Although, I'm feeling a bit restless just sitting at the table doing nothing. To be honest, I wanted to go and look through Horace's garden one more time. There are just so many species of flowers and plants out there that I haven't seen before."

"I reckon it's probably safer for you going outside during the day, but you still should take someone with you," Andrew cautioned warily.

"Well, I'm pretty much finished with my breakfast; how about I go with you?" Amy volunteered, setting down her utensils across her now empty breakfast plate.

"Sounds good," Becky agreed.

Finished with breakfast, she and Amy headed towards the back door of the house, out to the garden.

Tom and Huck watched their girlfriends exit outside, before staring at the empty plates on the table beside them in a look of befuddled surprise. "How in the world did they finish before us?" Huck asked aloud.

"Well, I can't explain that, Huck; but unlike them, I could definitely go for seconds," Tom remarked.

Horace's garden was simply exquisite. He probably had two acres of space devoted to growing beautiful flowers, some neither Becky nor Amy had ever seen before. There were many paths in the garden that they hadn't yet walked on. Each trail brought something new. To Becky and Amy, it seemed like a place fit for fairies and sprites. The botanist's paradise bloomed brilliantly. Bushes of lush, beautiful roses sprouted gorgeous red, white, purple, yellow, and orange blossoms. Exquisite hydrangeas commanded attention with their vibrant hues of blue, white, and pink. Opulent trees overflowed with picturesque plumerias and enticed the senses. The entire area wafted a gentle and relaxing aroma into the air.

Becky knew that she would certainly miss the overabundance of flowers when she went back home. But she had to keep reminding herself that they were at the inn because of the danger posed by Dead Eye Dan. Still, the week away from town had been a nice change of pace. With any luck, they might very well return in the future.

The girls spent perhaps 30 minutes in the heavenly garden, exploring. Amy asked countless questions about plants, that Becky more than willingly answered. Amy found herself impressed with the extent of Becky's knowledge.

"Seriously, that's amazing, Becky. How is it that you know so much about everything, anyway? I know that I pay just as much attention in school as you."

Becky humbly shrugged her shoulders. "Well, I definitely don't know EVERYTHING. I mean, I really don't know anything when it comes to understanding boys. The very first time I met Tom at school, do you know what he asked me? He asked me if I liked rats at all. And when I told him that I didn't, he said that he likes dead rats that he can swing around his head with a string!

Why would boys want to play with something dead and rotten? It doesn't make any sense. Why do guys have to be so gross?"

Amy laughed at her recollection. "That definitely sounds like Tom all right! When he and I first became acquainted, he offered me a can of freshly caught fishing worms! I can still remember almost throwing up when he gave me that present. He definitely takes some getting used to. Now, Tom was my boyfriend for a long time, and this might sound strange, Becky, but I kinda used to be like you, as far as being ladylike was concerned. However, early on, Tom showed me a more fun way to live, and I don't think I would ever go back now. I mean, me personally, I would rather not touch a rat if I didn't have to, but I certainly don't mind playing around in the mud. You may not like it when guys talk about and do gross things, but getting messy can be a lot of fun - so long as you clean yourself up afterwards."

Becky smiled, and then asked Amy an intriguing question. "Amy, a girl like you has got to be very popular among the boys. I mean, your red hair is so beautiful. How could any guy resist you? Why have I never seen you play with other guys besides Tom and Huck?"

Amy chuckled to herself a little as she thought about what she would share with Becky. "You would definitely think that. But some of the guys got the dumb idea in their head that my hair is only red because it's been cursed."

Becky tried not to snicker at this new revelation. "Cursed? How?"

Amy rolled her eyes good naturedly. "Cursed, as in they think my hair is red because the devil made it."

"What? Now who honestly thinks that?"

"Don't know. Could have just been a rumor started by one of the other girls at school. But it's ok. Tom and Huck are the only ones who never cared about how I looked. They just liked me the way I was. And I'll tell you something else, Becky: Tom is certainly a great guy, and you're lucky to have him. However, Huck also likes to have just as much fun as Tom, and he also cares for me a whole lot. I mean, there's no other guys I'd want to spend time with."

"You know, I think it sounds like we BOTH got really lucky," Becky smiled.

On the return trip back to the house, Becky and Amy found themselves gazing in wonder at an enormous plot of sunflowers before them. The stalks of the flowers towered over both girls, and the plants stretched for a couple hundred feet in all directions. It would be a great place for a game of hide and seek.

Amy, however, had other plans. "Hey, Becky, wanna race to the other side? First one out of the field wins!"

A look of fiendish glee crossed Becky's face at the prospect of a race. "Alright, Amy, you're on! Ready? Set? Go!"

Both girls set out at a fantastic clip as they worked to quickly navigate their way to the other end of the rows of flowers. Amy had a naturally aggressive ability to push through the rows of flowers, but Becky demonstrated grace and the agility to sidestep and almost dance daintily around the flowers as she raced towards the house.

"I'm gonna beat you, Amy!"

"Don't bet on it, Becky!"

Finally, after much determination, Amy emerged victorious, sprinting the final steps out of the field of flowers. Horace's home lay just ahead. She was eager to gloat in her victory and turned around to face the field once more as she waited for Becky. "Now that's something they don't teach ya in school, right, Becky?"

But Amy's question brought forth no answer; she was greeted with only a chilling silence!

"Becky?!" Amy felt confused. There was no way that Becky would have just let her win. Maybe she tripped? Amy peered into the rows of sunflowers, trying to look for some sign that Becky was okay. But the only sound present was the wind rustling eerily through the leaves of the plants.

Amy's heart began to race. What could have happened? Where was she? Amy hadn't heard anything, not Becky's body hitting the dirt, a cry for help, or even a scream. Becky may as well have vanished into thin air!

Quickly retracing her steps, she came back to the inn and found Tom, Huck, and Andrew sitting on an old couch in the kitchen, waiting for them.

"Hey, Amy, you and Becky were gone a long time. Thinking about taking one of those plants home with you?" Huck teased playfully.

Worry underscored the words Amy spoke. "No, Huck. Umm...have you seen Becky? Did she come back here? We were racing through the sunflowers, but she disappeared in the field and still hasn't come out."

"No, we haven't seen her," Andrew responded, now alarmed. "And if she came back to the house, we would have noticed. Tom, hurry, go check upstairs. Everyone else, stay close. I don't like this. I don't like this one bit."

———— ⚬⚬⚬ ————

As Tom swiftly ascended the stairs, Amy sat down on the couch next to Huck. Deep inside, she knew Andrew was right: Something was very wrong.

After checking the girls' rooms, which yielded nothing, Tom made his way to the attic, just in case. Again, no Becky.

The longer Tom searched the attic, the more convinced he became that looking up here was pointless. Becky hadn't ever come up to the attic before and wouldn't have a reason to be up here. Lost in worry, he was brought back to the present by the slight creak of a floorboard...but there was no one but him in the attic! Silently, he looked around, but saw nothing. A sharp worry danced in his mind, and the hair on the back of Tom's neck stood on end. Whipping his head around as fast as he could, Tom yelled out, "Andrew, if you're trying to play a joke on me, this ain't funny!"

But there was no Andrew. There wasn't anybody.

And there it was again - the creaking sound. Tom turned around, but not fast enough. Someone brought a cudgel down hard on the back of his head, and he crumpled to the floor! As Tom was losing consciousness, he spotted a blurred figure crossing his line of vision. And then, he passed out cold.

———— ⚬⚬⚬ ————

Downstairs, hearing a muffled cry of pain and the sound of a thud above him, Andrew stood up from the couch. "Did you two hear that?" he asked.

"Yeah, what was it?" Amy asked, gulping nervously.

"I don't know, but something doesn't feel right. I'm going upstairs to check on it. I'll be back soon. Huck, don't leave Amy alone!" Andrew yelled, as he dashed out of the kitchen and raced up the stairway to the attic.

"Huck, what's going on?" Amy wondered aloud.

"I don't know, Amy," Huck spoke uneasily. "I don't know."

Andrew checked the second floor and then hastily climbed the ladder to get into the attic; the room was bizarrely quiet. There was no sign of Tom anywhere. An initial inspection of the room told Andrew that nothing had been moved, and Tom's bed was just as messy as he had left it. The window on the far side of the attic had still been left open to allow the hot air inside to escape, enabling cooler, more comfortable, outdoor breezes to circulate inside the musty attic.

Andrew did notice two peculiarities, however: First, there were several fresh drops of blood scattered across the thick flannel blankets on Tom's bed! As far as Andrew knew, it would be almost impossible to injure oneself when sleeping to the point that blood got spilled.

The second peculiarity was a series of dirty boot tracks left on the wooden floor. Andrew had known Tom for a long time and was accustomed to Tom's usual footwear – which was no footwear at all! Tom never wore shoes unless he had to. At the inn, that was almost never. The boot prints on the floor were definitely not made by Tom. Someone else had been in the attic!

Andrew's mind was racing as he tried to figure out what all of this meant. At the same time, he began to look around for more evidence. Checking the closets and looking under the beds, he found nothing suspicious. Andrew even looked out the open window, but he still saw nothing out of the ordinary.

Just when Andrew was about to give up, he noticed the wooden chest at the foot of his bed. It looked the same as always, but out of curiosity, he undid the latch and lifted the lid. He was hoping that he might find something, anything, that could help him understand what had happened. Instead, what he found inside the chest was immensely more disturbing!

Tom's limp body lay at the bottom of the chest, curled up lifelessly like a broken doll, his forehead touching his bent knees! Scarcely daring to breathe, Andrew gasped when he noticed Tom's chest expanding and contracting slowly. He was still alive!

But that didn't explain how he got there or who put him in the chest. Andrew was now seriously frightened. The bizarre string of events since that morning were terrifying: First Becky disappearing, and now Tom getting knocked unconscious and stuffed in a chest! What should he do? He couldn't leave Tom in the trunk – he needed Huck's help – but there was no way he was going to leave Amy alone. Turning around to head back downstairs, Andrew stopped. His ears pricked up at the sound of new footprints lightly hitting the surface of the floor. He quickly swiveled his head to face whatever unknown foe waited for him.

But before he could turn all the way around, a pair of brawny, and quite hairy, hands gripped him tightly around the shoulders and pushed him towards the partly opened window! Andrew fought, but the other man fought harder. With a final grunting heave, the stranger pushed Andrew through the window to fall to his death!

When neither Tom nor Andrew returned, Huck and Amy became afraid. Huck was unsure if he should leave her to go look for the others. It had been almost ten minutes, and they hadn't heard so much as a peep. Suddenly, the haunting silence of the house was broken by a loud crash upstairs! Then, through the kitchen window, Huck chanced to see a large object fly past!

What?!

Concern got the better of Huck, and he dashed out the back door to investigate. But before he left, he instructed Amy to lock the door behind him.

The next thing Amy heard was Huck screaming hysterically. His panicked face appeared at the window a few moments later. He was wildly motioning for her to unlock the door.

Quickly, Amy unlocked the door and let him in. "Huck, what happened? What did you see?" She sat him down in a chair and tried to calm him down. But it wasn't easy getting coherent answers out of him.

It took Huck a minute to calm himself down enough to report what he had found. "It was Andrew! Andrew's hurt, unconscious, and there's broken glass everywhere! I think he was thrown through the attic window!"

Amy gasped, shaking. "Huck, what are we going to do? Someone **IS** after us. Is it Dan? Did he find us?"

"I don't know, Amy. But I've got to get Andrew. Lock the door, and don't let **ANYONE** in but me, Tom, or Becky. No one, you hear?"

Amy nodded quickly, and then Huck hurried back out the door.

He jogged the short distance around the house. As he rounded the corner, his stomach dropped. The broken pieces of glass were still there, but Andrew was not!

Huck began to panic. Andrew couldn't have just gotten up and walked away: He was unconscious when Huck last saw him. It just didn't make any sense. Even if Andrew had come to, he surely would have returned to the house!

Casting his gaze upwards, Huck scanned the nearby area, looking for something, anything, out of the ordinary. Just as he was sure that everything was exactly as it should be, something sharp jabbed him in the stomach! Groaning in pain, Huck placed his hands around a small dart that had pierced his abdomen! His eyes widened, and he tried to yell for help, but he couldn't form the words! With blackness enveloping him, he looked around desperately. But all he saw, before he crumpled to the ground, was the mocking glare of his assailant from the cover of some bushes.

───────── ∞ ─────────

When Huck didn't return within a couple of minutes, Amy grew extremely frightened. She didn't understand what could take him so long. So far, nothing that had happened that morning added up. Finding herself sitting frozen on the kitchen couch, she alternated between nervously biting her nails and twiddling her thumbs, as though either of those simple habits could speed up time. The sound of the front door creaking open caught her attention. She looked up from the couch, over the counter, and could see Huck's straw hat enter the kitchen, worn down over the eyes of someone's face.

That should have told her a lot. If Huck had been inside, Amy would have had to unlock the back door to let him in. But she hadn't. So, if that wasn't Huck, who was it?

Taking a deep breath, willing herself not to be a coward, Amy cautiously began, "Ummm…Huck? So, how is Andrew doing?" she asked, her voice higher than it had ever been. "And why didn't you try to come through the back?"

The wearer of Huck's hat glared up at her, revealing a frighteningly evil pair of eyes beneath the brim of his hat.

"Maybe it's because I'm not Huck!" the stranger growled menacingly from beneath a black bandana, which covered the lower half of his face and his mouth.

Amy was only faintly aware of the man dashing towards her before she understood what was happening. The assailant who had attacked and subdued the others was now coming after her!

She opened her mouth to scream for help, but the man covered her mouth with one hand and then gripped the sides of her neck tightly in his other hand. The edges of her vision began to turn black. She tried to fight, to get away; but slowly, she lost consciousness, until she was completely out cold in the arms of the stranger.

He had gotten them all!

CHAPTER 43

THE CREMATORIUM

When she at last awoke, Amy found herself roughly restrained. Her ankles were roped together, and her wrists had been tied firmly behind her back. She struggled around to sit upright on the dirt floor she was lying on. There was a bit of light coming from the small holes in the room's walls, but otherwise, the entire area was pitch black. "How'd I get down here?" she asked aloud.

She was startled to get a reply.

"Well, Amy, given the fact that we're one step short of hogtied, I'd venture to guess we've been kidnapped," Huck called out to her from close by. She could hear his frustration; it mirrored her own.

"Good guess," Tom's voice chimed in from the darkness.

As Amy quickly learned, she wasn't alone – not by a long shot. Huck, Tom, Becky, and Andrew were also there and had regained consciousness a while earlier. Though they couldn't physically see each other, by talking out loud, they were able to gain a general understanding of each person's current state of health. Despite his three-story fall, and with exception of a couple of cuts sustained on his cheek from his scuffle, Andrew wasn't doing too badly: He could have been a lot worse. Tom complained of a lingering headache but was otherwise unharmed. Huck reported no feelings of pain or injury, though he was slightly woozy. Becky claimed to have been spared any infliction of trauma at all. And despite her initial confusion as to where she was and what had happened, Amy herself had suffered no injuries. Except for a small headache, she felt fine.

In time, their kidnapper descended the stairs into the makeshift dungeon. In his hand, he carried a bright kerosene lantern that lit up the dark enclosure and chased away the shadows. With the light illuminating their confines, they realized what they all had suspected: They were sitting on the dirt floor of the mansion where they had last seen Dead Eye Dan. Each person sat confined in one of the many shallow dirt pits that branched off the main slope of the hill.

Looking up to face their abductor, there could be no denying that it was Dan that stood before them.

Looking triumphant, he hissed, "Trying to spy on my plans, were you? I thought I made it clear that no one ever escapes from me!"

The much-wanted criminal laughed at their dismay. "You fools should not have meddled with me," he warned. "I'm afraid I can't allow you to live after what you've seen and heard."

"Wait," Tom interrupted, trying to buy time. "How did you know where we were hiding?"

"I thought it was completely obvious," Dan sneered. "Phillip and I followed you. It was actually quite easy to guess your location since there ain't another usable building for five miles; I doubt that you could possibly have run as far as that."

From the dark staircase, Phillip's annoying voice followed Dan's as he came down to join his master. "Yeah, we saw you run into Horace's home, so it just came down to figuring out where everyone was sleeping. By the time you guys had run inside, we had already made it to the outside of the inn. Early in the morning, I ran around the house and grabbed a big ladder to see into the windows. I saw Tom, Huck, and Andrew on the third floor, and I knew that Becky and Amy had to be on the second floor because the curtains were closed on only two of the rooms."

Becky and Amy let out a sigh. They had closed those curtains to keep themselves safe and hidden, never realizing that such a simple action could give away so much information.

For a brief moment, 'Phillip the Incompetent' had redeemed himself.

"So, you really did spy on us through the attic window?" Tom remarked irritably. "I knew I wasn't imagining things!"

Dan broke in. "When Phillip had finished spying on you outside the attic, he accidentally fell off the ladder. I worried that we had lost the element of surprise, but he is a little more agile than he looks and was able to recover and hide quickly."

None of this was acceptable to Tom. How in the world had these two idiots taken them completely by surprise? He was not having it and demanded to know how it had been done.

Dan smiled and sat on a nearby barrel. "Well, first, kidnapping you all became much easier when everyone had split up. You know what they say: 'United we stand, divided we fall.' Becky was easiest to capture. While she and Amy were walking in the garden, I followed at a close distance, waiting for the right moment to ambush her. When Amy challenged Becky to a footrace, I knew I had her. The sunflowers were high enough to hide me. I swiped Becky without any problem. I had brought with me a rag soaked in ether. As soon as I snatched her, I held the rag to her nose till she passed out."

"You knocked me out with ether? That compound is dangerous!" Becky shouted irately.

"I couldn't take any chances of failing in your kidnapping: You're far too important of a bargaining token, you know, Rebecca," Dan smirked, and then continued. "Next was Tom. When Phillip told me his location, I climbed up into the attic through the open window, using the same ladder as before, and hid under the bed. I just had to wait for him to arrive."

"I don't usually spend the daytime up there," Tom interrupted. "How did you know I was going to come upstairs?"

"I didn't," Dan admitted. "I guess you could call it my lucky day. If you hadn't come up there, I probably would have had to leave the attic and ambush you another way. In any case, when your back was turned, I came out from hiding and struck you on the back of your head with my revolver."

"So that's why my head hurts so much," Tom groaned.

Dan looked at Tom. "Yeah, that usually happens when you knock someone out in that manner. I guess I hit you hard enough to draw blood. In any case, may I recommend some whiskey for the pain?"

Tom stared at Dan incredulously.

Dan went on. "After leaving Tom in the bedroom chest, I was about to go downstairs, but then I heard footsteps coming up; I guess I had made a little too much commotion. I quickly hopped onto a bed and hoisted myself up onto one of the wooden cross beams that supported the attic roof, so that I could hide myself. When Andrew wasn't looking, I dropped back onto the floor and shoved him out the window. It was his lucky day to land on that large hedge outside before he hit the ground," Dan mockingly sneered. "A fall like that should have killed him."

Listening, Andrew realized what had been bothering him. "So that's why there were dirty boot tracks on the floor; you were about to come downstairs."

Dan ignored Andrew and kept talking. "Next was Huck. Throwing Andrew out the window caused my ladder to fall away from the building. I needed another way to get down without being seen. I was peering out that window, when suddenly, I saw Huck discover Andrew and then run back around the house. So, without the ladder, I improvised. I climbed out the broken window and shimmied down the drainpipe. Then, I hid Andrew and waited for Huck to come back out. When he did, I shot him with my blowgun from the cover of some bushes."

Huck nervously asked. "Were you trying to kill me?!"

"Not yet," Dan remarked casually. "The dart I shot you with only contained a sedative. It just knocked you out. You were never in any real danger," he explained. "It wasn't your time to die...yet."

Huck didn't feel any happier after hearing the explanation.

"Finally, I dealt with Amy," Dan continued. "After swiping Huck's hat for disguise purposes, I walked in through the front door after picking the lock and ambushed her in the kitchen. She never suspected a thing until it was too late."

"How did you knock me out anyway?" she inquired, obviously not happy that he had attacked her, but genuinely curious.

Dan paused for a second to remember. "Your method of knockout was my personal favorite. I call it, 'The Boa Pinch'," Dan said. "I cut off the flow of blood to your brain by squeezing your carotid arteries. Doing this the right way causes unconsciousness very quickly."

"Wait, where was Horace when all this was going on?" Becky demanded.

Turning, Dan replied apathetically, "I went after him first, in the earlier part of the morning. A short while after he came back from town with groceries, and had made breakfast, he walked out the front door to mail some letters. I came up behind him and ambushed him, knocking him out with a brick. I can't have witnesses to my crimes. If you want to find his body, well, I left him unconscious somewhere in the middle of the woods. You're more than welcome to go visit him when you come back as ghosts."

At this, the five went quiet, the seriousness of their situation now clear.

Dan went on, unaware of the effects of his speech. "You five are rather interesting. Phillip here knows you personally, and he filled me in on each of you." He gestured to Amy and Andrew first. "Amy and Andrew Lawrence, brother and sister, and owners of the carpentry store in town. I suppose capturing you ain't the crowning achievement of my criminal career, but sometimes a man can't be choosy with his victims."

"No, but you could be choosier in picking assistants," Amy mouthed off. "I'm sure I've met a hundred people smarter than him," she said, nodding at Phillip. "Are you actually trying to get caught?"

Phillip, for all his lack of intelligence, certainly didn't lack emotion. A delayed expression of offense slowly materialized on his face: Amy had hurt his feelings.

"Trust me, if there were anyone better educated and willing to work with me, I would have picked him in a heartbeat," Dan muttered, before moving on to Huck.

"Well, Mr. Finn, I must say that it's been many years since we've seen each other," Dan spoke, in a fake-cordial manner. "How has your dad been doing? Still hooked on the drink?"

Huck glared daggers at Dan for even daring to bring up his father. "He's not doing much better than you, but he ain't on the run from the law right now!" Huck barked back.

Dan appeared almost taken aback, but quickly hid his shock. "You've inherited your father's quick temper. I'm sure he would be proud of who you've become," Dan sneered, as he circled to face Tom. "Now, here's a man I could foresee following in my footsteps: Thomas Sawyer. Phillip didn't need to explain much about you. Do you know why that is?"

"Because he's about as dumb as a bucket of mud?" Tom guessed sarcastically.

Dan briefly looked over at his assistant, but then returned his focus back to Tom. "We've already established that Phillip is the village idiot; can we move on now? And no, that's not why. Tom, your name, and tales of your exploits have spread throughout the entire state of Missouri – and even to neighboring states. Suffice it to say, you may one day be as famous as I am."

"Just not so stupid or ugly. I don't know what would be better: Covering your head with a bag forever or tying your whole body up in a sack and then throwing you into the river. Either way, we wouldn't have to see your creepy face ever again," Tom deadpanned. Dan turned on him quickly, but then decided against saying or doing anything more.

"Last, and most certainly not least," Dan continued, regaining his composure. "Rebecca Catherine Thatcher. How are you doing, my dear?" he asked, as he walked over and leaned close to Rebecca's face. With a long, grotesque finger, he touched her cheek.

Rebecca quickly recoiled and then spat straight into Dan's creepy face! His smirk faded as he wiped the wetness from his cheek. "You need to learn, Rebecca, to treat your elders with a little bit more respect," he grimly warned.

He raised his other hand into the air and brought it across her cheek in a violent backhand! She let out a pitiful, painful scream as she fell over.

"LEAVE HER ALONE!" Tom yelled at Dan, baring his teeth, like a wild wolf protecting his mate.

At first, Dan didn't react, but then he said, "Oh, it seems I hit a nerve with that, Phillip. Tell me something, Tom. What does she mean to you?" Dan taunted.

"More than anything else in the whole world, you lowlife scum!" Tom roared.

"Flattery will get you nowhere, Tom. And I suggest you remember her face; this will be the last time you ever see it!" With that, he yelled at Phillip, "Get the door ready; it's time that these meddlers met their maker!"

The children watched in anger and horror as Dan made his way up the sloping dirt floor, towards the stairs. The light from his lantern slowly faded, leaving them all in the dark again. Before climbing the stairs, Dan stopped and turned once more towards his captives.

"Goodbye forever, to all of you."

And with that, he picked up a small barrel lying next to the wall and began to pour something out of it. The liquid, which had a sharp odor, began to drain toward the five friends, who were unable to move. Slowly, but surely, the unknown liquid snaked its way down the hill, towards the bottom. But many smaller streams of the fluid also broke off the main path of the slope and entered each of their dirt pit areas.

Becky gasped. "Huck, what is that?"

Andrew responded before Huck did. "It's definitely kerosene, Becky."

Dan took that moment to enjoy the note of fear in their voices before uttering his final mocking statement. "Aw, there ain't no need to worry. I'm not gonna leave you in the dark."

He laughed ominously as he raised his lantern high into the air. Then, with a mighty swing, he threw the lantern down hard at the ground just in front of him. Crashing onto the dirt, and an enormous puddle of kerosene, the glass shield on the lantern shattered, and the flame from the lantern's wick ignited the oil in a large, explosive combustion! From there, the fire followed the streams of oil down the hill and also into each of the dirt pits, where the explorers still sat tied up! Each prisoner screamed and struggled desperately to scoot away from the flames.

With a last look at the captives through the climbing flames, Dan fled up the stairs and out of the mansion, laughing the entire time!

CHAPTER 44

ESCAPING FROM HELL

Dan had left the barrel of oil on its side at the top of the incline, which allowed the contents to continue slowly draining out. In the moments since Dan had left, the temperature in the air had risen about 15 degrees. Smoke engulfed the ground floor room.

Already breathing in the oily smoke, the five friends all began to cough violently.

Tom fought against his bindings, feeling around for a weak spot. But the ropes were as tough and strong as chains.

"Hey! Need some help there, Tom?"

Tom swiveled his head towards the sound of the voice and discovered Becky, free of her own bonds, standing over him!

"Becky, hurry up!" Amy cried in horror. "You've got to help us!"

Tom, though, was amazed. "How did you get free?" he asked.

Becky took a precious moment to think as she knelt down and began to fiddle with Tom's ropes. "It was something I learned from Joe Harper, I think. When someone ties you up, and you simply surrender yourself to them, escaping becomes almost impossible. However, if you flex your muscles right before they tie you up, the ropes will be loose enough to wiggle out of."

"I don't know what's weirder, Becky - that you actually asked Joe Harper for that kind of information, or that you were interested in such information at all," Tom joked to her, trying to distract himself from having a panic attack.

Becky was working her hardest, but despite the light from the flames, she had a really difficult time finding the knot holding Tom's ropes together. "Tom, what do I do?" she cried. "I can't find the knot!"

In response, Tom shouted. "There's a folding knife in the front pocket of my overalls! Find it and start cutting my ropes!"

She quickly found his knife, but the blade was impossibly blunt from its last use. Becky started fumbling again in the dim light with his rope, when a burst of flames illuminated the knot holding Tom's wrists together.

Despite the dangerous conditions, Becky almost laughed: Tom's ropes had been tied in a bow!

Becky chuckled to herself, figuring that Phillip had probably been the one to detain Tom in this manner.

But then, she had a brilliant thought: *Were the others tied up in the same way?*

Becky bellowed out to the others, "Guys, the ropes that were used to tie us up might have bows at the end! Try to get loose!"

Huck and Amy scooted closer to each other. Soon, they were back-to-back in the same dirt pit. Following Becky's shouted advice, they quickly achieved success. Both emerged from the fiery ordeal, coughing, and sputtering loudly.

Andrew, however, yelled out in pain!

He had wiggled backwards, towards the flames, and had been

able to singe off his ropes. He had burns on his hands, but quickly told them he was fine.

—⁂—

When everyone was finally free from their bindings, they looked desperately at one another: They needed to get out and get out quickly. Their air supply had begun to dwindle!

Huck ran towards the stairs first. "Let me see if we can get out this way," he shouted. As he raced up the dirt incline, his legs bumped into something heavy. Catching himself before he fell, he squinted in the smoke. The container's label read, KEROSENE. That was not good. Apparently, Dan had a second barrel of it. Huck guessed that the vessel was completely full. Fearfully, he raced past it, up to the wooden staircase. It was clear of any fire. Quickly, he called to the others to join him.

Hurrying up the first set of stairs, they sprinted along the narrow pathway, and then up the final set of stairs. At the top, Huck threw his whole weight against the metal panel in the ceiling, but no amount of pressure would open it. Dan had locked it from the outside!

Thick tentacles of smoke snaked menacingly up the stairway, like a demonic creature straight from the depths of Hell. They were trapped. In front of them was the locked panel, to their sides were sturdy, wooden walls, and the lower level was already engulfed in flames.

Panicked, they looked at each other. Becky began to weep. They had been left to die a horrible, painful death no matter what.

Everyone but Amy reached for Becky. But Amy's attention was somewhere else. *"Phillip and I followed you . . ."*

She was remembering what Dan had told them all. But what did it mean?

"Phillip and I followed you . . ."

Amy looked around her as she considered the implications of his message. The five of them had locked the trap door to this room last night, and still, Dan and Phillip had escaped.

They had followed them to the inn!

There must have been a second way out!

"Listen, everyone," Amy began, hurriedly explaining her theory of a secret escape route. In unison, they ran back down the stairs, to the bottom of the room, and began searching high and low for some kind of secret passage.

Huck found it first. His foot stomped down on something hollow. "Hey, guys!" he shouted, thumping a few more times. "This might be it right HERE!"

His statement ended in a scream. Right after kicking the floor, he fell straight through into what first appeared to be a pit!

They all dashed over and looked down into the hole, where Huck sat, uninjured. There had apparently been a piece of disguised wood covering the pit he had fallen into, and apparently, he had broken through it from his stomping. "This must be some sort of underground tunnel," he yelled excitedly. "Get down here, fast!"

Huck was now kneeling on the floor; the tunnel roof rose about a foot above Huck's head. There wasn't enough room to stand, but there was enough to move, and the air was clear of smoke. The others hastily dropped into the hole as Huck quickly crawled forward in the tunnel. Andrew climbed in last. Because of his height, he had a harder time keeping his head from hitting the top of the tunnel. It was important that he quickly figure out how to crawl through. If he damaged the roof of the tunnel, it might collapse on them all, and they would all be buried alive!

CHAPTER 45

LIGHT AT THE END OF THE TUNNEL

Crawling through the tunnel while avoiding a collapse took precious minutes. The entire tunnel wound into a circular shape. It was amazing that Dan had been able to dig this escape route without causing at least one wall to collapse. Aside from the indirect glow of the flames shining from behind them, only darkness lay ahead. Without any choice, they continued to crawl toward their elusive freedom.

Leading the way, Huck suddenly remembered the second barrel of kerosene he had bumped into earlier. If the fire reached the container, or if there were even the slightest of leaks, it could explode! "Guys, we need to hurry!" Huck called to the others. "I saw another barrel of oil in that room! We need to get out of here!" He warned loudly.

"Relax," Amy reassured him, as if she knew everything about fires. "It ain't like it's gonna explode or anything."

And that was exactly when the explosion happened.

KABOOM!

A deafening blast shook the tunnel, and an exponentially bright light flashed around them as the remaining barrel of kerosene combusted and burst powerfully into the air like an active volcano! To his horror, Andrew looked behind him and saw an enormous puddle of lit kerosene land on the dirt floor of the passageway! The kerosene from the exploded barrel was leaking into the tunnel! And worse still: The fiery oil began to slither down the slightly declined floor of the dirt tunnel after them! "MOVE IT! RIGHT NOW! THE FIRE'S FOLLOWING US!" Andrew yelled.

As fast as they could, they made their way through the tunnel. But everyone's hope of quickly finding their way out of the tunnel soon plummeted. Ahead of them wasn't one exit, but multiple exits! Left, right, or straight ahead? The wrong choice could mean the difference between life or death.

Leave it to Dan to try and confuse them. In any case, Huck made a decision right then and there. "We've got to split up!"

The others stared at him in shock, as if he had just told them all to commit suicide. Ironically, however, those that chose poorly could face that outcome.

He went on. "There ain't no other way. If we choose the wrong tunnel, we might never get out, and we all could get burned alive!" Huck reasoned. "If we split up, some of us will get out. Those that do can come back to get the rest of us."

The others agreed that this made sense and quickly put the plan into action. Huck and Amy took the path on the right, Tom and Becky took the path on the left, and Andrew kept going straight ahead.

"C'mon, Becky!" Tom encouraged. "We're so close to the end! Don't give up now!"

"I'm right behind you, Tom!" Becky called back, doing everything she could to keep up.

Going the opposite way, Huck and Amy continued deeper into their tunnel. Huck checked behind him every few seconds to make sure he hadn't lost Amy in the panic.

About 20 feet later, Tom and Becky's path abruptly ended in a solid dirt wall! There was nowhere to turn! They would have to go back! "Dead end," Tom muttered angrily.

Huck and Amy's tunnel ended in much the same way!

All four began backing out of their respective branches of the tunnel, but crawling backwards through the dirt was almost impossible. Worse still, the trail of flaming oil had reached the place where the tunnel had forked! Bent to the force of gravity, and the slightly lower angle of the side tunnels, the fire quickly split streams and chased after each of the couples in their inescapable dirt confines!

Spotting the danger, Tom gave their situation a minute's thought before he made what seemed like a drastic choice. "Huck! Pull down the ceiling of the tunnel! Collapse the tunnel!"

"What?! Are you crazy?!" Huck yelled back.

"Trust me! It's the only way to stop the fire!"

Tom also had a second reason for doing this: They were probably already out from under the house and maybe even close to the surface.

But Tom was really taking his chances. If his plan worked, they would get away. If it failed, they would slowly suffocate to death, buried alive. Truly a gruesome and horrible way to die, but they didn't have much of a choice.

Becky and Tom began scraping down the dirt at the top of their tunnel. Sure enough, an avalanche of soil dropped from above. It provided a solid enough barrier between them and the fire, and they had bought themselves a few precious moments.

They accelerated their digging. But something was wrong – the dirt never ended!

And then, out of nowhere, a sharp, steel blade jammed down through the dirt! It came within an inch of slicing into Tom's hands! The blade lifted away and took the dirt above them with it. Hope and sunlight shined through a new hole in their tunnel above them. Somehow, they were free!

Poking their heads out of the ground, they saw what had happened. A few feet away, resting comfortably on the handle of a spade he had found, Andrew grinned proudly. Next to him, Huck and Amy stood safely.

"Saw you struggling there and thought I'd help out," Andrew informed them, smiling broadly. "My tunnel let out near the bushes over there."

"Your timing couldn't have been any better, Andrew," Amy praised.

Huck and Amy ran over to help Tom and Becky out of the hole that had almost become their grave. Once out, Tom dramatically kissed the ground, immensely grateful to be alive. Becky rolled her eyes, wet with tears, at his silliness. Still, she said nothing; Tom's actions actually made sense.

They all turned to survey the damage.

Unbelievably, the house still stood. But surely it couldn't last for much longer. Smoke from the fire poured out of every tiny opening in the wooden walls of the room they had escaped from; flames were also beginning to shoot out through the cracks.

"When do you reckon the house will collapse, Huck?" Becky asked.

"No clue, Becky," he shrugged. "When the kerosene burns up, I guess. But maybe the fire will only burn through that one room. Regardless, there's not much we can do."

They all agreed it would be too dangerous to stay there, what with Dan on the loose. Walking quickly away from the mansion, they began the long trek back to the St. Petersburg village. Talking amongst themselves about what to do when they got back home, the five friends were oblivious to a focused pair of eyes watching them from the cover of a bush!

They were being followed!

CHAPTER 46

THE MASTER OF DISGUISE

July 4th rolled around just like any other ordinary day of the year, apart from the countless picnic tables, carnival-style games, and food stands being set up in the local park. Endless amounts of delicious food had been brought in, as well as a special crew to handle the fireworks show. Every business in town was closed, and so was the grain mill. Judge Thatcher had also locked the town bank and closed operations for the day.

Everyone in the village was gathered at the park to celebrate Independence Day. Plenty of homemade wine was available, as well as cold lemonade – a rare treat – for the children. The brass band that was playing kept everyone's spirits in a lively mood.

Becky, Amy, Huck, Tom, and Andrew arrived back at the village around 6:00 that evening, while the sun was still out. Foremost on their priorities was updating the sheriff on all that had happened and briefing him as to Dan's exact location. Additionally, Becky was anxious for her father's safety; now that Dan had presumed her dead, what was to stop Dan from also bringing harm to her dad? Talking to the sheriff was the best bet to protect Judge Thatcher.

They quickly arrived outside the small jail and entered

through the front door. Inside, a pair of rugged prisoners sat quietly on their cots in their cells. They barely looked up at the kids as they dashed in. Sitting at a nearby desk, with his feet propped up on the top surface of his workspace, and his hat slanted forward to cover his eyes, the sheriff snored soundly.

Urgently, they tried to wake him. But no matter their efforts, he just dozed on.

"Why ain't he getting up?" Huck asked, mightily confused.

It took Becky perhaps a minute of looking around to piece it all together. "Because he's not sleeping, Huck; I think he's unconscious."

Huck and the others looked at Becky. Was she right?

"How do you reckon it happened, Becky?" Tom asked.

She motioned to the lone, metal cup sitting by itself on top of the sheriff's desk. The aroma coming from it was just strong coffee. Inside, at the bottom of the mug, though, a thin, almost invisible layer of white powder sat collected together underneath the leftover coffee. She couldn't identify what it was, but her gut said it probably wasn't sugar.

"I think someone may have put something in his coffee. What exactly, I can't be sure, but I'd bet that either Dan or Phillip had something to do with this," Becky deduced.

"So...they decided to drug the sheriff but not kill him?" Huck queried. "That doesn't make any sense."

"Killing the sheriff would have been too messy and would have alerted the whole village to the fact that there's a killer on the loose," Becky reasoned. "Best to just make him sleep through it all. Dan is very strategic and doesn't like to improvise. He'd want his plan to run like clockwork; murdering the sheriff had too many downsides."

"That makes sense, Becky. He's clever, I'll give him that," Amy admitted. "He really thought to cover all his bases."

"So, what happens now?" Tom asked urgently.

Andrew gave it a moment of thought before devising a solution. "As long as we stay somewhere public, and as long as one of us stays with Becky, she will probably be okay. But she can't leave the crowds, and we can't let our guards down for even a moment!"

Well, at least it was a plan. Though all of them realized it was risky, they set out for the park, where the festivities were being held, and where the crowds would be the biggest. As they entered the park, a few people acknowledged their presence, but thankfully, they didn't attract too much attention. Content to avoid a scene with their parents, Becky and Tom selected a modest table of their own and invited the others to join. The empty surface of the wooden table soon became filled with numerous plates of slices of fruit pie from the dessert stand. Not having eaten anything since breakfast, they gorged themselves senseless on the decadent desserts. They were lucky: They just happened to be good friends with the woman who was the best pie baker in the village.

Half an hour later, unable to put even a bite more into their mouths, nearly everyone had stopped eating.

"I don't know about you," Amy sighed, after burping quite loudly. "But that's about enough pie to last my stomach for a whole year!"

Everybody at the table uncomfortably agreed.

"Can somebody go and bring me another glass of lemonade?" Becky asked politely.

"Oh, can I get another one too?" Amy added.

"Of course," Tom responded chivalrously.

"Sure thing, Amy," Huck echoed.

Tom left first, followed by Huck. Both trekked together to complete the same mission. Andrew held his stomach and moaned a little bit. He had eaten far too much pie. Hurriedly, he left to find an outhouse.

Amy wasn't going to leave Becky alone for anything. So, she moved away from the picnic table and just laid down on her back on the grass, basking in the fleeting warmth of the sun, and resting her arms contentedly behind her head. Becky soon joined her, comfortable in the knowledge that her safety was now assured. Not even Dead Eye Dan would dare make a move on her; she was in the middle of a crowded area. Besides, he thought her already dead.

At the lemonade stand, Tom and Huck had just ladled out their ladies' drinks and were beginning the trip back. However, out of the corner of his eye, Tom spied Sid sitting at a nearby table. Quick as lightning, Tom came up with a desperately clever idea. Just because it was a national holiday didn't mean that he couldn't cause mischief. He and Huck excelled at mischief.

Setting his cup of lemonade down on a nearby table, Tom returned to the stand and filled his front overall pockets with as many ice cubes from the lemonade bowl as he could hold. Huck quickly followed suit. Together, they slipped over to a nearby tree and quickly climbed up and disappeared into the branches. Tom found a concealed spot, high in the tree. Able to see clearly over the leaves, Tom reached into his back pocket and pulled out the wooden slingshot that had travelled with him on all of their adventures. Huck caught on quickly and brought out his own. Parting the branches ever so quietly, Tom took careful aim at Sid and launched the first ice cube!

Sid sat amidst the grownups. He was all dressed up in his miniature suit, doing his best to act like an adult. Among those seated at his table were Aunt Polly, Mr. Dobbins, and Judge Thatcher. Sid had just commented on how Aunt Polly was such a good mother to him and Tom, and how she had raised him (Sid) up in the right way.

After Sid was finished talking, he sat quietly, listening to the adults' conversation, and minding his own business. Suddenly, he winced in pain. Something hard had just smacked him on the back of his head!

Confused, he rubbed his sore head while simultaneously looking around. He didn't see anything weird or out of place. He did glance up at the nearby tree, but there was nothing there. But no sooner had he turned back to the table than was Sid hit by another projectile - this time on his back! Though he didn't know it, Huck had joined in on the fun.

Sid quickly turned his head around, suddenly realizing that

this second attack couldn't have happened by accident. Though Sid didn't possess a great number of friends – his tattletale reputation made it tough to keep friends – he had a hard time believing that one of the kids from the village would pull a stunt like this.

Could it have been Tom?

Turning his attention back to the adults, Sid played it cool.

And then, Tom's next ice cube shot through the air and stung Sid smartly - right on the seat of his pants!

Sid's reaction was instant: He leapt up, off his bench at the picnic table, shook his fist in the air, and angrily shouted out a very bad word! Looking around the whole park, he saw no sign of Tom. At this point, he didn't even need to question that Tom was behind this; deep down inside, he knew it.

Regaining his composure, Sid sat back down and smiled cheerfully at the adults, who all sat in shock at the unsavory word he had just uttered. Aunt Polly hurriedly apologized for Sid's manners before whacking him over the head.

———⚬∞∞⚬———

Not far away from the picnic grounds, near the front door of Thatcher Bank, Dead Eye Dan was working busily and chuckling to himself. He was very self-satisfied: Everything was about to fall into place. Wealth, revenge, a good life, and an even more infamous name stared him in the face. They were all just within reach.

Dan had arrived at the bank prepared to get his hands dirty. Thatcher Bank didn't have special features like thick glass or security guards. Judge Thatcher and his single key were all the

security the bank had. Up until now, it was all the security the bank had needed. But tonight, with the judge settled in at the picnic, Dan had hauled a thick burlap sack, loaded with tools, up to the wooden wall of the bank.

Having looked at the bank's floor plans, Dan knew there were limited options of entry. But he also knew about the bank's limited security protection. Tunnelling underneath would take too long, so he decided to take a more direct route to break into the building. The first thing he did was tap his fist on the wooden exterior of the bank. He was searching for a place in the wall where the wood had been weakened by rot. Patiently knocking every couple of inches, Dan traversed about three feet before his knocking revealed a hollow spot in the wall. Fishing around in his bag, he retrieved a long, sharp handsaw. Testing its sharpness against his finger, he grinned devilishly and set to work.

Becky and Amy were still lying on the grass, resting, and waiting for the boys to come back. Knowing both boys as well as they did, they suspected a mischievous detour may have occurred. It would not be out of character. They just hoped that Andrew's return would prove swifter.

In the dimming light, a large shadow darkened their view. Looking up, Becky saw a fat, old lady standing above her, wearing a ruffled dress and a very decorated sunbonnet.

"Pardon me, sweetheart," the woman spoke jovially. "But are you by chance Rebecca Thatcher?"

Amy flipped over from resting to observe Becky's visitor.

"That's right," Becky confirmed, nodding her head.

"Oh, I'm so glad," the woman answered. "Your father sent me to get you. He's fallen a bit ill from a fever and asked me to bring you home to help take care of him. Can you please come home with me?"

Becky quickly agreed. Her father did have a tendency to catch illnesses at some of the worst, most inopportune times: Measles on her birthday, the flu on Thanksgiving, and pinkeye on Christmas morning stood out as memorable examples. In some of the worst instances, Judge Thatcher would often end up getting HER sick with the infection as well!

Amy, however, was on guard. This was a pretty big coincidence. Becky needed to stay in the park, where the crowds still remained to watch the fireworks. But the lady had turned away from Becky and began to walk away...and Becky had followed. Not leaving anything to chance, Amy followed closely behind Becky to make sure she at least made it home safely.

∞∞∞

Back at the bank, Dead Eye Dan had finished sawing through the wooden outer wall. When the gap was just big enough, he squeezed himself into the bank. The depository was eerily silent. There was no one working, and the light inside was dim. Dan quickly set about finding the safe, which all banks had. This would be where Judge Thatcher stored all the money.

Dan eventually located it behind Judge Thatcher's desk. A cloth blanket had been draped over the safe to conceal it. Dan paused for a moment to examine the various articles on the judge's desk, looking for anything additional of value to steal. His eyes stopped on a small, framed, black and white photograph of the judge and Rebecca embraced in a loving hug. It was an opportune place for Dan to leave his calling card.

He unfastened the back of the frame and removed the picture. With a wicked gleam in his eyes, he proceeded to tear it down the center, right between father and daughter. Picking up the judge's fountain pen, Dan wrote a short message on the back half of the picture with the judge's profile on it and then replaced it into the photo frame. Quickly, he pocketed the other half and set to work getting into the safe.

Removing the blanket, Dan found himself confronted by a huge, steel lockbox, protected by a key and combination lock. He had anticipated this. Digging furiously into his sack, Dan brought out a couple of dynamite sticks. Wrapping rope around the safe, he positioned the dynamite directly on top of the locks. He then lit a match and set the fuses alight. Quickly, he dashed away and crouched a comfortable distance from the safe.

His timing was perfect. Outside the window, the sun had almost set. The fireworks had commenced! The explosions of the rockets would disguise the sound of the dynamite exploding.

A few seconds later, as both sticks of dynamite exploded, the safe rattled on its foundings! The explosion was enough to demolish the locks. The safe itself had borne the brunt of the blast, though a few extraneous scorch marks had defaced the nearby desk and chair. But nothing else had been damaged, and nothing had caught on fire. Dan couldn't have been happier.

Rushing over, he opened the door of the safe and grinned at

the enormous piles of cash and gold. Quick as a flash, he relieved the safe of all of its contents and then closed the door. He replaced the blanket over the front of the safe so that, at first glance, his handiwork would be invisible. Clutching his sack, he shimmied back through the gap in the wooden wall and was out as quickly as he had come in.

Meanwhile, elsewhere in the village, some distance from the festivities, the woman escorted Becky down the side street leading up to her house. But before they had reached Becky's house, the woman pointed them down a different direction.

This was a red flag to both Becky and Amy.

"Where are we going? My house is back that way," Becky advised warily.

"I understand, sweetheart," the stranger apologized. "But your father will need some medicine for his pain. I'm stopping by the pharmacy to get some. Wouldn't want to come in empty handed, you know."

"But the pharmacy is closed: Everything is closed for the festival," Amy pointed out.

The woman turned around to address Amy. "Well, normally, it would be on July 4th. But thankfully..." The stranger stopped walking and reached into the top of her dress, pulling out a brass key hanging on a string around her neck. "...as the physician's wife, I think I can make a special exception." With that, she turned to the left and kept walking, pulling Becky behind her.

"You mean the PHARMACIST'S wife," Amy corrected.

"Err...that's what I said, my dear," the female replied nonchalantly.

Amy's eyes went wide at the contradiction. Something definitely wasn't right. Quickly, she caught up to the stranger. As she did so, she intentionally crossed in front of the strange woman and looked her directly in the eye.

Amy stared at the woman for a long minute, trying to devise a plan. But then, she gave way. With a gesture of absolute humility, completely out of sorts with how she was feeling, Amy graciously motioned for the mysterious person to walk ahead of her.

It was time to put her plan into action: As soon as the woman moved in front of her, Amy very intentionally stepped on the back edge of the fat, old lady's skirt! With a loud RIPPPPP, the entire dress split apart to reveal a very familiar body and face!

"Phillip Morse!" Amy accused. "I knew it! I knew that no woman could be that ugly! Becky! Run!"

Becky turned around to look at Amy and Phillip, who stood there in a white wig and makeup, wearing work clothes under the dress (Thank heavens!). Becky should have run, but she couldn't help but laugh; without the full disguise, Phillip looked like a silly circus clown.

Phillip, on the other hand, was neither fazed nor embarrassed. With deliberate motions, he reached his hand into the torn fabric and pulled out a burlap sack. Quicker than they could imagine, Phillip Morse trapped Becky and pulled the burlap down over her body!

Becky struggled valiantly but, ultimately, wasn't strong enough to get away. Amy was too shocked at what was going on to do anything else but start to scream. For his size and shape, Phillip proved rather strong. He quickly hoisted Becky over his shoulder and started running away! Amy, who couldn't do anything to stop Phillip, dashed back to the festival, hoping to enlist the help of Becky's father, who clearly wasn't sick at home. Judge Thatcher, though, was going to be a problem.

"Judge Thatcher! Judge Thatcher! You've gotta come quick!" Amy urgently called out to him, as she spotted him in the crowd.

The judge clumsily turned his gaze away from the bright fireworks show to stare at the girl. "Save it for the end of the party, child! It's a lotta fun!"

Oh no! The judge was practically slurring: He had drunk too much homemade wine!

As she hurried around the park, trying to find other less-intoxicated adults, her heart sank at the abundance of wine glasses sitting on every table. Just by surveying the park and counting the number of empty wine bottles sitting on the serving table, she guessed that every adult there had probably drunk at least two glasses of wine, possibly more! Even if they weren't wasted, she needed sober adults to help her. In that moment, Amy knew where her only hope lay. "TOM! HUCK!" she yelled frantically, running through the park, looking for them.

Spotting her, and hearing the panic in her voice, they quickly dropped out of the tree and ran over to her.

"What's going on, Ames?" Huck asked.

"Becky's been kidnapped!"

"What?! How did Dan get into this party without Mr. Thatcher seeing him?!" Huck demanded, alarmed at how easily the crime had been accomplished.

Amy shook her head vigorously. "No, Huck, it wasn't Dan; Phillip was the one who kidnapped her! As for Judge Thatcher, he's had too much to drink to help us, and quite frankly, you could color me impressed if you found one adult here who's completely sober. I don't think a single grownup would recognize Dan if he had walked into the crowd carrying a giant sign with his name on it!"

"So, what do we do now?! And where's your brother?!" Tom inquired worriedly.

"I don't know, Tom. He doesn't know that Becky's been taken. Oh, Huck, what are we going to do?!" Amy wailed.

"Amy, I don't know," Huck admitted. "It's getting dark, and we need a plan. Let's regroup with Andrew and figure this out together."

Sometime later in the evening, when the party was through, the judge eventually returned to the bank. He vaguely remembered that he had left one of his suit jackets at work. In his hand, he clutched a kerosene lantern. Somehow, he had reached his destination without injuring himself. Clumsily, he pulled out his key ring. Choosing the right key, he let himself inside. Stumbling over to his desk, he grabbed his suit jacket off a nearby coat rack and then looked around at the inside of the bank itself.

Running his eyes across the top of his desk, he noticed the

torn daguerreotype in its frame. "Now how did that happen?" he asked curiously, still not alert to the danger. The judge opened the back of the frame to remove the photo. He fiddled with the picture in his hand, puzzled. Eventually, he turned it over. A spirit of horror and anger slowly possessed him as he read an ominous message inscribed on the back.

10 years of my freedom rotted in that miserable cell you locked me up in. But don't worry. You'll get to see your daughter one more time...at her funeral!

Consider us even!
Dan

Judge Thatcher was not sober, but the sheer terror of this horrible, new development brought him to his senses. Suddenly starkly alert, the realization that Dead Eye Dan had Becky, and that she might already be dead, simply overwhelmed him. Grabbing the picture frame in one hand, he hurled it at the wall with all his strength. The glass broke and flew everywhere, but the judge didn't care. All thoughts were on his daughter and how he might lose her forever. He broke down and sobbed, slamming his fist on the desk out of anguished sorrow. "MY DAUGHTER! MY BEAUTIFUL, PRECIOUS DAUGHTER!"

CHAPTER 47

NO TURNING BACK

Becky awoke the next day, groggy. Save for the small sliver of daylight seeping underneath what she assumed was a door, she was imprisoned in a completely dark room. Her hands were bound tightly behind her back. She sat on the floor; her legs were stretched out in front of her, and her ankles were tightly restrained. In her mouth was a thick wad of cotton.

How long had she been like this? She guessed that she had been dumped here last evening, and that it was already many hours into the new day, but she really didn't know. The sensory deprivation currently enveloping her prevented much logical thought. She was able to remember the events that happened the night before which led up to her kidnapping: Phillip had crashed the village's Fourth of July party, dressed as a very ugly woman, and then strong-armed her into a sack to stifle her cries for help. Whatever happened afterwards was mostly a blur, but she knew that Dan must be involved in some way.

She tried working out a plan to escape and clung to the hope that Amy had reported her current predicament to Tom, Huck, and Andrew. That hope would have to carry her through Dan's wretched plot.

An hour later, a burst of brightness made Becky recoil and squint into the light. It was Dead Eye Dan: The door had opened to reveal his silhouette. Dragging her out by her ankles, Dan left her laying on the ground and then sat down in a wooden chair nearby. Phillip Morse stood close by, awaiting orders. It appeared she had been locked away in a bedroom closet in Dan's house, or at least what remained of his house.

Dan nodded his head in Rebecca's direction, which prompted Phillip to bend down and remove the gag from her mouth. As Phillip did so, Dan made sure Becky looked at him. Drawing one of his trusty revolvers from its holster, he pointed the cold, steel barrel straight at her head. "If you so much as make any loud noise, I'll be repainting this room an interesting, new shade of red. Understand, my dear?"

Becky nodded but showed not the slightest sign of fear. "How did you even know I was alive?!" she hissed through clenched teeth.

Dan chuckled. "Well, I actually can't take credit for that knowledge," he admitted, shrugging his shoulders. With a nod at Phillip, he acknowledged, "Phillip brilliantly had an afterthought: He worried that one or all of you might escape from my fiery inferno, so he volunteered to stay behind as a lookout."

Phillip nodded, a stupidly unattractive grin adorning his countenance.

"Personally, I thought him mighty foolish for doubting my brilliance, but I have to thank him for delivering on his end of our bargain," Dan praised.

"So, I reckon that this is the part of your scheme in which you hold me as your prisoner for two weeks and then let me go when you receive my ransom money?" she asked hopefully, knowing good and well that this was all a part of Dan's revenge plan.

A tiny smile crinkled at the corner of Dan's mouth as he studied her. "So, you did overhear that part of my plot?" He nodded and smiled, acknowledging her attention to detail. "You're a very clever girl, very clever. I'm surprised that you don't remember what I said to Phillip afterwards, though. So, I'm going to humor you and tell you the answer: Yes and no."

Becky arched an eyebrow. "What?"

"Yes, you're right. I'm going to hold you prisoner. Unfortunately, the second part won't come true for you, I'm afraid, Rebecca," Dan laughed.

"What do you mean?" Becky queried, feeling a bit of a punch in her heart.

"Well, ever since you five discovered my presence on the island and told the sheriff, you've forced me to act on impulse and speed up my plans. And besides, now that I have all the money from your father's bank in my possession, I'm afraid that, even if he wanted to, he couldn't afford to pay a ransom. The entire money supply of the village doesn't even exist anymore – I've got it all: He won't have anything left to give! Also, there's no way I'm going to stick around for two more weeks."

Becky gulped and tried to quell the growing terror in her gut.

"What I mean to say, Rebecca, is that you won't be returning to your father alive; I'm going to have to kill you."

"You're a horrible man, Daniel," Becky muttered, her every word laced with venom.

"Well, you've certainly got a way with words, my dear; perhaps you could have written a book. Now, I suggest that it's time you go to sleep."

And with that, Dan brought forth another rag, soaked in ether, from the storage of his pocket, and pressed the polluted fabric firmly under Rebecca's nose.

Becky squirmed desperately, but the sedative took effect almost instantly, and her world was once again plunged into darkness!

"How are we supposed to rescue Becky now?" Andrew threw the question out in the air.

Hoping to find Judge Thatcher, but finding only a locked door at the bank, Tom, Huck, Amy, and Andrew had snuck through the gap Dan had sawed in the wall. They were sitting in a circle on the floor of the bank, trying to come up with a plan to save Becky. They had tried the sheriff, but he was still out cold.

"Becky's most likely being held captive somewhere, possibly Dan's house," Huck spoke.

"Maybe not, Huck. Knowing Dan's plans, he'd probably want to make a spectacle out of Becky's demise," Tom responded, barely audible. His face was buried in his hands. The truth was, he felt far beyond distraught over his carelessness. He knew Becky was incredibly crafty, and that she was trying to escape even now, but the thought was not much of a consolation. Dan and Phillip had botched their first attempt to kill her: They wouldn't be so careless this time. Tom stood up and addressed his friends. "What if we borrow ourselves some guns from the sheriff and storm Dan's house? If we catch him off guard, I think we could take him," Tom suggested.

Andrew chuckled briefly before shaking his head. "Tom, for one thing, Dan still has an enormous number of weapons. If he's keeping Becky hostage in his house, he'd likely just shoot her and then shoot all of us. There is nothing subtle about storming a house; spooking him could endanger Becky. And for another thing, how much training have you had with firearms anyway?"

"Well...I...um...not much," Tom sheepishly admitted.

"Meaning?" Andrew pressed for clarity.

"None at all," the brave hero confessed.

"That's what I thought. If you don't know how to aim and fire a gun correctly, you could end up shooting one of us or even Becky," Andrew replied, as he stood up from the ground and paced, trying to put the whole puzzle together. "Tom, how long did Dan plan on holding Becky hostage?"

"He said that he'd keep her alive for two weeks," Tom replied. "We ain't got much time."

Huck then offered a not-so-brilliant suggestion. "Why don't we wait to get enough ransom money together and try to reason out the problem with Dan?"

The others stared at him for a couple of seconds, almost as if inspired, and then broke into a loud laugh. Eventually, Huck laughed out loud too.

"That's the dumbest idea ever!" Amy declared. "I say we go rescue her right now!"

"It will be very dangerous, Amy. We could all get killed," Andrew cautioned.

"You got a better plan, Andrew?" Huck countered. "Who says that Dan would even bother waiting for the whole two weeks to pass?"

"Touché," Andrew agreed.

"Okay, you guys," Tom spoke and stood up, inviting them to gather around the judge's desk. "Here's what we'll do."

Becky woke up for a second time that day, lying on her back, outside, under a large bush. She was restrained once again but was also tied to something she couldn't immediately identify. Gagged, she couldn't make any sound at all. Her chest faced the sky, and her legs and arms were stretched out in a "spread-eagle" position. Her wrists and ankles were bound tightly. She had been laid out on top of something hard and rough. It was probably a piece of wood, she reasoned. Was she lying on a log?

Though she was surrounded by the thick foliage of branches, the hot sun made her perspire. In any case, Becky guessed that the time was close to 3:00. She lifted her head towards her chest to look down at her legs.

Becky's prison took the form of a log raft. Not too big; it was just large enough to carry perhaps three or four people comfortably. Large nails had been driven into four points on the raft, providing a secure place to tie the ropes which bound her hands and feet. A fifth nail had been driven and attached to a long rope, which bore a large noose on the other end, presumably for hauling the raft. She could see that nail number five had been positioned at the midpoint of the opposite end of the raft. Her head lay near one end of the raft, but she could tell that there remained quite a bit of empty space on the raft between the ends of her feet and the end of the raft furthest from her head.

Aside from her head, though, the rest of her body couldn't move at all. Dan had taken the time to properly ensure that Becky wouldn't escape again.

Without warning, the leaves and branches parted to let in more sunlight. The unmistakable silhouette of Dead Eye Dan appeared above her. "Are you comfortable, my dear? I hope so. You're about to go for one wild ride!"

CHAPTER 48

OFF THE EDGE OF THE EARTH!

Not wanting to alert Dan to their presence, Huck, Amy, Tom, and Andrew crept quietly up to his house. They didn't completely know what opposition awaited them, and they were completely unaware of Becky's location. Three of them were unarmed, but Andrew had brought along a loaded revolver, that he had borrowed from Judge Thatcher's desk, just in case they needed to protect themselves. When they arrived, Andrew urged them all to stay as quiet as possible. As they cautiously ascended the front staircase that led into the mansion, they checked left and right. Taking a deep breath, they crossed the threshold of Dan's lair.

⚊⚊⚊∞⚊⚊⚊

As the youngsters were sneaking into the mansion, Dead Eye Dan and Phillip Morse were sneaking down the road, dragging Becky and the raft she was tied to along the rough ground. Becky had no clue what Dan was planning, although she suspected they were going to set her adrift somewhere. Eventually, the raft stopped moving. Becky lifted her head up to take in her surroundings: They had parked her next to the edge of a side channel of the Mississippi River, where the width of the waterway was much narrower, and the water raced much faster.

Together, Dan and Phillip waded into the water, pulling Becky and the raft with them. Quickly, the two men were waist deep into the water. As they fought to stay upright – the current was fast – they were able to pull the raft down the bank, into the choppy water. Once the raft was in the water, and with a great heave, Dan threw his end of the rope with the noose onto the raft and gave the vessel one final shove.

"Unhappy travels, my dear," Dan called out darkly, waving his hand, before he stepped back and allowed the mighty river's current to do its job.

Back in the house, the search came to a stop. It had become clear that Becky wasn't there, nor was anybody else for that matter. Understanding that the danger to them – Dan and Phillip – was not there, they felt okay to talk out loud. "Where could Dan have taken her?" Andrew asked in frustration, as he opened and shut various doors, revealing nothing important.

But no one answered. Such was their concern for Becky at this point, that everyone realized the question was rhetorical.

"Hey, guys!" Amy called from a room down on the first floor. "I think this might be where they kept her!"

The others soon joined Amy in what looked to be Dan's bedroom. The old, wooden floor showed deep scuffs amid the filth. A single bedframe with four posts stood opposite the door. On the bedframe rested a dirty mattress, with an old pillow, and a couple of stinky bedcovers thrown on top. The room had a desk and a closet, whose door was open. There was one dingy window, in front of which Amy was standing.

"Look!" she called urgently.

Amy pointed to a path newly trampled into the grass behind Dan's house. It led into the nearby woods. Gazing down on the path, they all realized what they were looking at: The path had almost certainly been made by Dan and Phillip. Had they taken Becky with them? She wasn't in the house – they knew that for sure.

"C'mon! Let's follow the path!" Tom commanded, as he opened the window and climbed over the low-resting windowsill to the outside. "They've got Becky; I know it!"

But Becky's friends were too late. Already adrift, Becky was slowly floating down the Mississippi River. Once the narrow channel had slightly widened out, her raft trip grew tranquil and quiet. Becky couldn't understand why Dan had chosen this method of death – Death by a peaceful ride down a river? It just didn't add up.

Up ahead, though, loomed a change in the river. Only minutes after pondering a nap while floating in the afternoon sun, Becky's ears pricked up. Just faintly, she could hear the sound of rushing water. She didn't know it, but a great mass of large rocks interrupted the flow of the river directly in front of her. The current picked up. Her raft bounced hard over a few of the rocks but did not overturn.

Becky processed this information and tried to work out a reason why Dan had cast her adrift where he did. She knew that rocks are generally found where a river gets shallow...or where a river meets a waterfall.

A waterfall! That was it! She only knew of one waterfall nearby, but it was huge: Devil's Drop Falls! It was legendary. Trappers and traders spoke of it with fear. The river dropped 150 feet straight down into a small lake full of tall, sharp rock spires! She would never survive going over the falls!

Panicking, she thrashed against her restraints, desperate to loosen her bonds; but her fierce efforts changed nothing.

"Oh, Tom, where are you?" she wondered fearfully.

She knew her friends would move mountains to find her, but if they didn't get to her soon, she and the raft would go over the falls. She lifted her head as far as she could but could get no real idea of how close the falls were.

The sound of the water, however, was growing louder. Even if she couldn't see the falls, she knew she was close to the point of no return!

CHAPTER 49

BATTLE TO THE DEATH

Huck, Amy, Tom, and Andrew relentlessly trudged along the grassy path, but there was still no Becky. They had already walked quite a distance. Their hopes began to falter, but no one spoke of giving up. No one **WOULD** give up.

Suddenly, Tom's head snapped up. If Becky were in any danger, he would reach her faster by increasing his pace. He broke into a run. The others followed suit shortly after, putting their trust in Tom's instincts.

In minutes, out of the quiet calm of the woods, they emerged next to a side channel of the Mississippi River, which flowed with a quiet, but mighty power. They observed that the trail of footsteps ended at the edge of the bank, leading Tom to guess the obvious: Becky might be in the water.

Tom ran along the bank. Faster and faster he went, desperate to find Becky. The others followed on his heels.

Tom began to despair: Becky was nowhere in sight. Slowing down, he shaded his eyes with his hand, canvassing the river as far away as he could see.

Then, just for a moment, he thought he saw something

solid – something that was not part of the river – but it disappeared around a curve!

Tom redoubled his efforts and his speed. He didn't care if what he had seen was only a trick of the light – he had to know.

Bolting into a sprint, Tom ran harder than he had ever run in his life. And then, he saw it! It was a raft, and Becky was tied to it, helplessly struggling! Swimming out to her wasn't an option: The raft was moving too fast. But the raft wasn't far from the bank. He only had one shot! Immediately, he ran even harder than before. He was so close now! 40 feet, 30 feet, 20 feet, 10 feet, 5 feet, 4 feet, 3 feet. Then, with a giant effort, he flung himself from the edge of the bank and crashed onto the deck of the raft!

Bam! The raft took the hard impact of Tom's fall as he landed on his stomach. Becky stared in complete shock at what had just taken place. But then, her face showed immense fear. Gagged, and unable to speak, she motioned with her head and her eyes toward what lay ahead.

Tom's eyes followed Becky's gaze. He felt his heart leap into his throat. They were only 500 feet from the edge of Devil's Drop Falls! He had maybe two minutes left to get her free! He had to act fast.

He first removed Becky's gag, but his fingers were shaking a lot while doing it. Then, knowing his pocketknife wasn't sharp, he tried to remove her ropes by hand. Same problem. He was on the verge of complete panic, when suddenly, the raft shuddered!

Tom spun his head around and gasped as he stared into the wrathful eyes of Dead Eye Dan! Apparently, Dan wouldn't be allowing any chance of Becky getting rescued!

To their surprise, Dan reached not for his gun, but for the wooden handle of his Bowie knife. A murderous grin appeared on Dan's face as he pulled the razor-sharp knife free.

Tom took in the lethality of Dan's blade but kept his cool; his protective instincts triumphed over his fear. Quickly, he stood up and protectively placed himself between the criminal and Becky. Armed with nothing more than his fists, Tom decided to take a more defensive posture; Tom wasn't exactly the fighting type, but he reckoned he could dodge attacks better than he could dish them out.

Dan twirled the knife between his fingers, his venomous eyes never once leaving his prey.

"FORGET ABOUT IT, DAN! I FOUND HER IN TIME, AND I'M GONNA SAVE HER! YOUR FEUD AGAINST BECKY AND HER FATHER IS OVER!" Tom shouted.

Something like hellfire raged inside of Dan's eyes as he clutched his Bowie knife. His body visibly shook with an uncontrollable rage. "IT AIN'T GONNA BE OVER TILL I SPILL ALL OF YOUR BLOOD INTO THE RIVER, BOY! ARGGHH!"

Dan roared and lunged forward, thrusting his knife violently toward Tom's midsection. Tom jumped to the side, just barely managing to avoid becoming a bloody shish kebab. Annoyed at his miss, Dan then furiously swung his knife in a sharp arc at Tom, who ducked at just the right moment, avoiding the death strike to his neck.

Tied to the raft, Becky had no choice but to watch Tom fight for both of them.

As far as Tom knew, Dan didn't have any formal military training. But everything about the way he fought practically labeled him as a soldier! Tom jumped up off the deck as Dan swung his knife lower, this time aiming for Tom's legs.

Having missed entirely, Dan took the fight to a dirty level and furiously kicked Tom in the chest. Tom fell backwards and landed on top of Becky's legs.

Dan no longer cared what happened to Becky - it was Tom he wanted to kill. With a huge swing downwards, he angrily tried to slice Tom's head clean off! Seeing Dan at just the last moment, Tom rolled sideways, towards Becky's upper body, and out of the way of the swing.

And then, something quite surprising happened: Dan swung at Tom with such ferocity – and carelessness – that he accidentally sliced through the rope restraining Becky's right ankle! Becky joined the fight instantly, lashing out with her right foot. Suddenly, Tom had a little help on his side.

Seeing his blunder, Dan then screamed at the top of his lungs as he bent over and grabbed his crotch. Becky had kicked him there, hard! Wasting no time, Tom untied the rope on Becky's left ankle.

Now there was only 300 feet separating them from the edge of Devil's Drop Falls. In a little more than a minute, they all would plunge to their doom!

Becky, with both of her legs free, took on the job of keeping Dan busy from hurting Tom. Dodging Dan's wild swings, Tom leaped back, performing an excellent back-handspring over Becky's torso. Quickly, he bent down to free her upper body.

In a flash, while Dan backed away from Becky to avoid her kicks, Tom was able to remove the bondages on her wrists. Soon, Becky was able to swing herself up from the raft and stand on her own two feet again.

Dan was livid at how his plan was unravelling. With a loud, angry grunt, he swung his right fist in a powerful hook! Tom took the devastating blow in the face! Becky retaliated with a fearsome side kick to Dan's middle, throwing him off his feet, onto the raft.

That was the break Tom had been waiting for. Grabbing Becky's left hand in his right, the two of them jumped off the raft and onto the bank, tumbling onto the grass together. The raft was only 100 feet from the falls!

Dan, who had landed on top of the tow rope, wasn't about to give up his prize so easily. He quickly stood up and jumped off as well. With a mighty shout, Dan leapt through the air and fell onto the bank, landing face-down in the grass - but only for about two seconds. Catching his breath, he lifted his head up and voraciously bared his teeth, staring menacingly at the two before him.

"END OF THE ROAD, BECKY!" he growled.

Becky screamed.

Tom threw himself in front of Becky protectively.

Dan laughed like a demonic maniac as he used his Bowie knife and his free hand to slowly claw his way along the ground towards them!

And then, all of a sudden, Dan couldn't move another inch

closer. He suddenly lost his grip on his knife as he found himself being dragged backwards, back into the river!

Intent on killing Tom, Dan hadn't noticed that the tow rope with the noose had gotten snagged around his left ankle! Desperately, he fought to release himself from the rope, but he was well and truly caught.

And then, the raft sailed over the cliff, taking Dan with it just 20 feet behind!

No matter how much Dan screamed, struggled, and scraped at the noose which bound him to the raft, his body was yanked towards the falls.

With an angry, terrified scream – "I WON'T REST TILL YOU'RE DEAD, TOM SAWYER!" –– Dan was unwillingly pulled over the edge!

Tom and Becky would never forget the genuine fear of death in his eyes as he plunged down the long face of the cliff to his demise!

CHAPTER 50

YOUNG LOVE AND RETURNING HOME

Tom and Becky quickly raced to the edge of the bank that overlooked the falls. Peering down, they caught sight of the once sturdy, wooden raft, shattered into half a dozen large pieces on the jagged rock spires below. As for Dan, there was nothing. They didn't catch even a glimpse of his body and assumed it had been speared apart and pulled under the water below the falls. No human being could survive a fall like that.

Tom checked to make sure that Becky was okay and had not been hurt in any way. She was breathing hard from the fight but, other than that, seemed alright. Holding his hand to his face where Dead Eye Dan had slugged him, Tom tried to figure out what the damage was. The left side of his face had borne the brunt of the blow. Dan's fist had struck close to his eye, and Tom's nose had bled out a little bit. But the bleeding from his nostrils had mostly stopped, and the pain in his jaw would eventually go away. The only other injury would probably just be a black eye. Oh well, the way he figured, it would make a terrific battle scar and a great story to tell the other boys of the village. He knew how lucky he and Becky were.

Tom turned his full focus to Becky as he spoke every word

and feeling weighing heavily on his mind at that moment. "Becky, thank God you're okay; I thought I had lost you," he confessed, shuddering at the thought, and trying to hold back a tear. "I don't know what I would do without you."

"I knew you'd find me, Tom," Becky quietly reassured him. "I had faith." Here, she stopped for a moment and then smiled, "But next time, let's not cut it so close, alright?"

They then both embraced in the tightest and warmest hug they had ever given each other. When they separated, Tom was grinning from ear to ear like a lovesick puppy. Becky blushed bright red.

"Wow," Tom marveled. "I don't know about you, but I would have missed those hugs a lot."

Becky's loving eyes met his as the words left his mouth. "Oh yeah? Just my hugs?"

"Huh?" Tom stammered, as Becky leaned in and brushed her warm lips against his in a tender, pure, and magical kiss!

Tom's eyes went wide at first. He honestly didn't know how to think sensibly in a situation like this. All he could do was desperately enjoy the sweet taste of Becky's lips, feel the gentle softness of her hands, and realize, deep down inside, that she **WAS** the perfect girl for him. *"Thank you, God,"* Tom thought gratefully in his head.

They continued their embrace, whilst they tried to quell the flutter of the millions of tiny butterflies in their stomachs. All Tom could wonder was how Becky could make him go crazy inside, all with just a simple kiss.

Amy, Huck, and Andrew strode quietly up, suddenly noticing

what was going on as they approached. "Aw man, Tom's an awful lucky son of a gun," Huck grumbled quietly and smiled. He was happy for his best friend.

Amy turned her head as she heard him speak these words. She smiled when she saw the gentle look Huck gave the pair. Inching closer to him, she wrapped her arms around Huck's neck and closed in with an excellent, warm, and memorable kiss of her own.

Huck, taken completely by surprise at this show of affection, clumsily fell backwards onto the grass, taking Amy with him.

Andrew watched these events unfold and found himself rolling his eyes. "Teenagers," he muttered cynically, all the while remembering the girl that had stolen his heart when he was just a youth like them.

<hr />

The five friends eventually found their way back to the village. As they sauntered through the town, Amy noticed that nobody was in their homes, or even outside in their gardens for that matter. A ghostly silence covered the entirety of the village - no happy voices, no pleasant chirp of birds, nothing. The entire town appeared deserted. What was going on?

Turning the corner, they came across the missing town folk. They were all gathered in a circle, outside town hall, listening to a man speak.

Rebecca's father stood on a chair in the middle of the group, sober once more, speaking to everyone as the leader they had all come to recognize. The judge had assembled all the grownups together. At that moment, they were discussing a plan for a brave search and rescue attempt. They were on the brink of leaving to go find Becky and save her from Dan's clutches.

"Now remember, everyone," Judge Thatcher warned. "Dead Eye Dan's wishes must be met if we're ever going to get Rebecca back."

"Dad!" Becky shouted, from outside the crowd.

Judge Thatcher looked up for a moment but couldn't see his daughter, who was hidden behind the larger adults. Eventually, he went on talking!

Trying to reach Judge Thatcher, with Becky leading the way, the five friends pushed their way through the crowd.

"Dad!" Becky called again, this time tapping her father on the arm and getting his attention.

Judge Thatcher looked down at her and smiled. "Hello, dear," he responded casually, and then turned back to face the people.

An expression of stunned disbelief appeared on Becky's face. Did her dad need eyeglasses?

Immediately, the judge performed a double-take and gasped aloud in front of everybody. He stepped down from his pedestal to surround Becky with his arms. Hugging her close, tears started to flow forth from his eyes. "Thank God you're alright!" he shakily choked out and continued to hug her. "I thought I was never going to see you again."

Just to the side of Becky, her friends watched the tender moment. They were happy to see the judge's reaction. He was not usually a demonstrative man; clearly, he was moved beyond words.

Wiping his eyes, the judge stepped back a little bit, astounded at how, only hours before, his entire world had been stripped away, but was now being returned to him unharmed. "How in the world did you escape from that monster?" the judge inquired.

The rest of the village leaned in as the judge asked the question, equally interested in hearing her answer as well.

Becky said what came first to her mind: "I wouldn't be alive if it weren't for my friends," she answered, waving to Tom, Huck, Amy, and Andrew.

The village gave out many hurrahs and pats on the back for Tom and his companions. Even the judge thanked them, though he wouldn't let go of Becky's shoulders.

Though Amy, Tom, Huck, and Andrew didn't enjoy the excessive attention, they bore up under the praise. Eventually, after thanks and relief were expressed by all, the adults from the village began peeling off to return to their own lives...all except for Aunt Polly, who pulled Tom close in a hug. "You run off way too much!" she scolded gently. "But I'm so glad to have you back."

By now, Tom was used to her motherly lecturing and hugged her back without saying a word, grateful to be home again. In his mind, things couldn't have ended any better: Safe and mostly unharmed, Becky and the others would never again have to face the wrath of Dead Eye Dan, and their friendship with each other seemed to have grown even stronger than before.

"By the way..." Aunt Polly started to speak.

Tom gulped, knowing by now that those words never meant anything good.

"You'll have to answer me why you felt it necessary to steal my

Sunday luncheon ham and douse me with freezing-cold water, Thomas Sawyer," she ended her reprimand, eyes twinkling.

Tom retreated from the hug, scratching the back of his head awkwardly as he avoided eye contact with his aunt. "Um...it was summer vacation, and uh...we got hungry?" he sheepishly offered his answer, hoping her judgment wouldn't be too severe.

Aunt Polly stared at her adopted son for a few seconds, amazed at his ridiculous excuse. Eventually, she just smiled and turned to head back home as well. "Next time, don't take the whole ham, mister," she cautioned. "I swear you've become rowdier at 17 than you ever were at 11."

And with that, the five adventurers were left alone at Town Hall, enjoying each other's company.

Tom smiled. It was good to be back.

CHAPTER 51

THE FINAL PIECE AND A DARK, DANGEROUS SECRET

Still, I bet you're wondering, *"What ever became of the great treasure hunt?"* Well, the story's not quite finished yet.

The following week had brought more than enough time for everyone to rest and recover completely. On the seventh day, the adventurous five reunited. All were wondering the same burning question: Where was the treasure?

Unfortunately, after giving the topic a few minutes of discussion, nobody could think of any new leads to follow. So, instead, Andrew proposed another avenue of investigation totally unrelated to the treasure hunt – just something to keep them busy. "Now that Dead Eye Dan is no longer a problem for us, how about we head back down the road and explore his mansion again?" Andrew asked.

The opinions this question engendered were of a mixed sort. "I reckon I'll go. If that place hasn't fallen to the ground yet, it's bound to fall soon," Huck said. "But other than that, I can't think of another reason to go."

As everyone voiced their opinion, Andrew waited quietly.

Tom showed a little interest, as did Amy: At least it would be something to do. They were both bored, as were the others. Becky didn't very much feel like going back to their attacker's hideout, for understandable reasons. But in the end, the decision was made to go – carried mostly by their boredom. That day, they began hiking back down the road, and through the woods, to Dead Eye Dan's mansion.

"Well, we finally get to see what this place looks like during the day without having to fear for our lives," Becky commented cheerfully.

"Didn't think the sheriff would ever let us back in here," Amy chuckled. "He's been watching this place like a hawk in case Phillip, or God forbid, Dan, somehow came back."

"Well, after clearing out all of Dan's weapons and recovering the bank's money, I guess he decided that it was safe to leave the post after waiting for a week. Dan's as good as dead, and besides, the sheriff's got a lot of important things to do," Becky replied. "And don't scare me like that. I've made enough memories about Dan to last me my entire life."

As they approached the mansion, all were surprised to see that it was mostly still intact. They could see the burned-out wood around the room on the lower level, and there were trails of soot that climbed out from the cracks in the walls, up to the second floor. But, surprisingly, most of the mansion still stood: It looked like the fire had burnt itself out before consuming the entire place.

Tom chuckled to himself as they walked up the front stairs. They trapsed back through the open front door one final time, but this time with confidence and bravery. It was time to uncover the secrets of this deranged man and to find out all that went on in this mysterious house. When they had ascended to the second floor, Becky even worked up the nerve to push one of the gargoyles off of its pedestal, causing it to fall and noisily break into pieces.

"How could Dan have lived here for all this time and nobody knew about it?" Huck asked, as they investigated.

"Well, Dan probably bought this place using the stolen profits he made from his life of crime and then declared ownership under a false name. That can be the only explanation," Tom deduced.

In the main hall, they once again found themselves confronted by the numerous doors to various rooms, most of which had not been explored thoroughly. Each of them decided to explore as many rooms as they could: A ballroom, a kitchen, two bedrooms, and a guestroom were discovered. Still, nothing special was located.

Andrew decided to search the inside of the office again – the same office on the second floor they had been in the first night they discovered Dan's hideout. Eventually, the others found him and joined him in searching the room.

Becky got to work and meticulously looked through the various drawers in the desk, finding some old letters that Dan had kept. Some of them were bills, but others had been sent from some of his friends; Suffice it to say, the fact that Dan had any friends was nothing short of remarkable. In any case, Becky soon found herself snooping through the dead convict's mail.

As Becky glanced at the postage addresses on the envelopes,

she learned Dead Eye Dan's full name. Whoever had sent the letters had addressed them all to a Daniel William Lawrence. *"What an impressive name for such an unattractive personality,"* she thought.

Opening the first envelope, she silently read a long, boring letter from a friend named Cynthia. Nothing good in there! She set the letter down and went on to the next one.

Eventually, after all of the regular correspondence had been opened, Becky came across a package from a friend named Jason Rusher. The parcel contained several items. Among the first things she discovered inside was an assortment of aging photographs.

The first one showed Dan and another man – Jason? – standing next to a lush tree in front of a house. Becky didn't know who this Jason character was, but she guessed that he must have been close friends with Dan. Both men looked to be about 35 years old. Dan, who had apparently shaved for the photo, looked quite handsome without the scruff.

Photo number two showed Dan holding a smiling, little boy, probably no older than five, on his lap. Something about the young boy's appearance looked awfully familiar to her; Becky was sure that she had seen him someplace, but that was not possible.

Once Andrew finished going through the remainder of Dan's personal belongings, he stood up to leave. "I'm through with this room," he called to everyone.

Becky glanced up from the photo of the little boy to meet Andrew's gaze. And there it was: She made the crazy connection.

The little boy looked exactly like Andrew! The last name on the letters should have told her everything. Daniel William LAWRENCE – The same last name as Amy LAWRENCE and Andrew LAWRENCE! The young boy in the photo must surely be Andrew! His overall look hadn't changed much, and there was no mistaking Andrew's familiar, dimpled smile!

Andrew and Amy were related to Dead Eye Dan?! How could that possibly be? Becky thought about the picture – she was sure it was Andrew – and then thought about Amy and Andrew's family; or rather, she thought about their lack of family.

Slowly, she looked towards Amy, who was going through the bookshelf against the wall. "Amy? Can you spare me a moment?"

Amy gazed sideways. "Sure, Becky, what's going on? You're looking more pale than usual. You gotta get out in the sun more often," Amy joked good-naturedly.

Becky didn't even break into a small smile, and Amy felt an uncomfortable lump form in her stomach. "Becky, what's wrong?"

"Amy, how much do you know about your parents?" Becky nervously inquired.

"My parents?" Amy repeated. A frown crossed her face as she searched her mind. In truth, she knew very little. "Uh, from what Andrew told me, my mother died about a year after I was born; I think it was polio. As for my father, he left when I was only about four; I never really knew him – I was too young. Andrew's relationship with him wasn't solid either; he told me that dad left in an angry fit one night, and that was the last we saw of him. After that, we lived by ourselves, but Andrew managed to get a job working as the carpenter's apprentice to make a living for us both..."

Becky held up her hand to stop Amy from talking. Slowly, she passed the package to Amy and then pointed at the name it was addressed to.

"It's a package, Becky. What's that got to do with..."

But then, Amy noticed the surname of the recipient. Her eyes went wide with shock. "Well...huh...Becky...That's strange... You don't think...Well, surely that's just a coincidence. Lawrence isn't exactly a unique last name, right?" Amy stuttered, hardly believing the words she spoke herself.

Becky nodded as she also handed over the small, sepia-toned portrait for Amy to see. "That may very well be true, but this photo came with the box. Do you recognize the people in it?"

As Amy's eyes traversed the picture, her breathing became erratic and ragged. In seconds, she was in a full-blown panic attack.

Becky yelled loudly for Huck and Andrew, who both came running to Amy's aid.

"Amy, take it easy there," Huck gently urged. "What's come over you?"

Without saying a word, she shakily placed the box and the portrait into Huck's hands. Huck took a moment or two before passing the items along to Andrew in shock.

After gazing at the two objects for a whole minute, Andrew stammered, "I can't believe this. There's got to be some other explanation." His denial was firm.

"What? You reckon Dan was some sort of a distant uncle,

Andrew?" Tom questioned, now having looked at the package addressee and the photo himself.

"I don't know, Tom. This is just bizarre," Andrew said. "I mean, I knew that our dad had problems, but I didn't think he would turn into a criminal. I mean, is it even possible?"

"Hard to tell, unless you've got your birth certificates somewhere," Becky responded. "I don't reckon there's anything we could do to find that out besides ask Dan ourselves, and it's hard to ask for answers from a man who's been dead for over a week now. That picture is pretty hard to ignore, though."

"Well, it's been years since he saw either one of you. If it's truly Dan in this picture, I'd bet that Amy wasn't even born yet," Huck spoke in defense of Dan, having already considered Amy and Andrew's current ages.

"But Dan knew their names when he captured us, Huck," Tom pointed out uneasily.

Andrew closed his eyes and shook his head in absolute mental torment. "He's a wanted murderer, Tom. I guess if I were him, I wouldn't care who I killed either if it meant I wouldn't get caught."

"So, what do we do now?" Amy squeaked fretfully.

"Nothing," Andrew declared resolutely. "We're the only ones who know the truth, and I'm comfortable taking the truth to my grave. We've gotten along without him just fine before we began this expedition, and we'll get along just fine now: Nothing has to change."

"So, we're all in sworn agreement to keep this truth a secret, then?" Tom asked.

Everyone nodded.

"Should we sign our names in blood again?" Tom pressed the issue further, liking dark secrets.

Huck shook his head. "Tom, the last time we did that, Dr. Robinson had done been killed, and Injun Joe was still a free man."

Tom shrugged. "What's your point?"

"We're older, and the man in question is as good as gone," Huck explained.

"Okay," Tom surrendered. "I just thought it'd be fun to keep the tradition alive."

Tom peered into the parcel. Reaching in, he retrieved a large, heavy, sealed envelope that bulged in the middle. Quick work with a letter opener found on the desk did the job of granting them access.

The first items to fall out were several large, gold coins. As they clinked loudly onto the floor, Huck picked them up and examined them. Squinting his eyes, he tried to figure out the strange markings that ran along the outside.

After a short while, he managed to identify the origin of the currency. "Looks like Japanese 'Jibakurei Gold.' This here stuff was hidden by an elite tribe of ninjas around the 6th century. Sworn to protect it at any cost, they dedicated their lives to do nothing but guard it at all hours of the day and night. And, according to legend, the gold was also protected constantly by some very powerful, spiritual forces. It's a wonder someone actually got a hold of some."

The others stared at Huck, surprised, both at the outburst from him and at the knowledge he had about the coins. For once,

Becky found herself impressed: Huck knew something that she didn't.

Huck got defensive. "What? I've read a few books about other cultures; They're interesting, and I learn about other hidden treasure. There ain't nothing wrong with that," he justified.

The only item left inside the envelope was an old, folded letter. Gently unfolding the worn paper, Tom struggled to read the words that had faded over time.

Greetings, Daniel,

So much time has passed since last we met. As I sit back and reflect over my life's story, I can't help but remember all the adventurous times we shared together on the high seas. We could have spent many more great years together. The ship just hasn't felt the same since your departure. I hope that your family lives a happy life right now. Lord knows I miss my mother, father, and even my own wife. But what I lost in your absence, I have regained in respect and fear from others. Fate has acted rather mysteriously on my behalf. As the new captain of The Dark Mystery, many towns and villages fear even the mention of my name. Perhaps you would consider rejoining my crew? Maybe you can even be First Mate. We all accepted you and knew you to be a loyal companion and a deadly warrior. I trusted you more than I trusted my own mother and father. And so, I hope that the enclosed coins can help you. Guard them well: They cost me many lives and took me a very long time to get a hold of. My biggest *secret lies also with this letter I am writing to you. Never let anyone else get hold of it.*

Again, wishing you all the best,

Yours truly,

Jason Rusher (Red Beard)

The children stood in complete and impossible awe. What had they just learned?

"Wait," Andrew interjected. "What in the world was Red Beard getting at when he mentioned his biggest secret?" he demanded.

"Who knows?" Tom volunteered. "It seems he was pirate friends with your dad, but I ain't sure that tells us any secrets about Red Beard. Besides, I'm pretty sure that Dan didn't even know what Red Beard meant since this envelope clearly hasn't been opened before."

Amy reread the letter in her head. "No, Tom," she said. "Red Beard told Dan that the biggest secret lay **WITH** the letter."

"**WITH** the letter?" Becky repeated, trying to work out possible answers to the mystery. "Tom! Quick! Check inside the envelope!"

Tom inverted the wrapping, hoping that a hidden item might drop out. But nothing did. An even more thorough search proved the envelope was indeed completely empty.

Huck snapped his fingers as a surge of logic entered his mind. "No, we're looking at this all wrong. When he said, 'My biggest secret lies with the letter…,' he didn't mean that there was another item, inside the envelope, with the letter; he meant that there's a secret in the letter itself!"

All of them hurriedly scanned the words on the letter, looking for a hidden message or code. However, none of them noticed the torn edges around the sides of the paper.

"There's got to be something we're not seeing. There's nothing special in the message he wrote!" Andrew huffed angrily, throwing the paper into the air in frustration.

Tom watched as the paper fluttered down through the air, twisting and turning every way, until it finally settled quietly on the floor. He allowed a big grin to cross his face as he picked up the discarded parchment and brought it back to the others. "The reason we ain't seeing anything is because we're looking on the wrong side!" he deduced. He flipped the letter over to reveal that the other side bore no writing but, instead, was covered with an assortment of strange markings. Unfortunately, they had completely ignored the obvious: The message wasn't just a letter, it was part of a map!

It took them all one glance at the torn piece of paper to guess the answer to the puzzle: The big secret from Red Beard's letter was the location of his treasure!

Sure enough, in the upper section of the parchment, a dark red X permanently scarred the paper. After having waited for so long, the five friends could now discover the riches and treasures of the infamous Red Beard!

Huck, who was currently in charge of the map sections, now removed the other two pieces from his back pocket. Carefully, he placed them on the floor and fitted them all together along their respective, torn edges. Becky found a glass bottle, filled with glue, lying on Dan's desk. She handed it to Huck, who lost no time in reconnecting the sections together. Huck soon had the original map back in one piece, which led to a resounding cheer of triumph from the other four. All of them were eager to embark on the final exploration for the treasure.

Unfortunately, by the time they had finished in Dan's office, night was upon them. There would be no treasure hunting that day. A fair share of grumbling about the untimeliness of the sun going down occurred, but in the end, they realized that they had already learned so much that they could wait until the following day to continue.

"All right, then," Andrew agreed. "See you guys tomorrow!" He and Amy left the mansion, followed by Huck, who made sure to grab the map and the gold coins. Tom and Becky were the last to leave. The climax of their adventure was imminent, and none of them possessed much more than an ounce of patience.

Sleep didn't come easily for any of them that night, but who could blame them? The exciting final leg of their adventure lay just on the horizon!

CHAPTER 52

A LITTLE TOO CLOSE TO HOME

Morning took forever to arrive. When it did, none of the kids had anything else on their young minds; only the enticing smells of breakfast could temporarily distract them. By mid-morning, everyone had gathered in Andrew's carpentry shop to study the map. They all were focused on finding the treasure.

Huck placed the reconnected map onto a table in the middle of the room and gestured for everyone to gather around.

As Tom had pointed out earlier, the map did indeed include an illustration of Jackson's Island. In addition, the map also encompassed the western edge of Illinois, near the forest where they had found Gregory and Wesley. Interestingly, the map also bore a wide enough radius to include the approximate area near where Horace's inn and Dead Eye Dan's mansion were. However, the path to the treasure started out not from these distant environs, but from the boat dock down near the river.

The treasure was in the village!

Anyone with even a minimal amount of cartographical expertise could navigate the map. The route to the treasure had been clearly marked with a series of inked dashes, which led to the treasure's location. Becky cleverly figured out that even though the final piece of the map had the X on it, the rest of the map wasn't useless. Without having the other pieces of the map, one could never have figured out that the buried treasure location was somewhere in Missouri. The map showed only geographical borders – no names. The illustration of the village appeared a little bit out of date, as there were only a few buildings plotted on the paper. Nowadays, there were dozens of new homes and buildings. In any case, the red X marked a point somewhere past the center of the village.

The only difficult mystery to them was that the X wasn't touching any buildings or plants. Either Red Beard had hidden his treasure somewhere not many people knew of, or he wanted to protect the identities of whoever happened to live or work there.

Huck knew enough about treasure maps to decode the markings on the paper. Each dash representing the trail to the treasure was about 50 feet of walking distance: Huck said that was the general rule for treasure maps.

In a flash, they hurried to the quiet edge of the dock, eager to complete this wild goose chase.

"Okay," Huck announced triumphantly, holding up the map. "The trail from the edge of the dock to the X shows exactly 30 marks. That means we walk about 1,500 feet."

Becky, Amy, Tom, and Andrew all nodded in agreement. It all came down to the last 1,500 feet; if they were right, at the end of the trail they would find the location of Red Beard's treasure!

Of course, measuring 1,500 feet precisely would prove to be quite difficult. A quick discussion eliminated the possibility of using a wooden ruler: It would be impossibly tedious, and they would almost certainly lose track of their measurements.

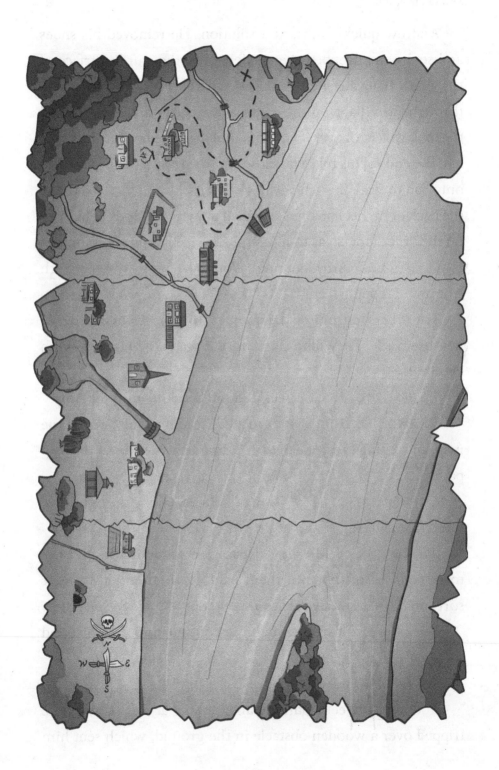

Andrew quickly devised a solution. He removed his shoes and socks and dropped them safely onto the sturdy surface of the wharf. Then, he went to the edge of the dock, where the trail through the village on the map appeared to start. Since he had the longest feet of everyone there, the distance between his heel and the ends of his toes was closest to the length of one foot. He only had to walk in such a way so that each time he took a step, the back of his heel on one foot lined up with the ends of his toes on the other foot, so as to measure each step as one foot long.

"1…2…3…," Amy counted aloud, keeping in sync with Andrew's stepping feet.

The others murmured the numbers to themselves in order to not lose track. They followed Andrew, watching his steps with precision.

"…204…205…206…," Becky counted, taking over for Amy.

"…508…509…510…" Huck recited, keeping a close eye on the map, and telling everyone to turn occasionally whenever the map path curved.

"…1,045…1,046…1,047…," Tom calculated, taking the figurative torch from Huck.

By now, they had trudged past the schoolhouse and the town square. But none of them paid much attention to their surroundings, lest they lose count. No one wanted to start over.

The number of steps remaining continued to dwindle, and soon enough…

"…1,497…1,498…1,499…AH!"

Andrew had been counting and looking at his feet when he tripped over a wooden obstacle in the ground, which sent him falling to the ground nearby. Tom looked up – he had been staring at Andrew's feet too. Needless to say, the final destination threw everyone into a state of absolute confusion.

They were standing outside of Tom's very own house!

The stumbling block that had caused Andrew to fall turned out to be Tom's own cellar door! The last step would have put them right **ON** the cellar door! Becky, Tom, Amy, and Huck all realized this at the same time.

"I'm ok," Andrew said, as he got to his feet and dusted himself off. "What in tarnation just happened?"

Becky turned to look back at the cellar door. "I think we just found where Red Beard buried his treasure."

CHAPTER 53

RICHES AND REVELATIONS

"Golly, there ain't no way that...I mean, could it be?" Tom queried aloud, rubbing his head confusedly.

"Only one way to find out, Tom," Huck summarized.

Tom hurried to pull open the heavy cellar door, which put up quite a resistance at first. Eventually, he got it open, and Huck climbed in first. Down the old, wooden stairs he went, followed by Becky, Amy, Tom, and Andrew.

The entranceway was bright enough, but the rest of the cellar was just too dark to explore. Quickly dashing up the stairs, Tom sprinted back to the house. A minute later, he returned with a lit kerosene lantern.

Stepping back down into the darkness, Tom continued the exploration with the others. Outside, the lantern's flame hadn't made a big impression, but inside the dark confines of the cellar, the tiny light shined unbelievably bright. Many storage barrels lined the walls of the cellar; some of them contained sugar, flour, or salt. They also discovered a dozen clay flowerpots. Five or six gardening tools with long handles leaned against the dirt walls, while a number of bulgy burlap sacks holding who knows what sat nearby.

As the search continued, Andrew discovered a wooden door built into a faraway wall of the cellar. Grabbing the knob, he pulled with all his might, but the door didn't move at all. "Tom, where does this go? It's impossible to open!" he groaned awkwardly.

Huck went behind and wrapped his arms around Andrew's midsection, pulling with him to provide more force for opening the door. Still, the stubborn door refused to budge. Finally, Amy and Becky threw their weight into the battle as well. To no avail, the door remained shut.

Tom sighed at the sight of his idiot friends. "You know, guys," he began, trying not to snicker. "Sometimes you need to work smarter, not harder," he said, as he twisted the knob and gave it a gentle push, causing the door to open effortlessly.

The others all looked away in awkward embarrassment.

"Oh right, **NOW** you become smart," Becky joked sarcastically.

Tom rolled his eyes and went ahead into the secret room, with the others following closely behind. He never actually went down into the cellar, except on very rare occasions when twisters sometimes blew through the state. But even when he did come down into the cellar, he had never explored this particular room before.

Everyone squinted their eyes as the light of the lantern was reflected back at them a thousand times – It was bouncing off of countless, shiny objects in the room. As Tom moved the lantern slightly, everyone's eyes widened at the enormous pile of gold coins completely covering the dirt floor of the tiny chamber!

Shock and amazement filled them. They were rich! They had

finally found the treasure that they had pursued for so long. And it was here, in Aunt Polly's cellar?

Though they couldn't tell exactly, Becky estimated that the glimmering pile probably rose to nine feet high at its tallest point! Stretching to fill the small 20-foot by 20-foot room, a large assortment of different kinds of treasures, including gold crowns, pearl necklaces, and sterling silver chalices regally decorated the entire pile!

After filling his eyes with the scene, Tom put down the lantern, scaled the pile of gold, and retrieved a small, wooden chest that sat atop the heap. Handing it down to Huck, Tom then made sure that everyone could open it as a group. "Ready, guys?" he asked, allowing each of them to place a hand on the wooden lid.

The group nodded. "1...2...3..."

The top came off, and everyone shrieked in excitement.

Inside lay the most amazing, royal assortment of rubies, sapphires, emeralds, amethysts, diamonds, and other jewels! Ultimately, they would have to go to a jeweler to have their value appraised, but the general consensus was that the contents of the box would probably sell for thousands of dollars! Maybe millions! They couldn't even fathom a million dollars!

Tom was beyond ecstatic. "We're rich! We're rich!" he crowed happily, as he triumphantly jumped up and down.

"You're already rich," Becky pointed out, though she too was grinning from ear to ear.

Tom nodded, and then quickly changed his chant: "We're even richer! We're even richer!"

Becky burst out laughing.

"Well, let's not just stand here cheering about it; let's get this fortune out of here!" Andrew insisted.

Each of them grabbed a single handful of the gold coins and filled up the empty spaces of the chest with them. Then, they piled it high until the lid almost couldn't close. Of course, now, because of the weight increase, Huck had a harder time supporting the box.

Andrew, seeing Huck struggle, graciously offered to carry out the chest himself. Huck was only more than happy to be relieved of the burden, and they all began to exit the cellar together into the midafternoon sun.

As they emerged from the dark cellar, Aunt Polly, hearing their excited voices, beckoned to them from the front porch.

"Guess what, Aunt Polly?" Tom rejoiced. "We found Red Beard's fortune! It's been hidden in the cellar this whole time!"

However, much to the surprise of everyone, Aunt Polly looked at them fondly and then said, "How nice for you."

It was as if they hadn't said anything unusual. In the same normal tone of voice, she blithely continued, "Have you all been out having a good time today? The weather's beautiful, isn't it?"

Huck and the others looked at each other, totally confused by her reaction. Eventually, they all shrugged their collective shoulders.

"You don't seem excited that we found ourselves a collection of treasure," Huck deduced suspiciously.

"Well, I've actually known about that treasure for many, many years," she answered, showing the slightest hint of a smile.

"What do you mean?" Becky questioned.

Aunt Polly looked them all in the eye. "You do know who placed that treasure there, right?"

"Yeah," Huck replied. "It was Red Beard."

Aunt Polly shook her head. "I meant his real name."

Amy thought back to when they had all read the letter from Red Beard to Dead Eye Dan. "His name was Jason Rusher, right?" She guessed.

Aunt Polly nodded. "I knew Jason Rusher for a few, wonderful years of my life, and then, one day, I learned that he had died at sea."

Aunt Polly became very quiet. A single tear trailed down her cheek. She glanced away from them and looked down at her feet, bringing her hands together.

Just then, Tom noticed her frail hands gently, and almost unconsciously, caressing an old, faded ring on her finger!

A single thought coursed through Tom's mind at that moment, one he hadn't considered before: *"Had Aunt Polly ever been married?"*

Andrew had the exact same idea and turned to the woman he had only ever known as Polly. "Ma'am, can I ask you what your last name is?"

She looked up and smiled sweetly. "It's Rusher."

"Wait!" Amy had difficulty coming to grips with this. "So that means…"

Aunt Polly nodded. "Yes, Jason Rusher was my husband."

For about 10 seconds, no one spoke.

"No way!" Huck finally exclaimed. "You were married to Red Beard?!"

Tom just stared at his aunt, finding himself at a loss for words.

"Tell us about that!" Amy begged, speaking for the rest of them.

When Aunt Polly nodded at them, the five quickly scrambled onto the porch and sat in a circle at her feet. They couldn't comprehend that Aunt Polly and the mysterious wife of Red Beard were one and the same person.

With a small smile on her lips, Aunt Polly sat down, took a moment or two to compose herself, and then began with her story.

CHAPTER 54

'TIL DEATH DO US PART

"I was only 25 years old when I met Jason at my church. He was new to the area, as I recall. And though he was several years older than me, we quickly became great friends and had the grandest time together. Oh, how we would pretend to be pious, while we stole the neighbors' tomatoes and skipped them across the lake. I really don't know what inspired us to make a tradition out of something like that, but he sure knew how to show a girl a good time."

Here, Aunt Polly stopped to think about just how much of her private life she wanted to share with the kids. Eventually, she continued. "Anyway, one year later, I went off to visit my grandparents, who lived in Europe, and I didn't end up seeing Jason for four very long years. When I did return to America, and we saw each other again, there were so many emotions - excitement, longing, sadness, even brief tears of joy. We courted for perhaps two months before he worked up the courage to ask me to be his wife. I can still remember everything the way it happened that day."

Aunt Polly paused as she mentally returned in time to the day it happened. A sweet smile crossed her face as the memories rushed back. She went on, describing the day in vivid detail.

"Jason! Jason! Where are we going?" Polly laughed, as Jason led her by the hand through the cool, silent woods of Missouri. The year was 1803, and Polly was 30 years old. Jason was older than her, but still young at heart. He had taken her out for a peaceful picnic lunch by the river. Throughout the course of the meal, however, Polly could tell his mind was on something else.

The second she finished eating, Jason took her hand in his and led her deep into the woods. Eventually, when he felt that they were far enough away, he located a sturdy log for her to sit on. He knelt down on one knee and took her by the hand. At once, she understood what was happening; still, she couldn't believe it.

"Polly Anne, in the time that I've known you, your very presence in my life fulfilled me, while every second I spent away from you hurt me immensely. I now know what I feel inside is true love. I know we were meant for each other. This may be a new experience for you, but it's new for me as well. I'm ready to face the future with you, whatever it may bring. Polly Anne, I love you more than anyone I've ever met. Would you please spend the rest of your life with me and become my wife?"

With every tender word he spoke, she felt surrounded by his love. Tears of joy welled up in her light-green eyes, and she felt happier than she ever had been in her entire life. "Yes," she sighed happily. "Of course I will, Jason."

He smiled at her as he pulled a small, velvet-covered box from his pocket. "This is my eternal promise that I would sooner die than love any woman other than you."

He opened the lid of the box to reveal a dazzling, star-cut ruby, set on a 24-karat, solid-gold ring, and surrounded by 10 small diamonds.

She practically fainted at just the sight of it. "Oh! Jason, it's so beautiful! Wherever did you get this?"

At this, Jason's eyes shifted away from hers. "I...umm... worked many years to find a treasure as beautiful as this."

In all the years she had known Jason, she never knew what he did for a living. Somehow, though, it had never seemed important to her to ask him.

"Of course, all the treasure in the world isn't even close to as valuable to me as you are," he assured.

She became overwhelmed with joy when he placed the extravagant ring on her finger.

"I will never let anything get in the way of the love I have for you, Polly," Jason promised lovingly. "Never."

———∞∞∞———

Leaving the flashback behind, Aunt Polly continued speaking to the children. "We eloped shortly after and settled down here in St. Petersburg, with the intention of starting a family. And after a short while, we were blessed with my daughter, Mary, who lived with me until she recently got married and moved away. But sadly for me, Jason didn't stay in Missouri for very long after our marriage. I'll never forget the day he left. He told me of an amazing merchant opportunity he needed to pursue. That day, the day that he left, was the last time I ever saw him alive. Thirty years later, I learned he had died while at sea. The remains of his body were later recovered by the U.S. Navy off of a ship that sank near the coast of Cuba.

It was called <u>The Dark Mystery</u>. At the time, it was reported by a local newspaper that Jason had been involved in piracy. I didn't believe it at first. But later, a second newspaper company received information that Jason had, in fact, been the notorious Red Beard."

Aunt Polly briefly looked up from the children to casually motion at the nearby cellar door. "He always told me that if anything were to happen to him, I could live off of what he had stored in the cellar. Granted, until something did happen to him, he had forbidden me from ever going in there! He even put a large, sturdy padlock on the door to that inner room. And I never went in there, until, that is, I found out he had died. At that point, I figured it would be okay to go in. So, after I broke the lock off, I discovered that he had stored a great collection of treasure underneath our very house. I put some of the gold coins away in the bank, but you saw what was still down in the cellar."

She began to chuckle. "Can you imagine what would have happened if I had brought all of the treasure to the bank? People would have started talking, and I wouldn't have been able to live here in St. Petersburg, which has been my home for a long time now. Jason and I had married in secret, and even though the whole town knew of his death, they couldn't tie Red Beard's crimes back to me because our marriage wasn't public. In any case, I've kept my married name a secret and have been living off my savings ever since."

Tom was at a loss for words. His aunt? The unassuming mother figure of his life? The woman who tried her hardest to keep him out of trouble? THAT woman was, in fact, the widow of the legendary man he practically idolized?

"Does Sid know about any of this?" Tom inquired curiously.

Aunt Polly shook her head. "No, Tom, Sid isn't aware of my history with Jason, and frankly, I'd rather keep it that way," she spoke deliberately.

"Why?" Andrew asked.

With a laugh, Aunt Polly remarked, "Andrew, honey, I'm not an idiot. Sid has the biggest reputation in the village for being a snitch. It doesn't take a genius to figure out that snitches are the worst secret keepers. I tell Sid, and the whole village might as well know too!"

Laughing out loud, Aunt Polly had to take a moment to catch her breath. "Tom, you remind me very much of Jason. Though he's not your father by blood, I guess he's kind of your father in spirit."

Tom couldn't help but give a small nod of affirmation and a smile at hearing his aunt's words.

Huck found himself stunned at all the new revelations. "So, does that mean that you knew the treasure was down in the cellar the whole time we've been searching for it?" he queried.

The slightest trace of a grin curled on Aunt Polly's face. "Of course I knew it was down there. How do you think I take care of myself and three children? I think the real question is, 'How did you all know it was down there?'"

Tom chuckled. "Well, we actually found a piece of Red Beard's map buried in a chest in the dirt of your garden, Aunt Polly. That day you gave me the seeds to plant was when we found it. After that, we decided to search for his treasure, and eventually, we were led back here. Did you know that Jason hid part of the map so close by?"

"No," Aunt Polly shook her head. "It's just a coincidence that you all found the map piece on my property; Jason never told me about a treasure map."

"How did you know that we were searching for his treasure, anyway?" Becky asked.

Aunt Polly let out a chuckle. "If I know my godson at all, looking for treasure is his passion. I doubt he even does it primarily for the money – he's already got all of that money from the gold he found in the cave. If I had to guess, I'd say he mostly looks for treasure just to be able to say he found it. I knew you all were on some sort of a quest, so it was probably about treasure. But I didn't want to interfere; you're all growing up so fast now."

As everyone pondered her words, they realized, despondently, that the treasure, which had consumed them for the last month, already belonged to somebody else.

"It's like we had this adventure for nothing," Becky sulked.

"Yeah," Amy echoed forlornly.

Aunt Polly, observing their disappointment, said nothing - at least not at first. Her next words, however, soon filled them all with happiness again.

"Andrew," she began, pointing to the chest, "Open that box for me, please."

Andrew obeyed, showing Aunt Polly the glittering jewels and the sizeable amount of gold coins inside.

"I'll tell you what: For all your hard work, I'll let you keep whatever is inside that box right now."

Tom's eyes popped to the size of oranges. "Are you serious, Aunt Polly?"

She nodded. "And, if you need money every now and then," Aunt Polly went on, "I don't see why you can't have some access to my treasure trove. For now, you can all consider me your private banker."

"Really, Aunt Polly?!" They all gasped with joy.

"Of course. I don't see why not; it's not like I have an interest in spending such a large sum of money by myself. Until otherwise decided, this will be our little secret," she announced to them, as she stood up from her chair and walked over to the chest. "Alright, everyone," she called, gesturing them all over, "Let's see what wonderful treasures are in here for each of you!"

And with that, all five best friends, together with Aunt Polly, knelt down around the pirate's chest and began excitedly digging for beautiful gems and shiny gold coins!

CHAPTER 55

FRIENDSHIP IS FOREVER

The day that Dead Eye Dan went over the edge of Devil's Drop Falls, Phillip Morse went into hiding. Due to his deadly shenanigans with Dan, Phillip would never be a free man, and he knew that he could never return to St. Petersburg.

After Dan went over the falls, and after Tom and his friends left the falls to return home, Phillip, who had been watching from the cover of a large bush, snuck down to the base of the waterfall, intending to pay his final respects to his dead master. His attention was drawn to the pieces of the broken, wooden raft, which floated on the surface of the water near the bank. Phillip quickly found the piece with the rope attached to it and made quick work drawing it out of the water.

In no time, he soon had the other end of the wet rope in his hands. He dreaded what was on the other end: The last he had seen of his boss, Dan had been trying to free the rope from around his ankle. But as Phillip pulled the end of the rope with the noose out of the water, the loop came up empty: It was no longer tied around the ankle of Dead Eye Dan!

Phillip found himself more perplexed than usual! He gave the matter a few seconds consideration as he stared into the murky water: Since Dan had indeed gone over the edge, what had happened to his body? Who had released Dan's ankle from the rope?

Phillip was overwhelmed. He simply couldn't figure out where the body had gone. There was no way that Dan, or anyone else, could have survived the impact on the rocks from a fall that high. Phillip glanced quickly at the sharp rock spires jutting out of the water at the base of the falls, but there was no body there either. Tossing the rope back in the water, he stood up to leave.

But before Phillip could walk away, a cold, wet hand shot out from the water and grabbed hold of his ankle!

Screaming hysterically at the top of his lungs, Phillip lunged away, startling dozens of birds, but not achieving freedom. From the depths of the lake, a second hand burst out of the water to help hoist up the entire rest of the body that followed: Dead Eye Dan!

He had lived through the fall!

Once on the bank of the lake, Dan roughly covered his hand over Phillip's mouth. "Would you quit screaming?! You're gonna get us both caught!"

"B...B...B...Boss? Is that you?"

Sure enough, the creature who climbed out of the water was none other than Dead Eye Dan, in the flesh and unharmed!

Phillip could not have been more ecstatic. He wrapped Dan up in the biggest hug he could give, while Dan just stood there, breathing hard. "How on earth did you survive the fall?" Phillip asked joyously.

Dan smirked. "Did you really think that I could be killed that easily? I'm Dead Eye Dan!"

Phillip looked completely confused. "How did you do it?" he asked.

"When I fell, I pushed myself away from the raft so that my body wouldn't fall on the rocks. Then, I used this." Dan held up a hollow shoot of bamboo about 18 inches long. "I snatched up one of these – they grow by the base of the waterfall. I simply stayed underwater, breathing through this for about half an hour. I knew that the kids would think I was dead and leave."

At that point, Dan himself got curious. Staring at Phillip with more than a little amazement, he asked, "How are you still here? I thought the sheriff would have gotten you for sure," Dan probed.

Phillip grinned. "What can I say, Boss? You've taught me more than you think."

Dan grinned back and let loose with a deep laugh.

Phillip eventually joined in, laughing as well. "So, Boss, what are we gonna do now? Should we go after those kids and deal with them for good this time?"

To his surprise, Dan shook his head. "Nah, those kids are a lot smarter than they look. I don't want to take any more chances with them. Besides, if I do show my face around here, I'd be caught for sure. Best that we keep a low profile. I do, however, have other plans in mind."

"Like what?"

"Well, it may take us some walking, but we can still catch the train out of here. If we're lucky, we'll make it as far as California; you know, I hear talk they discovered gold down in those parts."

"You mean we're gonna be rich after all?"

Dan nodded. "We just might. Right now, I think it's best if we take a little break from our crime spree. After we strike it rich, then maybe we'll see about making our way to Europe. I hear the Queen of England wears a very valuable crown, and I'd only be more than happy to liberate her of it."

"Well, whatever you decide, Boss, I'm with you," Phillip enthusiastically promised.

Dan started walking. "Come along, Phillip! The train waits for no one!"

About the same time that Aunt Polly was telling her history, another wondrous story was playing out. At the western border of Illinois, Gregory and Dr. Wesley were about to get a most pleasant surprise of their own.

While lighting a fire to start cooking dinner, Dr. Wesley noticed two men approach their campsite. As the gentlemen drew near, they held out their empty hands in a gesture of peace. Dr. Wesley didn't recognize them, but that was okay. He gestured for them to come closer.

As they got closer, Gregory emerged from his tent. Taking measure of the two men, he thought he recognized something about their appearance, but he couldn't quite put his finger on what it was. One man was tall with reddish-brown hair, while the other was shorter with light-brown hair and freckles.

"Hello, sir," the tallest of them called out. "We don't mean to bother you, but would you have any spare food? We've been traveling for quite a long time, and our supplies have almost run out."

Gregory and Dr. Wesley were happy to accommodate the request. Not only did they round up some food for the travelers, but they also cordially offered to let them spend the night. The two weary travelers were more than happy to accept the generous offer.

That night, thousands of beautiful, bright stars came out to light up the sky. The men took turns naming the constellations, a skill they all seemed impressively good at. The heat of the campfire's blaze kept them warm and happy as they laid on their backs, making small talk to pass the time. "So, what brings you two strangers out here to these parts?" Dr. Wesley inquired.

This time, the shorter-statured man spoke up. "We're heading up the river on our way to Iowa. We know a friend up there who wrote to us, telling of an opportunity for employment; but we ran out of supplies quite a ways away from our destination. We got off the river to find a town, and then we ran into you two."

"I see," Gregory nodded. "Well, I must say that it's a pleasure to get to know you, Mr..."

"Goldman," the man voiced. "My name's Cody Goldman."

Dr. Wesley quickly sat upright, not believing the words he had just heard. It couldn't be. "What's your name?" the doctor asked incredulously.

"Cody Goldman," the stranger repeated.

The doctor crawled over to examine the man's face in the firelight. As he did so, Wesley's eyes widened, and his mouth dropped open in astonishment. "Cody, is that you?"

The moment these words were uttered, Cody sat himself upright instantly. "Wesley?"

The doctor nodded, stunned beyond belief.

It was his brother! Only a moment passed before the two men locked themselves together in a warm hug. Tears flowed freely down their faces. Who would have thought that after all these years, these two brothers would have the luck of being reunited once more?

"Wesley?" Cody asked, shocked. His voice grew warm and thick with affection and disbelief. "It's been decades. I never thought I'd see you again. How are you?!"

"I'm alright; time has treated me quite well. I've missed you for the longest time. You look quite good," Wesley complimented.

By now, Gregory and Cody's traveling friend were listening in on the heartfelt conversation. "Well," Gregory sighed happily. "I never would have thought that Wesley would see his brother ever again."

"Well, you never know, do you?" the stranger remarked good-naturedly. "Time has a way of bringing old friends back together."

Gregory nodded. It was true.

The stranger put out his hand. "I should probably introduce myself too. I'm Aaron MacCarthy. Pleased to meet you."

Gregory stopped dead in his thoughts. All of a sudden, Gregory's eyes went big, and then, meeting the stranger's gaze, he asked if Aaron had ever been the son of a cook.

"Well, yes, but how would you know anything about that…" He stopped speaking as Gregory locked eyes with him. "Gregory?"

Gregory nodded as well.

Aaron and Gregory quickly stood up, engaging each other in an enormous, long-overdue hug. It had been many years since all four of the men had seen each other. All of them had stories to share. Cody and Aaron were shocked beyond belief when they learned about Red Beard's untimely passing.

"It's bad luck that his ship sank," Cody offered his condolences. "You know, Gregory, you would have made one heck of a pirate captain."

"Yeah," Aaron concurred. "I could see that happening to you."

Gregory chuckled to himself. "Ok, yes, maybe that might have worked out, but I think I'd still be a happier man, here on land, with you guys."

They all wisely nodded. And then, Aaron spoke up. "Why don't you two come with us to Iowa?"

Gregory initially shook his head. He had lived in the woods most of his life, as had the doctor. It was their home. But what were the odds that their two old friends would come sauntering back into their lives? Perhaps he should be more open to change? They could always come back. "Wesley, what do you think?" he asked.

"Well, I suppose I could move my practice further north, but I'd have to start all over," Wesley said.

"Sure, but we'd all be together again. C'mon, what do you say? Red Beard's Fearsome Four all together on a new adventure?"

Gregory and Wesley took a moment to whisper a few words to each other, and then both said the same thing to Cody and Aaron.

"Count us in!"

EPILOGUE

THE ADVENTURE LIVES
ON IN OUR HEARTS

Thomas Sawyer, Huckleberry Finn, Rebecca Thatcher, Amy Lawrence, and Andrew Lawrence soon had their collection of precious gems and gold coins assessed for its value, which later totaled to a grand sum of over $100,000! Having had their tiny collection estimated at such a shockingly high amount of money, Tom and the others could only imagine the worth of the remaining fortune, hiding unused, in the bowels of Aunt Polly's cellar. In order to be able to spend the treasure, they brought the gemstones and coins to the city of St. Louis to exchange the precious materials for an equivalent cash sum.

Eventually, they brought their hard-earned money to Thatcher Bank, where Judge Thatcher set all of them up with their very own premium savings accounts. To this day, he remains shocked that they once again discovered treasure. Granted, Tom Sawyer was known for having amazing luck when it came to discovering fortunes. In any case, the judge divided the currency up evenly with more than $20,000 in each of their accounts. Thatcher Bank paid an annual rate of six percent interest.

With their share of the fortune, Amy and Andrew Lawrence eventually sold their old dwelling and moved into a new, bigger home, down by the Mississippi River. The carpentry shop still remains open for business, but Andrew usually closes up on the weekends. At Amy's urging, Andrew finally began courting his former high school sweetheart.

Tom and Huck remain best friends. They still manage to regularly cause an abundance of mischief. Even though their escapade was over, they still head down to Jackson's Island every year to reminisce about their adventure. The island has also become the place where they occasionally go for a vacation to escape from the annoyances of everyday life.

Huck and Amy's relationship has become even closer as they continue to mature. Every now and again, Huck likes to steal her away from whatever she happens to be doing to surprise her with romantic picnic lunches down by the river! But more often, Huck and Amy just like to enjoy a peaceful, quiet afternoon down at Old Man McCabe's dock, fishing together, hoping that someday, they'll both catch a really big fish, possibly worthy of newspaper headlines.

The money that Dan stole was eventually recovered and returned to Thatcher Bank, and from that moment on, Becky's relationship with her dad grew even closer and stronger. He has become a more emotionally involved father to her and allows her to make more of her own choices. Some people say that the judge even lets Tom take her out every now and then for dinner or dessert! Tom reportedly has even had discussions with Becky's father about marriage when he and Becky get a little older!

Speaking of Becky and Tom, it seems that Tom has become more thoughtful to his girlfriend! Every year, on the anniversary of when they first became boyfriend and girlfriend, Becky always receives a bouquet of freshly cut roses! Now, it could be Becky's imagination, but the flowers bear an odd resemblance to a certain type of rose that only grows down near the Riverfront Inn, where they vacationed. However, that would surely mean walking a long way down, back to the inn, to ask Horace for the favor. But I think we all know that Tom would move mountains just to make Becky happy.

As for Dead Eye Dan and Phillip Morse, no one knows what really became of them. They were reported to have been seen alive on multiple occasions, but no one seems to have any real evidence. Phillip's ingenuity for creating disguises seems to have helped them to remain incognito.

Gregory and Dr. Wesley moved up to Iowa with Aaron and Cody, but every now and then, they return to the forests of Illinois; and when they do, the kids often drop by to trade stories and say hi.

Mr. Dobbins still has trouble with Tom; but he has begun to notice a slight maturity occurring in his behavior, which is good news, as adulthood lies just around the corner for Tom.

Aunt Polly, Tom, and Sid still live quite happily together. And while Sid still plays the part of the innocent victim who never does anything wrong and likes to snitch on others, Aunt Polly has gotten wise to his wiles. It's such a shame that Sid remains clueless as to Aunt Polly's big secret, but maybe it's for the best.

Now, even though Tom and his friends won't live around

here forever, you can still always witness the living spirit of them whenever you see an adventurous boy or girl. They exist to remind us all that you're never too old to enjoy life, have fun, and become a kid again.

THE END

ACKNOWLEDGEMENTS

This book has been a long awaited project of mine for almost 15 years now. As such, there are several people that I would like to thank for their help in making this dream a reality.

- Mrs. Susan Lubinski: Growing up through junior high and high school, you've taught me so much about the English language and about the abundance of amazing literature that came before me. Thank you for having a ridiculous amount of patience to both believe that I can always get better and to craft my English and grammar skills to an enviable level. I can still remember how, in my first year of college, my peers weren't even close to writing at the same level of excellence you had gotten me to. I humbly apologize for all the times I complained about the homework assignments and every time you would pull out a red pen to correct my work. You made such an impression on me that I can't help but feel that I wrote this book partly as a way to give back to you for all that you contributed to my development. Thank you so much for allowing me to present you with a rough draft of my work to once again critique and review. Maybe, if you think they would enjoy it, you could recommend it to your current students. I would love to give back to the younger generation. Once again, thank you from the bottom of my heart for how much you gave to me in love and dedication. Very few words can describe the impact with which you've changed me and become a large part of my life. Thanks for shepherding me on the journey!

— Mr. Russell Allred: When I was still in some of the early stages of completing the rough draft, I had presented you with a very primitive, final copy of the book. Out of your limited time for yourself, you willingly offered to read the story all the way through and shared many tips of practicality and realism. Those were immensely invaluable towards developing a believable story. You saw my passion for the story and characters and helped me turn it into a world that I know Mark Twain himself would have been proud of. Thank you for helping to point me in the right direction. And more importantly, thank you for giving me guidance for seeking out a publisher and a professional editor for my story. Without you, I don't think many people would have the opportunity to read my work! From a young age, I admired how you were able to have fun with the world of imagination and write your own published stories. This has been a long time coming, and I have a much greater appreciation for the level of dedication that you put into your stories. From one published author to another, I can only say, "Thank you for showing me the way. You've taught me so much!"

– Mrs. Katie Hall: After bringing this literary accomplishment to the best quality that I could make it, I was strongly encouraged to seek out the assistance of a professional editor to make the story into a higher quality product to entice more readers. When I began to look for the right person, I had two desires in mind: One, since my story borrows from the legacy of Mark Twain, who grew up in Missouri, I wanted to make sure that I hired an editor who both lived in Missouri and could add some accurate local dialogue and idioms into the story. And two, I wanted to recruit an older editor, since I knew that someone older would be more willing to treat the characters of classic literature with the respect they deserved. I had no frame of reference for the wonderful contributions that a professional editor could add to an author's final edit, and I didn't think you could do much more work with my story. Boy did you prove me wrong. Having revised and edited the story from beginning to end about 5-10 times myself, I had grown bored and sick of reading my own work. You went above and beyond everything I had hoped you could do for my book. You were so much more than just a "glorified red pen and highlighter." You condensed the book and made the language more concise; you offered advice on technologies available at the time of the older, fictional world; you even did some ghostwriting and added original material – a lot of which I ended up keeping in the story because it was better than anything I had thought of. You met me at my financial constraints, as far as hiring an editor was concerned, and you breathed fresh, new life into the project I had created. When I look over the story after you finished, I almost don't recognize it: It's like you helped me to write a completely different book! And more than that, you helped to guide me on the right path to seeking out a literary agent as a brand new author. I have so much to thank you for, both as an editor and as a person. I will never forget the contributions you made to help me out. Thank you for staying with me till the end!

— Lillie Joe: Hi, Sis! We started out working on this project together during the first year, and I was sad to lose your contributions before the first year was even up. I would have loved to have written the entire book with you from start to finish, but you had your own life to lead, and I have nothing but respect for you for making your own path. Thank you for the illustrations you did for the characters early on; I've received nothing but lavish words of praise from the people I've had the privilege to show them to. I'm sorry that the story changed enough to where the drawings wouldn't have made sense. But I still love them, and I'm sure I'll find a way to archive them with the original draft. At the start of the process, my enthusiasm for this story was as high as it could have been, but without your contributing hand in the story, I might have been at a loss for imagination and given up. I hope that you enjoy where the story has gotten to and that you'll like the finished version with illustrations and everything. Take care of yourself however you choose to live your life! You're still my closest friend, and nothing will ever change the fact that you're my sister and I love you!

— Mom and Dad: You've been there with me throughout the highs and lows of life. You've shown me how to take care of my own needs and the needs of others. And you've been there for me whenever I needed something, whether that meant offering me sage advice tailored to my exact needs and situations or holding me close and letting me cry on your shoulder in times of despair and sorrow. You've put up with a lot of my faults and weaknesses and tried to make me into the best version of myself that I can be. There are no other parents I know of who can love, care for, and protect me with the determination that you do. God couldn't have made us a more perfect match for each other. I've always hoped that someday, when I finish, that I would get the privilege and honor to read this book to you, like how you've read countless books to me and Lillie when we were younger. I hope, more than anything, that you fall in love with the story I wrote, and that this opportunity brings us even closer together than we are now. I love you both with all of my heart!

— And last and most importantly, God: Throughout the 15 years of writing and revising this story, you've been there with me through it all. You've given me a great imagination and a determined spirit to not give up easily. Over the years, I've sometimes lost interest in this story one day, only to rediscover the interest another day. You've given me a cornucopia of brilliant ideas and ways to change the story for the better. I've found myself in awe of how much the story has changed and adapted into an amazing work, from the first year when I was 13 years old to now at 29 years old. I can't be more grateful for the ways you've taken care of me, both while writing the story and while working away from the story. I never thought in all my dreams that this project would become the magnificent work that it is today. Thank you so much for the inspiration for the book as well as for bringing the right people into my life to contribute their skills. Forgive me for the ways I've put you in second place to put myself on top of the trophy shelf of my life. And thank you for being the ultimate Father, who I can run to when life doesn't go my way and cry out my heart to. You've always loved me deeply– no matter what; and I'll never forget it! Thank you for helping me to bring a satisfying end to this project and for constantly breathing fresh air under my wings of imagination to help me soar!

ABOUT THE AUTHOR

Sebastian Joe grew up in Southern California, attended California State University Long Beach, and received a bachelor's degree in communication studies. For more than 15 years, Sebastian has written stories for readers of all ages, authoring everything from action/adventure tales, to teenage spy novels, and even detective/mystery stories. He has starred in musicals, done voiceover work for radio dramas, and plays rock guitar with his friends in a local band.